Written in Stone
Tales of the American Indian

By Paul Schanen

Published by
Lauric Press
McKinney, Texas

ISBN: 978-1-932113-93-8 paperback

ISBN: 978-1-932113-94-5 digital

For Mom

Table of Contents

Disclaimer: This book makes references to cultural traditions of face painting in specific colors. Some painted themselves for religious or clan identity reasons, but, more often than not, it was part of a scare tactic. When you met your foe in hand-to-hand combat, you held an advantage if your opponent was afraid of your appearance. White was made using lead oxides from galena that was mined in SW Wisconsin, black was made using charcoal, red was made using iron oxides, particularly from ground hematite or red ochre. They may have made other colored paints from other materials as well, but these were favorites. These are not references to skin color or race. During ancient and not-so-ancient times face painting became deeply embedded in many cultures, not just Native American ones. Face painting continues today among many tribes including those in Panama. The references are not intended to be either racist or derogatory in any way, only reflective of the time. To omit them would be to omit a critical element of the culture of these people and it's the author's intent to represent them as accurately as possible even in a work of fiction.

Introduction

For more than 10,000 years people lived out their lives in the very same places that we do now. Long before we all became infatuated with the latest piece of technology or worried about meeting the demands of our busy lives, people were here. They built houses in many of the same places that we do now, they raised families here, they had deep spiritual beliefs, they laughed here, they fought here, and they died here. Their houses, like their bones, have long since returned to the earth from which they came. Their footprints have been blown away by the winds of time, and in fact, very little remains to remind us that they were ever here except for a few things. A handful of little stone arrowheads, atl-atl points, and stone tools stand in stark defiance of the years, reminding us all of our own mortality.

Most of you probably know someone who at some point found one of these ancient stone artifacts, maybe while weeding the family garden, or perhaps while plowing some farm field years ago. Some of you might remember a grandpa or uncle who had a display of these curious stone arrowheads upon the wall. A small number of you may have even found one or more yourself. Most people who find or examine one have the same thought cross their minds. They wonder what the person was like who made, used, and lost the point. They often wonder what it was used for, and they almost always wonder exactly how the stone and its owner became separated to begin with.

The stories that follow are for anyone who has ever wondered how these little ancient reminders of days gone by came to be lost.

– Paul Schanen

Chapter 1: Boy Warriors

Yellow Thunder and Keokuk slipped quietly from the edge of the village as the first hints of light began to ease the darkness. Already, the air felt thick, warning of the hot day to come. Thin tendrils of smoke still rose from the previous night's campfires as the boys silently crept along the edge of the river just below their village. They traveled farther than needed before daring to utter a single word. They had snuck out of their family's bark houses against the wishes of their parents. If their parents caught them now, they would be in more trouble than either one cared to think about.

Yellow Thunder had seen 10 summers and Keokuk only nine. No longer children, yet not quite men, both boys longed to reach the age of acceptance and respect enjoyed by the men of their clan. Both dreamed of becoming strong warriors like those they had descended from, both daydreamed together of a time when their people would sing songs about their heroics. Nothing could more readily propel a young man or even boy from being just that; a man or boy, to a respected warrior faster than taking the life of an enemy. It was with this thought in their minds that Yellow Thunder and Keokuk formed their plans earlier that spring.

Their people moved south along the Great Spirit River at the start of the hot season each and every year. The river offered an oasis, a bastion of resources, in the hot days of summer when the prairies farther inland became more difficult to survive. It was this place along the river, however, where Yellow Thunder's and Keokuk's people also lived in danger because not far to the south lived a band of people whom they called the Ojibi-nak-ton. Their people and the Ojibi-nak-ton both claimed the resources of the river in the summer months. Generation after generation it became this duel claim to rights of the river which ended many times with the river running red with blood. The conflict with the Ojibi-nak-ton was the subject of many songs and stories. The boys grew up hearing stories of horrific clashes between their people and the Ojibi-nak-ton. Yellow Thunder's grandfather proudly told the story each year of how he killed three Ojibi-nak-ton with his war club in a single ambush. There were also many stories of their own people being killed or captured as well. Keokuk's uncle had been captured by the Ojibi-nak-ton just two seasons prior while out tending his nets in the river. Three days later they found his body badly mutilated and stripped naked lying at the edge of the village.

Because of this perpetual conflict and close proximity to the Ojibi-nak-ton the boys decided it was the perfect time to go on a war party of their own and ambush some Ojibi-nak-ton. They envisioned nothing less than complete surprise and total victory. Their conversations had been more about the number of enemies each of them would kill, or what songs would be written about them, than about the possibility of defeat or any sense of danger. In fact, even as the boys snuck south along the Great Spirit River in the haze of the early morning light, they still felt no fear or sense of danger. They only saw visions of grandeur.

When they were more than a mile from their village the tension associated with being caught started to ease somewhat and Yellow Thunder finally dared speak. "Did you bring everything?" he asked Keokuk. Keokuk smiled and nodded holding a bow and quiver in one hand and a large leather bag in the other. Keokuk had his father's bow and arrows as well as a bag containing some dried venison.

"Did you?" Keokuk asked of Yellow Thunder even though the answer appeared obvious. Yellow Thunder padded the sheath on his hip where his father's large war knife now hung and swung his other hand around bringing his grandfather's cherished war club within inches of Keokuk's face. As the war club whooshed by Keokuk's face he flinched in surprise and that elicited a large toothy grin from Yellow Thunder.

"Let's take the high trail," Yellow Thunder said and then turned and started up the riverbank. That section of river cut deeper and deeper into the land so the boys could follow the water's edge. The riverbank continued to grow and grow, eventually turning into sheer bluffs as the river cut through the ancient sandstone. By taking the high trail along the riverbank they would have a bird's-eye view of the river and any Ojibi-nak-ton who might be in it.

Both boys knew that once their families woke up and found them missing a search party, if not a war party, would be organized; and now, as they hiked down the trail, both boys occasionally looked back over their shoulders to see if they were being followed. They continued to chat on and off about who would be the first to kill an Ojibi-nak-ton, but as they walked and as the night fully gave way to dawn a certain sense of reality started to set in. By mid-morning the boys reached the beginning of the hill country where the river started to cut its way down into the land and the banks became increasingly difficult to follow. Giant valleys with small streams dipped down to meet the river only to give way on the other side to a steep hill towering over it. This up and down terrain was a sign they were quickly approaching the end of their traditional territory and knocking on the Ojibi-nak-ton's front door.

Realizing they were getting close to their quarry, Yellow Thunder suggested they stop for a bite to eat. Both boys backed up against the trunk of a giant white pine along the river's edge and each chewed on a tough piece of venison jerky in silence. Neither boy really felt hungry at all, quite the opposite in fact, but neither boy wanted to demonstrate the slightest hint of fear. And so both chewed on in silence. After resting for a few minutes, they resumed their journey.

By noon the boys had traveled several miles farther than either one of them had ever dared go before. Their talk became less frequent now and increasingly hushed. The speed of travel also diminished as they stopped with eyes wide open, and ears finely tuned to every noise in the forest. Fear began to take hold of both the boys' hearts as each one silently pondered the outcome of a face-to-face visit with the Ojibi-nak-ton. Yellow Thunder now paused occasionally to wipe the sweat from his hand that held the heavy war club. Likewise, Keokuk stopped wearing his father's bow over his shoulder and now carried it in front of him with an arrow already knocked. The full heat of the day started to take its toll in addition to the growing sense of danger. Like several others they had already crossed, they came to a deep valley with a small ice-cold stream trickling down it toward the river. There they stopped to drink.

Yellow Thunder pointed up the hill on the other side and said, "We should take a break in the hot part of the day like this, save our energy."

Keokuk nodded as he sipped water from his cupped hands.

"We'll rest up there in the shade of the trees," Yellow Thunder added.

Pine needles covered the hill with occasional boulders of sandstone sticking out from the landscape. It took the boys a full 15 minutes to climb up the steep hill. They were both surprised to find that the hill was indeed high, but quite narrow. Only a short distance through the woods the hill again dipped down into another steep valley fed by a small cold creek.

"This is as good of a place to rest as any," Yellow Thunder said.

Exhausted by the hike, Keokuk made no objection.

Both boys laid down at the edge of the hill so they could watch the valley below just in case any Ojibi-nak-ton should happen to come through it. Only a short way down the valley and to the right the landscape fanned out into a sand bar and the main body of the Great Spirit River.

Keokuk dozed off to sleep. Yellow Thunder became completely lost in thought at first, and then sank down on the verge of sleep himself when a bit of movement down on the sand bar caught his attention. It took a moment for his eyes to focus on the objects because the sun glared in his eyes off the surface of the water. When he realized what he saw were people and not just a passing herd of deer, his heart began to beat hard, and his veins started to fill with adrenaline.

"Keokuk!" he said excitedly. But Keokuk remained motionless. Finally, he poked at him with a stick, "Keokuk!" he uttered again.

Keokuk finally came to his senses and looked at his friend through sleepy eyes. As Keokuk began to wake up he immediately became aware of the wide-eyed look of fear on Yellow Thunder's face. Keokuk slowly turned his head to follow the gaze of Yellow Thunder down the valley out toward the river. It took his eyes a moment to adjust to the glare of the river as well, but he could clearly see four people walking across the sand there. The boys' excitement turned to sheer terror as the four people changed directions and started to walk toward the little valley above which they now perched.

Both boys laid their heads flat against the pine needles and earth hoping to avoid detection.

"What should we do?" Keokuk asked Yellow Thunder.

"I don't know; there's too many of them!" he said in a subdued but excited whisper. "You should shoot them with your arrows if they come close enough," Yellow Thunder said as he nodded toward Keokuk's bow lying on the ground between them. Keokuk could already feel his heart beating hard and his hands trembling, however, and doubted his ability to hit anything in such an excited state.

"I can finish them off with my club," boasted Yellow Thunder. Keokuk remained wide-eyed and didn't answer; he simply shook his head ever so slowly back and forth in disagreement. After a few minutes passed, Yellow Thunder again raised his head and peeked over the ledge to check on the whereabouts of the Ojibi-nak-ton below.

Yellow Thunder suddenly didn't feel so brave. Directly below their perch he could plainly see the men now. All four of them were Ojibi-nak-ton warriors, and all of them looked like evil spirits come to life. All four wore their hair shaved except for a single tightly woven braid hanging down the back of their necks. Two of the warriors attached a single eagle feather atop their braid signaling they had taken the life of an enemy, and one of the men had two feathers, one split down the middle, signaling that he had taken the life of many enemies. The last of the four appeared not much older than Yellow Thunder or Keokuk and wore no feathers. All of the men wore large ear spools, and one had a necklace of white shell beads that stood out in stark contrast to his darkly bronzed skin. Yellow Thunder watched as the four men stopped to drink from the small stream. The oldest of the four appeared to notice something in the mud by the stream and pointed to it. The others all looked and began to talk excitedly. Yellow Thunder couldn't tell exactly what made the tracks in the mud but thought perhaps those of an elk would likely create such excitement. Though once plentiful, Elk had, in recent years, been hunted to near extinction. Anyone who found an elk to hunt and possibly killed it created a reason to celebrate in his own clan. Yellow Thunder figured the Ojibi-nak-ton shared this sentiment.

So focused on the activities below, Yellow Thunder hardly noticed Keokuk inching up toward the edge of their peak to have a closer look as well. Now both boys watched side by side as the four men made a plan to hunt and kill the elk who left the tracks. The boys could only understand some words that they used. Others were foreign, so the verbal plan was difficult to follow. However, the older warrior of the bunch, the one with two feathers, liked to talk with his hands. It became clear to both boys through his gestures that part of the hunters plan was to send one of their own up the hill where the boys were now hiding. Upon realizing that they might soon be discovered, both boys again laid their heads flat and looked at each other wide-eyed. One of the boys slowly started to push his body backward away from the edge of the hill and the other boy followed suit. When they had pushed themselves backward far enough from the edge so they could not be seen, they both stood up, crouched over, and started to retreat through the woods and down the valley on the other side back in the direction from which they had come. As they climbed up the other side of the little valley, their careful and quiet retreat soon gave way to a full out panicked run for their lives.

Neither boy tried to say anything or make any excuses for their retreat; both ran as though chased by a pack of wolves. Both boys slipped or fell down along the way many times. As they ran Keokuk's quiver slid lower and lower on his back until it risked dumping all of his dad's fine arrows out on the ground. At one point, a low hanging branch snagged one of the arrows from the quiver and pulled it out as Keokuk ran. The fine arrow landed in pine needles without a sound. Keokuk adjusted the quiver on his shoulder a short while later so he wouldn't lose any arrows, but it was already too late. The boys ran almost halfway home and were again on the flat land of their own territory before they slowed down enough to talk.

"Wow! That was close!" Keokuk sputtered, still trying to catch his breath.

"I can't believe you took off running like a scared prairie chicken!" Yellow Thunder said, taunting Keokuk with his facial expressions.

"Me? Run?" Keokuk dropped his father's bow and now stood still. "You were the big prairie chicken that took off running!" he yelled back at Yellow Thunder.

Both boys sprang at each other and locked arms in battle, wrestling in the dirt of the trail and yelling at each other as they fought. Suddenly a giant hand reached out and gripped Yellow Thunder from his perch atop Keokuk and ripped him off, flinging him to the grass beside the trail. Both boys now sat bloodied and silent as their fathers and 20 other warriors from the tribe stood around them, all painted with war paint and armed with bows and clubs.

Some of the warriors appeared to wear smirks of appreciation as the boys attempted to explain themselves, but not their fathers.

Both boys were forced to haul water for all of the village's houses for the remainder of the summer. That meant making more than 50 trips to the river and back each day. Eventually the boy's fathers forgave them and some even laughed at the story once the boys told them all the details. To the day they died both of them accused the other of being the one who ran first, but in time it became less important. As the years passed both Yellow Thunder and Keokuk became respected warriors who eventually did have real run-ins with the Ojibi-nak-ton. Just as the boys had dreamed about in their youth, songs were sung about them. One song in particular remained a thorn in their side, however. It was called "The Tale of Prairie Chickens" and was about two wolves that fled upon coming face to face with four prairie chickens. The song mentioned no names and made no reference to Yellow Thunder or Keokuk, but all of the people in the village knew who the song was really about; and they all laughed while they sang.

It was over 980 years later when two friends decided they preferred fishing one day rather than attending school. After their parents left for work, the boys took their dad's fishing gear and cut through the woods and a cornfield on the way to the river. One of the two boys found an arrowhead in the cornfield as they approached the river. They spent a good portion of the rest of the day looking at the finely crafted stone arrowhead and openly wondering about its origin. Both boys thought it must have been lost while hunting wild game, or perhaps even during some ancient battle fought right there on the banks of the river eons earlier. But of course it was the same arrow that had fallen from Keokuk's quiver as he and Yellow Thunder ran for their lives from the Ojibi-nak-ton all those years earlier.

Chapter 2: Two Bears

Two Bears had lived a thoroughly good life. Not an easy life by any means, and it certainly contained its fair share of heartache, but throughout he rarely experienced times of famine or war. From this birth onward, the area flourished in a period of relative peace and prosperity. He and his family rarely needed to travel far for what they needed. The dense forests to the north and the marsh lands to their east provided rich hunting grounds for all sorts of game. The prairies to the south offered an abundance of deer and buffalo; and the river, which formed their western boundary, provided good fish and clams all year long. This small 50 square mile area represented Two Bear's entire universe and offered him nearly everything he needed to survive.

The only exception to Two Bears all-inclusive realm was the sacred hill known as O-Chi-Nok-Kuknuk from which Two Bears obtained the stone needed to make all the hunting points and knifes he used. The sacred hill rested many days walk to the northwest of Two Bear's normal hunting grounds; and he, as well as other members of his small group, made the trip there every other year to obtain raw material. Two Bears' father taught him the route as a young boy and told him the hill would provide him with all the tools he and all his offspring would ever need through this world and the next. Two Bears had seen only eight summers when he went there with his father for the first time and started to learn how to knap the stone into the projectiles and knives he and his people used. When Two Bears grew older and began to raise his own family, he took his own sons to the same sacred hill and taught them to knapp as well. Now gray and plagued with a slight limp, Two Bears intended to return yet again to this same sacred hill in his 60th summer.

Two Bears could no longer make the journey to O-Chi-Nok-Kuknuk in just nine days like he had once done. Two Bears had developed a slight limp caused by pain in his hip, and he guessed the trip might take him twice as long since he needed to stop frequently to rest. His wife and sons worried the trip to the sacred hill might simply prove too much for him now, but Two Bears insisted it was not more than he could handle. As a clan elder the others could voice their opinions to him, but he had the final say either way. Two Bears' eldest son offered to make the trip with his father to ensure his safety and well-being, but Two Bears declined his son's offer because his son now had a family of his own and simply could not afford to take a long, slow trip when his family needed him at home. His wife and son both pleaded with Two Bears, but he remained unflinching. He silently admitted to himself that he would like company on the trip. Not so much because he needed help, but because on a long trip he enjoyed someone to talk to. Two Bears' gaze shifted from his wife and son to just a few yards behind them where one of his grandchildren now sat whittling a stick by the fire.

He interrupted his wife in mid-sentence and called out to his grandson, "Red Moons, would you like to make a trip to O-Chi-Nok-Kuknuk with your grandfather?"

The look on Red Moons' face said it all; and as Two Bears' wife and eldest son turned to look at Red Moons he stood up and eagerly accepted the offer.

So it was arranged, Red Moons, who was in just his 10th summer, would travel with his grandfather to put his dad's and his grandmother's mind at ease. Two Bears felt happy that he would have company for the trip and secretly looked forward to telling stories along the way. He knew such a trip provided a good opportunity to pass along legends of old to his grandson before it was too late. Two Bears and Red Moons began to get ready for the trip that same day, both eager to begin. Red Moons viewed the trip as an opportunity to hunt buffalo as he had not taken one himself yet and yearned to prove his hunting prowess to his father. Because Red Moons focused more on the potential for hunting than the trip itself, he packed precious little that pertained to anything else.

Two Bears however knew there was no guarantee they would see any buffalo at the current time of year and did not feel keen about getting one because he didn't want to haul all that meat and heavy hide home with only his young grandson and himself to carry it.

Two Bears also planned to take his atl-atl and several good straight spears but spent most of his time packing other gear that years of experience taught him would come in handy. He laid out a large elk skin hide and in it he placed a tightly wound bundle of dried venison, a large bladder bag of dried blueberries and hazelnuts, his fishing net, his flintknapping tool kit, some dried medicine plant leaves mixed with honey in a small bladder bag, and his lucky amulet. From his belt he hung his best remaining hunting knife fixed to a sturdy antler handle. Though only late spring, the mosquitoes already flourished, but other than their nuisance he found it a beautiful time of year to travel.

Two Bears and Red Moons started off at the break of dawn the following day. The morning felt slightly chilly to Two Bears, but the cloudless sky combined with the slight westerly wind told Two Bears that the day would warm up soon enough. In the distance a coyote yelped a complaint that the night had already given way to the start of a new day as Two Bears and Red Moons entered the shallow waters of the Great Spirit River. Together they walked the ankle and calf-deep gravel lined river. This close to home both Two Bears and his grandson knew exactly where the deeper waters of the main channel cut down through the gravel making those places to avoid.

For most of the morning Red Moons carried on excitedly about all aspects of hunting buffalo and spoke as though he had several lifetimes' worth of hunting experience. Two Bears simply smiled and listened to his stories, impressed and perhaps slightly jealous of the young boy's energy and enthusiasm. They followed the shallow waters of the river north all day. Just as the late afternoon sky gave off the first rose hued hints of evening Two Bears and Red Moons came to a large sand bar in the river that divided the main channel of the river from the old channel. Two Bears told the story of how the river had flooded so badly eight seasons earlier that it changed course at this very place. He related how he used to walk the shallow gravel bars on the opposite side of the big sand bar on which they now made camp.

As Red Moons went about collecting wood for a campfire, Two Bears set his fishing net out in the pool of water cut off from the main river channel. By the time Red Moons collected enough wood for the night and started the fire, Two Bears had already caught enough fish in his net to feed them for days. He caught so many in the little pool that he threw some back in. They spent the evening talking, but Red Moons, having talked all day of buffalo, now started to listen to his grandfather tell stories of old. Two Bears told his grandson the legend of how the river had come to be in that place, how it had come to be filled with all the different kinds of fish. He told the story of how

O-Chi-Nok-Kuknuk had come to be. When the fullness of night had vanquished all remnants of the day, Two Bears unrolled his elk skin and covered up. Both the old man and the young boy slept soundly through the night. Birds started singing high up in the tree tops along the river-bank before the first hint of dawn appeared; and by the time the sky started to glow with the first rays of the morning sun Two Bears and Red Moons again headed north along the shallow waters and gravel bars.

This cycle endured through the entire trip. As the days passed and the distance from home increased Two Bears became more and more impressed with his grandson. And in those few days Red Moons gained a tremendous amount of respect for his grandfather, and he began to listen intently to every word and every story he told. The new-found respect did not go unnoticed with Two Bears either, he returned the respect by taking extra care to tell the old legends in as much detail and as accurately as he could, pausing to even add sound effects here and there where needed. Sometimes, when the day became too hot, or Two Bears' hip began to hurt they would take a break in the shade of the trees along the riverbank. Red Moons would always take the time to pick out a place comfortable for his grandfather, and he would run off to chase down some small game if he felt hungry. One day he brought back a rabbit for lunch and on another a large turtle.

On the 11th day Two Bears and his grandson came to the place of many rocks in the river. Two Bears knew from experience that this place provided the best and safest opportunity to cross the Great Spirit River. Both Two Bears and Red Moons used walking sticks to keep their balance among all the slippery rocks there and crossed without incident. On the other side of the river rose a steep bank that took Two Bears quite some time to climb. From the top of the bank the ground rose still farther to a rocky outcrop high above the land. After making the climb, both Two Bears and Red Moons sat on the edge of the rocky outcrop to rest and admire the incredible view. In front of them they could see the Great Spirit River in all of its glory stretching out across the landscape for miles to both the north and the south. When they turned to look the other direction, a huge expanse of prairie grass stretched out before them broken only by an occasional clump of ancient oak trees and rocky outcropping similar to the one they now sat on.

Two Bears picked out one of the three or four rocky knolls they saw in the distance and pointed to it. "That is First Hill" he said as he traced its outline with his finger in the air. "It is the first rock that our people climbed to view the land after the Creator put us here. It is there that our ancestors built our first village and from there we hunted buffalo for generations," he said.

Red Moons listened intently and tried to make a mental note of which hill it was. Two Bears and Red Moons then spent the rest of the afternoon walking from their rocky outcrop along the river to the one in the distance that Two Bears pointed out. At times the prairie grass grew so tall it prevented them from keeping an eye on the hill, but from instinct they managed to keep heading the right direction. In one place they came to a large swath of land where the prairie grasses looked trampled down by the buffalo, and Red Moons could again see the rocky outcrop where they headed and felt surprised at how large it appeared as they drew close to it.

Two Bears and Red Moons crossed the great northern prairies and savannah from rocky outcrop to rocky outcrop. In the evenings they camped by the rocks for shelter and during the day they waded through a sea of prairie grass. From each vantage point Two Bears pointed out the next one in their journey and told Red Moons its name and how it got its name. From each vantage point he used his finger to draw a line in the air of the outline of the next rock. For five suns they walked from outcrop to outcrop in this fashion. In all, they stopped at more than a dozen places that Two Bears named and talked about. Late on the day of the fifth sun they climbed yet another vantage point; and in the distance Two Bears pointed to yet another rocky looking hill. This time he smiled as he pointed and traced its outline in the air with his outstretched finger. "O-Chi-Nok-Kuknuk," he said. That night they camped at the sacred hill's base.

Two Bears stirred from half asleep when he heard the sound of Red Moons gathering more firewood. Red Moons felt so excited to finally arrive at the sacred hill that he could not sleep well and awoke earlier than usual. He saw only a handful of trees at the sacred hill, but Red Moons managed to supplement the morning fire with buffalo chips he found scattered about the creek that ran below the sacred hill. After a quick morning snack and a prayer offering to the gods, Two Bears began teaching Red Moons what to look for on the sacred hill and how to find the best material. After they quarried several large slabs of raw stone, he showed Red Moons the methods used to reduce them down to manageable sizes. Then he taught Red Moons the basics of percussion flaking and lastly the methods used to do the fine work along the edges and notches.

Two Bears and Red Moons spent all day, every day, working on lessons in crafting stone tools. For several days the old master passed on the tricks and tips he learned over many seasons from his father to his grandson. Two Bears watched with a careful eye as Red Moons began to make his first large blades. Two Bears offered advice and tips every step of the way. Two Bears also made a few blades, but as he did his hands began to ache and in the end he left much of the knapping work to his grandson. When Red Moons made a blade that looked a little too thick, Two Bears used his expert hands to fix Red Moons' mistakes and hand it back to him to finish. The two of them produced many finished points and knives as well as many blank pre-forms that could be finished into whatever tools they needed later on. The lessons continued until they had more stone points, knives, and blanks than they could carry. A number of them they buried by a large old oak tree upon Two Bears' advice.

"When we come back next time, we won't have to work so hard," he said. "Some of our work will already be done." He added as he covered the hole filled with blades back over. "But nobody needs to know this but us," he said when he finished. Two Bears wondered silently if there would be a next time for him to return. The aches in his hands, hips, and gray hair reminded him that, like the leaves on an oak in the fall, soon he would fall to the ground. Red Moons helped his grandfather stand up, and the two went about packing up for the return trip. Now Two Bears' large elk skin no longer contained a big bundle of venison, but instead a large bundle of fine points and blades. All together they would bring home more than 100 fine atl-atl points and even more knives and blanks.

The trip home unfolded more slowly because of their heavy load. Red Moons carried the heaviest part of the load for most of the trip; but still Two Bears tired easily. They seemed to stop more often on the way home than they had on the way there. Two Bears uttered the name of each outcrop along the prairies as they returned trying to firmly implant the names and route into young Red Moons' mind. At some of the outcrops Two Bears only climbed high enough to see where the next point was rather than expend the energy required to climb to the top of each one. It wasn't necessary to point out each outcropping to Red Moons because their trail through the prairie grasses was still visible enough for them to follow home. Getting back to the shallow gravel bars and water of the Great Spirit River brought some relief to both of them because the water allowed them to cool off more easily when it became hot in the afternoons, and it made finding food much easier as well.

Two Bears felt impressed with Red Moons' ability to produce a wonderful variety of food each and every night, "From river tubers to turtles and nuts and berries to clams and fish, each night one feasts when one travels with young Red Moons," Two Bears said.

As the days passed and the pair once again walked in familiar territory both of them seemed to slow their pace. Outwardly it was under the guise of Two Bears' age, but in reality both Two Bears and Red Moons felt somewhat saddened to approach the end to the adventure and felt reluctant to sleep again in their houses.

All of the family seemed happy and relieved to see Two Bears and Red Moons return home. Red Moons' father in particular looked pleased once Red Moons showed him all of the fine points and blades he made for him. It meant he would not need to make the long trip himself for at least another year or two if he took care with the tools. Two Bears gave one large and very fine knife to his wife and kept one for himself, then he made rounds about the small village and gave gifts of one or two nice knife blades to some of the widows and other elders so they would have an easier time as well. After he gave away many of his blades, he buried the remainder into small caches by his house. One he buried to the east and one on the west side.

For the next year and a half Two Bears would go to his caches and remove a blade only when he could no longer sharpen the previous one. When good hunting abounded and he managed to kill many deer and buffalo he went through knives quickly, but in the summer when he focused on gathering edibles and fishing, they lasted much longer. After a year and a half, however he again started to run low on stone knives and points. As winter approached, he decided to conserve his last blades whenever possible; and when the warm southern winds blew the winter away planned to again travel back to the sacred hill. He thought perhaps Red Moons might again accompany him.

Late that winter Two Bears felt anxious for the spring thaw so he could retrieve the last nice knife buried by his house. But the thaw didn't come in time for Two Bears. He developed a bad cold that settled in his lungs, and he grew gravely ill. As the first of the warm southern winds melted the snows, Two Bears died. The loss represented a significant tragedy to his family, but they recognized it as part of life. Two Bears lived longer than many and represented a store of wisdom they could not easily replace. Because many looked up to him and he acted as a patriarch for so long, members of his group gave him a special burial. They painted Two Bears red and wrapped him in elk skins. Red Moons and his father carried the frail old body and loaded it in a canoe and then they paddled upriver along with the rest of the village to the place of many stones. The spot served as a point where the trail to the sacred hill diverged from the river to the prairies; and Red Moons remembered it as the same place where Two Bears told him the story of how the sacred hill and river came to be.

High on top of the rocky outcrop which overlooked the river and the prairies they built a large pile of firewood. On it they laid the lifeless body of Two Bears and surrounded it with offerings of hides, berries, nuts, venison, bone needles, digging sticks, nets, and all of the other things he would need in the afterlife. They burned his body and the offerings high on the bluff there and tended the fire until it consumed everything and turned it to ash. All of the village members worked together to carry baskets full of dirt up the steep hill to cover over the ashes from the fire. As the years passed and Two Bears' son and grandson grew into old men, group members burned and buried them too in the same location, each time covering them over with more earth. Over the generations others were buried there as well, and in time nobody could even recite the name of the first person buried there in that way. Like Two Bears' name, that burial custom eventually faded from memory, but that mound still overlooks the river to this day.

Two Bears indeed lived a long and very good life, but he never retrieved that last stone knife from the cache by his house that spring. A little over 3,000 years later a farmer's plow wrestled loose that knife from its long resting place. When the spring rains came, they washed away the thick covering of dirt and exposed the silvery stone to the light for the first time since the day Two Bears buried it for safe keeping. Two friends looking for arrowheads in that same field found the unusually large and well-made knife. The friend who picked it up felt delighted to find such a treasure and noted how much better it looked than the small and used up knives they usually found in that area. One of the two friends decided that it must have served some great ceremonial importance to the owner while the other thought perhaps it represented nothing more than a knife maybe lost before its owner ever used it.

Chapter 3: Dancing Bear and the Sleeping Bear

Dancing Bear's timing seemed off that day. Up to that point in his life he made his winter house near the rest of his family. But earlier that spring both his mother and father fell ill and passed on to the next life. According to the custom, once the mother and father passed on, the children set out to make lives for themselves and raise their own families, free from responsibilities and care for their parents. In the past when he, his two brothers, mother, and father all worked together they always produced a surplus of food to put away for the winter. The only exception happened a few years earlier where Dancing Bear and his two brothers needed to do a little extra hunting to supplement the winter stockpile.

This year represented the first year Dancing Bear and his family would make their winter house far from the others. The further apart they settled, the easier it became to find game. Dancing Bear, in spite of 20 years' experience, found himself slightly nervous at spending his first winter alone with just his wife and daughter so far away from the others. Many things could go wrong, and he tried to prepare for them all. His biggest concern remained food, and he and his wife worked hard to put away as much as they could. Together they filled large clay jars with dried berries, nuts, acorns, and tubers. They gathered so many walnuts he needed to dig a storage pit in the floor of their house to store them all. The ceiling of their small house hung thick with dried venison, elk, and turkey as well as fish. The constant smoking from the fire preserved the meat.

Despite all of his hard work preparing he found himself caught completely off guard by the severity of the winter when it came. Dancing Bear awoke in the middle of the night to the sound of the cold northern winds blowing. The trees cracked and small branches broke and fell to the ground in the nearby forest. The wind plucked the last of the fall leaves from the trees, and they, combined with millions of others, whipped about the forest floor before settling around Dancing Bear's house. That night the snow began to fall a full month earlier than ever before, and it didn't let up for days. Dancing Bear understood hunting in the snow; in fact, he found it the best time of year to hunt because animals left tracks he could see more easily. But the bitter cold made the snow thin and wispy. When the snow blew in wisps, tracks filled quickly with snow eliminating the normal advantage it provided. And when the wind blew it caused nearly whiteout conditions. On top of the other disadvantages of wispy snow, it became exceptionally difficult to hike through. Dancing Bear had a fine pair of snowshoes that he wore to stay on top of the snow, but the wispy snow didn't support his weight even with his snowshoes. The bitter cold, wispy snow and high winds all combined together to force Dancing Bear to stay inside the safety of his winter house most of the time. Worse yet, they had no choice but to start eating the winter's food supply much earlier than normal.

Despite the exceptionally harsh conditions Dancing Bear and his family tried to maintain an optimistic attitude. Each day, at least once a day, Dancing Bear dressed up in all of his winter clothing and went out hunting. He felt lucky one day to find a rabbit frozen to death outside its borough for some unknown reason; and he managed to find and kill a hibernating raccoon in an old hollow log, but other than that he met with little success. Most years he and his family relied heavily on the good winter hunting and only supplemented it with the stored winter foods, but this year it quickly became the opposite, and they were forced to eat the stored winter foods and only supplement those with Dancing Bear's occasional hunting success. As the days passed, the winter stores dwindled quickly. The snows continued to pile up, and before long Dancing Bear found himself tying extra pine boughs to his snowshoes just to walk short distances from his house. The worse the conditions became, and the longer the winter went on, the more Dancing Bear grew obsessed with his winter stick.

The winter stick represented a trick his father taught him. He carved a single hash mark into the stick the first day it snowed in earnest, and then one mark for each day thereafter. By counting the marks on the winter stick he could accurately predict how much longer the winter would last and could predict the first thaws of spring well in advance of any hint from the weather. Now, by the dim light of a small fire, he counted the hash marks repeatedly, obsessively.

He spent hours considering the amount of the various winter stocks that remained against the number of marks on the winter stick and against the number of marks he thought he might still add. No matter how many times he made the comparison the results came out the same, they would run out of food well before the spring thaw. Dancing Bear did not utter a word about the stick or their food stores to his wife, but she no doubt shared his worries. She could see by the look on his face and the constant shifting of his eyes from the winter stick to the dried meats hanging from the ceiling that she had reasonable cause for concern.

Days started to drag on and seemed to double in length; nights dragged even worse. At one point, not even halfway through the winter, Dancing Bear suggested they start to ration the remaining food supplies. He also renewed his efforts at hunting but found no success at all. Days turned to weeks and Dancing Bear, his wife and his daughter, all spent as much time sleeping as they could to conserve energy and help them deal with the gnawing hunger and boredom that was quickly consuming them all.

Depression set in and Dancing Bear knew he needed to find food, or they might all starve to death. He tried again to hunt, but he found the colder than average winter made it impossible for him to stay out as long or travel as far because he quickly grew tired. One day, upon returning home from another unsuccessful hunt and letting his eyes adjust from the blinding white of the winter back to the dark confines of his wood and bark house, he noticed his wife's and daughter's faces appeared gaunt and showed clear physical signs of starvation.

He lay awake all through the long night thinking and again counting the hash marks on the winter stick. He considered food sources he would not normally consider in the dead of winter. He knew where he could find a large patch of wild plants that produced many starchy-sweet tubers, but they lay all frozen solid in the ground now, and their location involved a considerable hike; so he abandoned the idea. He thought about fishing along the Great Spirit River, but the frozen surface offered no easy place to set up his nets. He thought perhaps the rapids far down the river to the south might still remain open and fishable, so he decided to go there, despite the long distance. If all went well, he might bring many fish home to fill their stomachs for another week or two.

He told his wife and daughter of his plan when they woke; and though they knew the trip presented potential danger, they greeted the idea with enthusiasm, placing their trust in Dancing Bear. That evening Dancing Bear instructed his wife and daughter to prepare a meal with no rationing, a full meal that would fill them all. He would need the energy for the trip, and it would go a long way toward lifting all their spirits as well.

Early the next morning Dancing Bear dressed up in all of his winter clothing. Around the outside of his winter robes, he cinched a belt tight; inside it he tucked a hunting knife. On his feet he tied extra pine boughs, and along with his fish net he gathered his atl-atl and a bag full of points for it. His wife prepared a small bag of nuts and jerky to take with him, but he declined, insisting it stay there with them in case he should not return—a thought that caused his young daughter to cry. Dancing Bear's wife hushed the child and recited a prayer as Dancing Bear left the dark confines of the winter house and stepped out into the blinding brightness of a winter morning. He noted that the sun shone and the wind had died down which relieved him considerably. He would at least manage to travel a while without the constant beating of a cold and vengeful winter spirit upon his back.

Dancing Bear headed straight south following the Great Spirit River in places and cutting across land where it offered a shorter and more direct route. The place he headed contained many rocks and falls in the river, he thought that it might offer a chance to fish, but he also remembered the many ravines carved deep into the land just north of the falls. He wondered if any of the deer, elk or bear that normally roamed these forests might seek refuge there through this long and harsh winter.

He continued south all day; and when the short winter day gave its first hint of darkness he stopped and started to break off pine boughs before placing them in a big pile. When he had a heaping pile of them in a sheltered spot by a giant white pine he climbed inside of the mound and quickly fell fast asleep.

Dancing Bear awoke before full light. The picture of his wife and daughter huddled together in the relative darkness, eyes sinking into their faces with hunger, now pushed him to move on in spite of his tiredness and hunger, or the cold. When he crawled out from his pine bough shelter, he found the bitter cold had returned. With no other choice, he simply moved on, trudging through the snow southward. At mid-day he came across a slight gully in the terrain. He knew from years gone by in his childhood that this gully headed toward the Great Spirit River, and with each footstep it cut deeper into the land. By the time it spilled out into the Great Spirit River hundred-foot sandstone canyon walls towered on either side.

He paused there in the freezing snow to remember a summer he knew as a young boy in which his family stayed in that gully all summer. His dad experienced great success fishing, and he loved how the deep gully stayed cool and comfortable, even on the hottest of days. A brief smile broke out on his face, but quickly faded as his wind dried lips threatened to crack. He again wondered if animals might take shelter in the deep gully in the winter not at all unlike how he and his family had in the heat of the summer. He stood there a long while. He knew the falls and fishing offered his best chance for food, but on the other hand he knew that taking the gully way would carry him out of the wind; and he knew an off chance existed that he might find a herd of deer or elk down deep enough in the ravine where it couldn't get out, and he might slay one. After several more minutes he decided to check the gully for game, he would still have time to make it to the falls and fish if he had no luck.

He changed course and started to follow the shallow

gully west as it slowly sank into the landscape. Not far into his trip down the gully he crossed deer tracks. He did not choose to follow them because the tracks looked old, and he thought the deer were likely miles away by now. But it renewed his spirits just the same and made him more hopeful about what he might find deeper in the gully. As the gully slowly transformed into a canyon with ever increasingly impressive walls on either side of him, he slowed, looking all over for any sign of game, but found none. When the Great Spirit River came into view up ahead and it became clear that the gully held no game, his heart sank heavy in his chest. He walked all the way out to where the gully emptied into the river and found ice well-formed far out into the river, but not entirely across it. He found the ice too thick to break up and fish through and too thin to trust walking on. His head lowered; he silently said a prayer that death might find him swiftly. He turned around to head back up the gully to the highland before continuing south, but the tiniest thing caught his attention from the corner of his eye.

Halfway up the steep sandstone gully wall a bit of movement caused him to stop and look. He froze, completely motionless and stared at the area where he thought he detected movement. Then he saw it again, it was the smallest wisp of steam. He sat there a long time staring and watching as every minute or so a tiny wisp of warm mist turned visible in the cold winter air. Finally he realized that somebody, or something, rested on the sandstone ledge above him just out of view. Not knowing what rested there his heart beat faster. He moved cautiously to rid himself of his extra baggage. The snow in the gully remained fairly shallow, and his snowshoes hung lashed to his back where he placed them some time ago. Now he carefully removed his snowshoes and his outside robe. He also temporarily discarded his atl-atl and took only his knife as he slowly climbed the steep sandstone slope. He did not have to climb far before he found himself standing at the entrance to an overhang, a bit of a cave really which sank far back into the wall face. From this dark void in the sandstone, he saw the occasional wisp of warm breath coming out to meet its frozen end. All at once it dawned on him, a hibernating bear!

He paused only briefly before working his way carefully over toward the little cave. He proceeded with intense care because the thin layer of snow remained wet down in the gully, and it made the stone there quite slippery. Twice he nearly slipped on the steep slope before reaching the ledge by the little cave. He peered into the darkness but found it difficult to see. He concentrated to focus out the noise made from the wind and birds in the distance, and tried instead to listen more carefully for sound under the ledge but heard nothing. He inched closer, allowing his head and shoulders to enter the small space as far as he dared. With his head and shoulders blocking most of the light his eyes slowly adjusted, and as they did the large black heap in the back of the cave took the shape of a bear. He felt as though the noise from his pounding heart might betray his presence at any moment as he slowly backed away from the confined opening. He made his way back down the slippery wet stone wall with difficulty because his legs and hands shook with adrenaline.

He sighed with relief when he reached the flat ground of the gully floor again, and there he pondered his next move. The cave provided no room for him to throw his atl-atl. He briefly considered throwing darts at the bear from the gully floor but knew the angle made it all but impossible to hit the bear. His still pounding heart and shaking legs told him to just go fishing, but he stood fast with images of his wife and daughter firmly entrenched in his mind. He took long, slow, and deep breaths of the cold winter air in an attempt to calm himself. He perspired heavily beneath his winter clothing, so he removed one of his several shirts. Next, he weighed his odds of success if he simply climbed up there, crawled into the cave, and slit the bear's throat. But he abandoned that idea before it completely formed.

He finally decided crawling into the overhang and stabbing the sleeping bear with one of his atl-atl darts provided his best choice because it kept him at least a short distance away from the bear, but also ensured a direct hit. When he picked up one of his atl-atl darts he realized the six-foot shaft felt much too thin and flexible for him to use in such a fashion. The design worked best when thrown like a giant arrow, not used as a traditional spear. Eventually he settled on the stabbing idea but decided he simply must make a spear just for that purpose.

Dancing Bear climbed partially back up the gully to find a piece of wood suitable for the task. He worked on the spear for quite some time before finishing and lashing his sharp hunting knife to the end of it. The short winter day already showed signs of retreating in the deep gully as Dancing Bear started to make his way back up the slippery slope. Even before he reached the little cave his heart and shaking legs doubled their attempts to derail his resolve. Dancing Bear mustered every last shred of courage he could as he again slipped under the overhang just far enough for his eyes to adjust to the darkness.

Once the outline of the bear became clearly defined he moved his makeshift spear into position and aimed it at a spot just barely behind the front shoulder blade where he knew he could hit not only both lungs, but also the heart, giving him the best chance at killing the beast humanely and quickly, but also the best chance of doing it without becoming a victim. Once he aligned his spear satisfactorily, he inched his way back to a position as far out as he could, yet still retain his ability to deliver a killing blow with the spear. He again fought to control his breathing and his heart rate before closing his eyes just long enough to say a prayer to the creator. His mind briefly flashed back to his wife and daughter before he thrust the spear forward with every bit of strength he could muster and screamed a primal call. As soon as he felt the stone knife plunge through the bear and hit the stone wall behind it he retreated. Halfway down he slipped and rolled down the rest of the way badly bruising his side along the way but not even realizing it until much later.

When he stood up at the bottom of the gully, he instinctively reached for the knife that he usually kept tucked in his belt but felt only the sheath hanging there. His eyes opened wide when he saw the handle end of the spear poke out over the little ledge that concealed the bear's winter den. He watched in horror as it moved farther out until the bear too emerged and focused its gaze on Dancing Bear. Dancing Bear reached for his atl-atl but struggled to find it because he could not take his eyes off of the now enraged bear. Panic nearly overtook him as he watched the bear, with spear protruding from its side, start to try and climb down the stone ledge to come and take revenge. The bear took only two or three lazy steps however before slipping and tumbling down the steep stone walls throwing blood out in wide spattering arcs as it crashed to the gully floor. Dancing Bear's legs gave out from under him, and he plopped down to a sitting position on the gully floor. His head spun as though he might fall asleep, but he did not.

Dancing Bear sat there for several minutes staring at the heaping black mass just a few yards from him as well as the growing pool of dark red blood that gathered by its side. When he stood up he felt as though he no longer had weight, as though he could float over to the bear. He checked twice to make sure the bear no longer lived. The bear was indeed dead. He pulled the broken spear from the bear's side and started to untie the lashings that kept the knife attached. He found the tip broken slightly, probably from impacting the back of the cave wall, but the damage did not distract him from the task now at hand. He immediately began to build a fire on the gully floor and went about butchering the bear. He used his knife expertly to make quick work of removing the skin and organs. He started to quarter the bear up as he cooked a portion of the heart and liver on a stick over the fire. When he finished butchering the bear, he wrapped all of the meat, the rest of the liver and heart, and one of the bear's paws in its own hide and tied it shut tightly using his fishing net to hold it all together.

Before he ate, he offered prayers of thanks for his good fortune. The freshly roasted flesh tasted better than anything he could remember eating in all his life. After he ate, he went about making a temporary shelter for the night though he didn't put as much time or effort into it as usual because the temperature down in the gully felt nowhere near as bad as it had up in the forest. He found it difficult to sleep with such a prize in his possession. He felt like he wanted to run rather than walk back to his wife and child. He dozed off for a short while, but rose, packed up and headed back out of the gully toward his waiting family before daylight the next day. He made a crude sled from two saplings and lashed his black bear package to it. He found it easier to pull the bear meat attached to the makeshift sled than to carry it all the way home. He didn't realize it at the time, but he had inadvertently left his knife lying on the rocks beside where he butchered the bear. In all of his excitement, he simply forgot to pick it up.

He found the weather no more favorable than when he headed south, but with a full belly and high spirits he made much better time going home just the same. He followed his same trail through the snow which also made things much easier. He didn't even need to spend a night in the forest because by nightfall he found himself within ear shot of his home. When he came close enough to know his wife and daughter could hear him, he started to sing an old hunter's song that his father used to always sing when he returned from a successful hunt. His face felt numb from cold, but he continued in high spirits knowing that he would have plenty of good bear grease to sooth his face and lips later. From inside the house, he heard shrill calls of joy, the same as his mother would make when she heard his dad return home after a successful hunt.

Tears greeted him all around as he entered his home carrying the big black bundle of fur.

"A bear!" his wife exclaimed. They all sat down for a meal, and Dancing Bear reached for his knife in his belt so that he could cut the heart and liver into pieces to share with his wife and daughter. Then he realized, feeling the empty sheath, that he left the knife lying in the gully where he butchered the bear. While not a big deal, because he had more knives, he still felt sorry because now he believed the knife to possess a special luck of some sort. He decided when summer came, he would take his wife and daughter to the gully to show them where he found the bear and to retrieve the lucky knife.

The huge haul of bear meat, along with the remaining food stocks, ensured Dancing Bear and his family would survive the winter. When spring finally broke, he along with his wife and daughter traveled back to the traditional meeting place where the rest of the family came together each spring. There he learned several members of his extended family had passed away from starvation or illness over the long winter. During such a harsh winter food proved hard to come by for others as well, and the elders of the group decided they should collectively move north along the Great Spirit River to the area where the white pines grew thick. These pines offered substantial protection in even the worst of winters. The people found elk and beaver plentiful in the forest. Dancing Bear, as well as his family, went on to live long and happy lives, never again facing such a hard and cruel winter, but Dancing Bear never did go back to get his knife.

That knife stayed there on the gully floor for thousands of years. Leaves and soil covered it up, sometimes for hundreds of years at a time, and sometimes, heavy rains would flush the gully out again exposing the stone knife to the sun. Sometimes for hundreds of years it remained exposed just beneath the leaves. The cycle repeated itself until 2012 when a father went hiking down that same gully showing his young daughter the beauty of nature. During that hike he noticed the stone knife lying partially exposed in the sand and rocks. Picking it up he examined it and noticed the tip looked broken, and he wondered if someone discarded it because of the damage.

His daughter found the knife interesting as well, and asked him, "Dad, do you think that Indian had a daughter to?" Her voice echoed in the gully.

"I don't know hon, he sure could've had a daughter, but I doubt she looked as beautiful as you," he said with a smile. She laughed out loud, and the father daughter duo continued their hike.

Chapter 4: Running-Elk and the Forgotten Boy

Running-Elk's mother gave birth to him on the Oak Savannah. To the north, the savannah soon gave way to the thick northern forests and the lands to the south thinned out and turned into vast expanses of prairie. Here in this middle ground between the thick forests of the north and the broad prairies of the south Running-Elk and his people thrived on a rich variety of wildlife for countless generations. His people remained a proud and successful people, and from birth Running-Elk became part of the prestigious Eagle Clan. Like his father, he expected to one day gain acceptance into the tribal council among the other elder warriors of the Eagle Clan. Now, in Running-Elk's 20th year, a new and terrible enemy emerged from the great northern forests.

They spoke a different language and painted their faces black with charcoal. They made no attempt at smoking the sacred peace pipe with the Eagle Clan, and they did not come bearing gifts or trade items as custom dictated. They brought only violence and death and threatened the very domain Running-Elk's people had controlled without challenge for countless generations. The year before, Running-Elk heard whispers of a strange and new people from some neighboring tribes to the east, but now the Black-Faced Ones made their presence known to all. They came at night with no warning. Running-Elk awoke to the sound of a woman screaming and chaos ensued. They came on a moonless night and killed five warriors and took three women with them including Running-Elk's aunt.

The morning light revealed the severed head of one of the elders and they found another elder impaled on a wooden spike used for stretching hides at the edge of camp. Running-Elk and his people had experienced war with others before, but never with a foe so savage and ruthless. Two days later the Black-Faced Ones struck again ambushing a hunting party of six, killing five.

After the second attack, the elders called a council meeting. All of the elders from the various clans gathered in the great lodge to share in the sacred pipe and make plans for defense and retribution. All of the young warriors from the Eagle Clan gathered outside the great lodge, most of them spoke in hushed but excited tones about the war party sure to come. Running-Elk did not feel as excited as many of the other warriors of his clan. His people had not fought a war since he was a very young child and he had not known war growing up. His role in the Eagle Clan had been largely symbolic and ceremonial up until that point, and he knew that was about to change. He secretly favored peace, but because he found himself the eldest son of one of the most respected warriors in the entire village, he could say nothing and tell no one how he truly felt.

The elders stayed in discussion for what seemed a very long while. By the time they emerged from the great lodge most of the village had gathered to hear their decision. Running-Elk, stood at some distance from the others and could not hear the announcement directly. But other members of his Eagle Clan shouted shrill war calls and he gathered the cries meant war.

His father found Running-Elk among the mass of people and explained, "We will send a war party out with the start of the new moon in three days. Older more experienced warriors will stay behind to defend our village. Elders nominated you to lead the war party, Running-Elk."

Running-Elk's face remained as emotionless as his father's. Running-Elk's father then handed him a full quiver of some of his best arrows.

"Thank you, father," Running-Elk murmured. The elders choosing him to lead a war party came as a great honor to Running-Elk. He and all the others knew it signaled his rise through the ranks.

The next couple of days Running-Elk fasted and meditated. A few of the young ladies tried flirting with Running-Elk now that they knew the elders had chosen him to head the war party, but he would have none of it. He remained focused exclusively on the Black-Faced Ones and their actions. He prayed for the men they killed, and he prayed for the women they took captive. Hour by hour he replaced the feelings of hesitation and indifference with a seething rage and anger. The day before the war party planned to leave Running-Elk made red and white war paint and restrung his favorite bow with a new and stronger string.

When the time came, Running-Elk lead a band of young warriors that numbered more than 50 away from the village and headed north. After the last attack, scouts followed the Black-Faced Ones' trail far to the north and east, and Running-Elk took the war party that direction to search for them. Through their actions they must make these invaders understand they could not push Running-Elk's tribe around. They could not push them from their lands nor could they capture or kill their women without consequences. As they left the outer edges of the village each warrior said a single word out loud, "Hok-nota-shu" which meant revenge.

Running-Elk took his war party north along the banks of the river until they came to the first of several large feeder creeks. On the opposite bank, in the tall grass, they could still see the old trail of the black faced intruders. So, they all crossed at the same point and continued north. A few miles farther up the river, the party came to a second feeder creek, this one they called Cranberry Creek. Here, in spite of searching long and hard, they found no tracks on the opposite bank, and so Running-Elk made the decision to follow that stream farther inland to the east.

He had hunted these lands for many years and knew the headwaters of Cranberry Creek originated in a large marshland rich with wildlife. Sometimes he and his family made winter camps there on some of the many little hills that dotted the marsh. Several miles farther east they started to see fresh tracks in and around the creek. In one area they could see where somebody recently dug clams from the creek. To draw closer to their enemy without detection they slowed down to a crawl and listened intently in all directions. They found it imperative to surprise their enemy to avoid allowing them time to prepare and to also strike fear in the heart of the Black-Faced Ones as they had done to them.

Suddenly, up the creek a way, Running-Elk heard sounds of people talking and splashing. He signaled for the rest of the war party to remain still and quiet while he snuck ever so slowly forward to investigate. He knocked an arrow on the bow string and carefully crept farther forward still. Up ahead he found two boys speaking the Black-Faced Ones' language and spearing frogs. He watched them for a minute and noted they did not appear the offspring of some ferocious animal as some said, but rather the same as many boys in his own village. Both boys appeared perhaps nine or 10 years old, not yet old enough to serve as warriors, but that time would soon come.

Running-Elk slowly drew back his bow and took aim at the larger of the two boys. Just as his fingers loosened ready to let his arrow fly, a third boy, Running-Elk had not noticed up on the creek bank, let out a warning call to his friends. Both boys turned and looked at their friend, and Running-Elk released his arrow. Two of the boys turned and ran, but the one that Running-Elk took aim on paused, momentarily, just long enough for Running-Elk's arrow to catch him directly in the chest.

The boy looked down at the arrow now protruding from his chest in wide-eyed bewilderment as if he could not believe what his eyes told him. The boy stumbled forward two steps before his knees buckled, and he fell into the creek. Running-Elk let out a shrill war call and the rest of his war party came running forward.

Running-Elk paused by the boy he killed and grasped the arrow sticking out of the boy's chest and pulled. The shaft of the arrow came out, but the arrowhead caught on bone and remained inside the boy's chest. Running-Elk threw down the now useless arrow shaft disgusted before running up the steep creek bank with the rest of the warriors.

All of the warriors stopped dead in their tracks as they crested the creek bank and came upon the shocking view now stretched out in front of them. Where once stood only forest now spread grand fields of raised beds filled with corn, squash, and beans. The fields looked unlike anything any of them had ever seen before. Running-Elk and some of the others vaguely knew about corn, but elders forbade them to plant gardens like these because they said such efforts belonged to lazy hunter's. The warriors all stood in disbelief, shocked at the diversity and scale of the fields. They watched as the two surviving boys ran to a large imposing structure in the center of the fields. Like the garden beds, none of Running-Elk's men had ever seen anything like what they now gazed upon. In the center of the fields an enormous wooden structure stood. It looked like trees had grown tightly together to form a large, perfect circle. Each tree appeared pointed and sharpened at the top. From inside this massive fortification a visible cloud of smoke drifted up indicating a large number of hearths inside.

Running-Elk felt he could not allow the other warriors to hesitate and so let out another war call and started to run toward this strange structure in the center of the fields. As he ran, he purposely pulled corn up and trampled the crops. When he looked over his shoulder, he could see the rest of the young warriors following suit and leaving a wake of destruction through the gardens. Running-Elk turned his attention back to the imposing structure and started to look for the entrance as he neared it. Without warning he heard a "whoosh" sound fly by his head. Moments later he heard another. When he looked up, he understood why. From on top of the pointed trees Black-Faced Ones shot arrows down on the war party. He desperately looked for a doorway to the inside but found none. With arrows flying all around him he started to retreat. As he retreated, he tried to gather his warriors to do the same but found the decision came too late. Many of the younger and most ambitious warriors, eager to prove themselves, ran up to the base of the wooden walls and started to shoot their arrows up at the Black-Faced Ones. Running-Elk lost several of his warriors in this fashion before he managed to pull the rest of them back toward the creek and out of range of the Black-Faced Ones' bows.

Running-Elk then found himself surrounded by the remaining warriors all looking to him for direction and leadership. Frustrated and needing time to think, he instructed his men to pull up all of the Black-Faced Ones' crops that they could without bringing themselves within range of their bows. While he watched them go about the destruction of their fields he came up with a plan. After the crops were cut he had his men start peeling strips of bark from the white pine trees that lined the creek and instructed others to build bonfires. By nightfall the warriors had peeled the bark from the branches of a large number of pine branches and the branches oozed copious amounts of sap. Running-Elk took one of his arrows to one of the pine branches and covered it in sap. "When night falls, we will light our arrows and burn down their house of wood," he said. Several of them let out shrill war calls; and all of them copied Running-Elk by covering their arrows with as much of the oozing sap as they could.

When darkness fell completely, they moved forward with torches and bows in hand. All around the fort they launched their flaming arrows in high arching shots that mostly landed inside the wooden walls. Some stuck in the walls in places and started to burn in a couple of spots. They could hear screams and yelling from inside. The Black-Faced Ones shot back at the points of light all around them in the darkness and struck several more of Running-Elk's warriors. When Running-Elk and his men had shot all of their arrows into the wooden fort they retreated back into the darkness of the creek bottom and started to work their way down stream toward home. He had left home with 52 warriors and returned now with 42 and no enemy scalps to show for their efforts.

Upon returning home early the next morning many of the older warriors greeted them with war calls, but those calls soon mixed with calls of sorrow and grief as families found out that not all of the young men returned. Running-Elk quickly went into the sacred lodge, and the elders asked about his serious losses and the outcome of his raid. After he explained it all in great detail the elder warriors seemed to understand but seemed rather suspicious of Running-Elk's description because none of them had ever seen anything like what he described. Upon exiting the sacred lodge, elders declared Running-Elk's raid a great success, and the village as a whole celebrated the raid.

While Running-Elk's people undertook preparations for a feast in his honor, the Black-Faced Ones inspected the damage from the previous night's attack. They had been lucky because, unknown to Running-Elk, most of the Black Faced warriors had been out on a raid of their own when Running-Elk's group attacked. Had all the warriors remained at the village, they likely could have overwhelmed Running-Elk and his men. In the end, the damage to the fort combined with the loss of nearly all of their crops forced the Black-Faced Ones to pack up and move back to their grand village several days walk to the north and east.

After a few days passed one of the young warriors who accompanied Running-Elk went back, at the direction of the elders, to scout the scene. He found the Black-Faced Ones gone and that they left their fort and garden beds in ruin. News of his report caused yet another celebration to break out in Running-Elk's village, and elders again declared him a strong warrior and protector of his people. Running-Elk did not feel like a victor, but upon hearing that the Black-Faced Ones had moved he felt considerably better. In a solemn ceremony a few days later elders accepted Running-Elk as a full member of the sacred lodge and gave him a seat among them and the elite warriors of his people, but the success was short lived.

The following year the Black-Faced Ones returned to the area in even greater numbers and over the course of the summer they raided, killed, or captured many of Running-Elk's people. Two years later a small and dejected group of survivors packed up and left their traditional hunting grounds in the Oak Savannah and headed out into the vastness of the prairies in hopes of escaping the wrath of the Black Faced people. Running-Elk eventually starved to death during the winter. He and his people were lost in the vastness of the distant, strange prairies where once they only visited.

More than 680 years later a farmer's son found an arrowhead lying on a gravel bar in the creek that ran behind his father's barn. The arrowhead was the one Running-Elk shot into the boy's chest. The Black-Faced Ones packed up and left, never finding the boy. His flesh and bones soon lay scattered by animals and weather, but the arrowhead eventually pulled free in his chest and remained in the creek. The farmer held the point in his hand and remarked how it looked similar to the ones they usually found in the big potato field just east of the barn along the creek.

Chapter 5: He-Who-Speaks-To-Trees

He-Who-Speaks-To-Trees first saw daylight while his family traveled on one of their seasonal moves. They left their fall camp far in the east and ventured halfway to their winter camp in the rich lowlands of the west. They stopped to make camp for the night on a small knoll above a quiet spring-fed creek. The skies gave no warning that day of the violent storm to hit that night. It caught every-one off guard as it came much too late in the season for this kind of weather. He-Who-Speaks-To-Trees' mother gave birth in the middle of the storm; her cries of pain drowned out by the howling winds that blew their way through the forests.

When the morning light finally succeeded in pushing the darkness of the sky away, everyone found the forest devastated. The wind knocked trees flat on both sides of their temporary camp. Only the trees around the little wig-wam in which He-Who-Speaks-To-Trees drew first breath remained standing. For nearly as far as they could see to the east and to the west the forest lay flattened, and so in this way he got his name. From the very beginning his people knew him as a medicine man for clearly, he had a strong spiritual connection with the forest which kept him safe.

When He-Who-Speaks-To-Trees turned 10 years old his family sent him to live with his uncle, Speaking-Turtle, to learn the ways of a medicine man. Speaking-Turtle pos-sessed a great deal of patience and seemed happy to have somebody to pass his knowledge along to. Every day they took long walks together through the forests, the creek bottoms, the marshes, and even the dry sandy areas to north and west. Each area flourished with its own unique set of resources and Speaking-Turtle pointed out the useful parts of the plants found in all these areas. As the seasons changed so did the plants available.

When the winter winds came, Speaking-Turtle gave lessons in how to make the various plants into medicines, salves, poultices, and even medicinal soups used to treat everything from the common cold to severe infections. He-Who-Speaks-To-Trees learned fast but, none the less, the lessons continued, season after season and year after year. After Speaking-Turtle taught him every single thing he knew, he declared the now 16-year-old He-Who-Speaks-To-Trees ready to serve as medicine man all on his own.

Speaking-Turtle prepared a medicine bag for his nephew that contained all the basic tools he would need before sending him back to his home village. He-Who-Speaks-To-Trees returned home to a lavish feast of beaver stew, nuts, tubers and maple syrup. Things went well for He-Who-Speaks-To-Trees. He spent several years treating close friends and family when they fell ill or developed some other problem a medicine man could help with. He helped many sick people regain their health and slowly, over time, built up a reputation for himself as one of the most skilled medicine men in the whole region. As the seasons rolled on and his reputation spread, people sometimes traveled great distances to seek his help, often bringing him exotic gifts from afar to coax him into helping them. He-Who-Speaks-To-Trees and his family enjoyed many good years in the lands between the Great Spirit River and the lowlands.

Early one spring, when He-Who-Speaks-To-Trees was in his 50th summer, a messenger from the east came with an urgent message for him. The messenger, while still out of breath, explained that many people of the great Sau-nee nation had fallen ill in recent days with some strange spotted sickness. He explained there were so many sick that they could not all make the trip, and he came instead to retrieve the best medicine man in the entire region. Up until that point He-Who-Speaks-To-Trees never felt afraid, but now, with a sickness that could make an entire people sick, he started to worry. He agreed that he indeed needed to go to his neighbor's side and try to help the Sau-nee, but he needed to make a spirit quest first. The messenger thanked He-Who-Speaks-To-Trees and departed a moment later in the direction from which he came.

Spirit quests were reserved for only the most serious of situations, and He-Who-Speaks-To-Trees believed this situation demanded a spirit quest. Prior to this time, he had only gone on a handful of quests, and he didn't care for the process. But it always led him in the right direction, and he felt no reason to believe that such a quest would not provide insight this time as well. Early that morning He-Who-Speaks-To-Trees traveled deep into the forest and found the vision quest mushrooms and picked leaves from the vision quest plant. He took the mixture to a place called "Sitting Rabbit" bluff and sat down on a small rock platform high above the surrounding landscape. He ate all of the sacred mushrooms and vision quest plant leaves. He remained there praying for three days.

The first spirit he visited appeared in the form of his great grandfather, Little Bear. Little Bear, however, did not behave as his usual calm self but instead looked nervous and worried. Little Bear said nothing but made He-Who-Speaks-To-Trees feel uneasy. Next, He-Who-Speaks-To-Trees visited with the turtle spirit famous for his great wisdom. But when he approached the turtle he refused to come out of his shell for fear of catching the spotted sickness. Lastly, he went to visit the spirit known as Teywa-

Tewa, Teywa-Tewa was the spirit guide who guided people between this world and the next. When they came to the ancient burial grounds, they found many fresh graves and many more people walking around the graves with spotted sickness. He-Who-Speaks-To-Trees became very afraid, and he continued to pray for guidance, but none came. On the dawn of the third day, he left the place known as Sitting Rabbit and returned home to prepare for his trip.

The people of his small village asked him what news his spirit quest had brought him, but He-Who-Speaks-To-Trees would say nothing of what he had seen and instead packed his medicines and tools in silence. He wrapped all of his most powerful medicines into a bag and took a blanket with him because the trip to the Sau-nee people's village took several days. As soon as he was packed, he left for the Sau-nee village. He continued to pray the ancient prayers all the while he traveled.

Even before he entered the Sau-nee village the air smelled thick with death. No children ran around the wigwams playing, and he heard none of the usual sounds associated with village life. When he entered the village, a single lonely dog barked at him. He picked a wigwam at random and called inside but got no response. When he pulled the door cover open, he found the house filled with death, and he stumbled as he backed up. In the next house he found a young man and woman lying together on their bed, the woman already dead, but the young man still hung on. Both of them showed signs of the spotted sickness the messenger spoke of.

He-Who-Speaks-To-Trees immediately went to work saying prayers above the man and forcing him to take strong medicine. Within an hour of He-Who-Speaks-To-Trees' arrival, the man died. He-Who-Speaks-To-Trees continued to go from wigwam to wigwam seeking, and finding, those still alive. In spite of his best efforts, he could not manage to save any of the Sau-nee. He found one boy in the village that did not catch the sickness, and He-Who-Speaks-To-Trees questioned the boy in an effort to find out what he had done differently, or if perhaps he possessed some medicine of his own, but the boy offered no clue. He-Who-Speaks-To-Trees went on to the next Sau-nee village and found the same conditions there; again he did not manage to save any of the people.

He-Who-Speaks-To-Trees went from village to village and along the way fell into deep despair. For the first time in his long life, he completely failed. He wondered if the spirits somehow stripped him of his medicine. Eventually he made his way back to his own village where several people immediately came up to him excited for news, fully expecting to hear of his success. But the look on his face and his silence soon gave away what really happened. The next day one person from He-Who-Speaks-To-Tree's village fell ill with the spotted sickness. When they called He-Who-Speaks- To-Trees to treat the sick person he did not take any medicine but rather only took his pipe which he smoked with the sick person and said the prayers usually reserved for funerals. The next morning, He-Who-Speaks-To-Trees awoke feeling warm and with the first hints of spots on his arms and chest. He knew that his days now numbered less than the fingers on one hand.

He-Who-Speaks-To-Trees quietly gathered up his medicine bundle, a blanket, and a knife. He left the village without saying a word to anybody and without saying goodbye. He slowly made his way to a place he had not visited since childhood. He and his parents once made a camp one summer on a high grassy knoll above the Great Spirit River. He-Who-Speaks-To-Trees always wanted to return to the place because he held fond memories of it.

Now he found himself once again in that special place, and he laid out a blanket in the shade of an old oak tree there. He began to slowly cut his arms in long deep cuts, he let the blood fall to the earth there, and he prayed that his blood might satisfy the angry spirits who killed so many. He prayed that at least his clan, his people, might escape the sickness by this sacrifice. An hour later He-Who-Speaks-To-Trees drifted off to eternal sleep.

He passed from this world to the next without ever knowing what happened to his beloved people and it was probably a good thing. In the days and weeks that followed He-Who-Speaks-to-Trees' spotted sickness spread throughout the land and soon sent nearly all of his people to the afterlife like so many from other clans. Over 400 years later an old man out looking for arrowheads on that little knoll high above the river found He-Who-Speaks-to-Trees' knife that he used to take his own life. The man paused, turning the stone knife over in his hand, studying its style and craftsmanship on one side, and then the other. He held it tight in his hand as he stood back upright; he gazed down at the river and wondered about the knife's prior owner.

Chapter 6: Dark Days

People knew Sharp-Knife far and wide for not only his hunting prowess, but also for his great skill in making arrows and bows. He had harbored an obsession for flintknapping and bow making ever since he was a young child. By the time he reached his teens he had mastered these skills, and now, later in life, he garnered quite the reputation. He shot so well with his bow that he seldom lost any of his arrows. From time to time, young men of the tribe challenged him to games of skill with the bow and though they were less than half his age they never beat him. In mid-summer Sharp-Knife was sitting by the fire when he first heard one of the elders note the vivid colors in the evening sky. He thought he detected some tone of worry in the elder's voice but didn't pay much attention.

Lack of good snows and spring rains, combined with an early summer and lack of rain, had resulted in one of the driest years anyone could remember. Now, the deep oranges and reds that accompanied the sun in the late afternoon and followed it to bed caused the elders to feel alarmed. Sharp-Knife could not remember, nor did most of the village, but a handful of the oldest among them spoke of a time when the Earth and skies looked burnt for as far as the eye could see in all directions. They said that in the days prior to the great fire the sky looked alight with oranges and reds similar to the way it looked now. Sharp-Knife still didn't feel too alarmed as some of the elders showed a tendency to exaggerate stories, but when he noticed several of them going about burying their most prized possessions deep in the earth for safe keeping, he started to wonder. Over the course of the next two days the oranges and reds in the sky grew more prominent through most of the day and on the third night a faint glow arose on the horizon.

The elders said the glowing horizon at night meant the fire spirit could be upon them with all his fury in less than a day. Near panic ensued as some villagers decided to start moving east toward the Great Spirit River while others began digging holes in which to bury their belongings. Sharp-Knife's children had already grown up and moved out on their own, two years prior his second wife died. Now, alone, he did not possess many belongings to worry about. He buried his stash of extra arrow points as well as some of his cooking vessels but possessed little else to worry about. He helped some of the elders pack their belongings and offered to carry some of it to lighten their load. By morning everyone finished packing. Most of the village's food lay buried deep as well as most of the people's personal belongings. Elders said to pack lightly because they might need to move not only fast, but far. As they headed out to the east the dry prairie grass crunched beneath their feet and dust rose into the air as if a herd of buffalo moved across the earth. The elders began to tell stories of old about how the Green Earth God-dess reclaimed the lands from the Fire Spirit and how great herds of buffalo followed behind to browse on the fresh greens. The stories made the trip seem less difficult and went a long way toward helping calm the children. In the dry summer air, the faintest hint of smoke began to fill Sharp-Knife's nostrils.

When they finally arrived at the banks of the Great Spirit River the women and children went across first, car-ried in some instances by the men. The extended period of drought allowed for people with sufficient strength to wade across the river. Most years a crossing at the same place required rafts and canoes. They made the crossing quickly and efficiently, losing neither people or belongings. Once on the other side the group began to move out again.

After the crossing two of the elders approached Sharp-Knife. "We hope the Great Spirit River, though weakened, will do battle with the Fire Spirit when he reaches this place. If the Fire Spirit wins and burns over the Great Spirit River, our people will need to keep moving. If the water spirits win the fight and stop the fire spirits here as we hope, our people may find safety. Will you stay behind here, at the banks of the Great Spirit River to watch? We will set up our temporary village at Fish Creek two days walk from here. If the fire crosses the river you will need to run as fast as you can to let us know so we have sufficient time to pack up and keep moving. If the water spirits win, you can take your time walking back to meet us with the good news. We must have somebody stay behind for this purpose Sharp-Knife. Because you are wise and without wife or child to look after, we have come to you."

Sharp-Knife set down the pack he carried and looked at each of the elders. "Of course, I will do this for you," he said. Sharp-Knife found a friend to carry the things he carried for one of the elders and then made a small campfire on the banks of the river as the rest of his people disappeared over the horizon in a cloud of dust.

Sharp-Knife knew many stories about the various spirits, but he never before occupied a place where he might actually watch two spirits come together like this. Not prone to weakness or fear, as he stood on the banks of the Great Spirit River he suddenly felt very alone, very small, and very afraid. He had no way to know when the Fire Spirit might make his appearance, and so Sharp-Knife decided to stay occupied. He stood by his small fire and briefly considered making some kind of offering to the Fire Spirit, but he knew not what to offer.

Finally, he decided he would simply spend his time fishing the river with his net until the Fire Spirit came. Sharp-Knife slid down the sandy bank of the river and out into the gravel bars and water. He found the deeper channel there and cast his net. He did not possess great skill with fishing like he did with his bow and arrow. But he still managed to catch a number of fish in short order. It seemed that the lower water levels concentrated the fish in places.

Back on the bank Sharp-Knife roasted his fish over the fire, looking up and watching for the Fire Spirit that he expected to see at any time. Though the middle of the day crept up on him, skies grew darker. He sometimes stepped away from his cooking fire to smell the wind. It carried more and more smoke by the hour. He prayed his people might make good time to their new camp, and he also prayed that the water spirits might win out over the fire spirits. He continued to occupy himself through the day and late into the evening by working on some arrow shafts by the fire and continued his fishing. That night the horizon glowed brightly across the entire expanse in front of him. As he waited, night turned nearly into day tinged by the far-off glow of burning forest.

Near morning it grew difficult to tell time. A few fine flakes of ash started to fall around Sharp-Knife. He stood on the banks praying and soaking in the bizarre sight. Though it felt very warm, the sky and earth looked as if a fine covering of fresh snow had fallen. The very sky looked on fire he thought to himself. While he could not predict the exact moment the Fire Spirit might arrive, he now packed his few things knowing it would not take long. He extinguished his small campfire and hung his bow from his back along with his full quiver of arrows. He took to pacing up and down the riverbank in nervous anticipation then a faint rumbling sound suddenly attracted his attention. He slowly grew aware that he could both hear the fire…and feel it.

Alarmed, he froze in place, removed his bow, and put an arrow against the string. If the Fire Spirit came after him, he would shoot it, he thought. Over the next couple of minutes, the rumbling grew louder and stronger. Perspiration formed on Sharp-Knife's brow, and his muscles tensed as the rumbling intensified.

Suddenly some movement on the opposite bank of the river caught his attention. He watched in fascination as a single bull calf buffalo stumbled awkwardly down the sandy bank on the other side of the river. Sharp-Knife and his people rarely saw any buffalo anymore. For several years now they normally did not travel this far east. Now, in spite of the immediate danger posed by the Fire Spirit, he found himself getting his bow ready, not for the spirits, but for this buffalo. Buffalo constituted a prize seldom encountered, and their bodies offered a plethora of, not just food, but also leather for blankets and bone for tools.

Suddenly a second buffalo appeared on the opposite bank, a large old bull. As the old bull started to make its way down the bank numerous other buffalo also appeared along the bank. Before Sharp-Knife even realized it a full out stampede of buffalo threatened to engulf him. Buffalo herded by the fire moved his direction, just like his own people were also herded by the fire spirits.

Now they crossed the waters of the Great Spirit River with eyes wide and nostrils flaring. Sharp-Knife suddenly remembered some advice once given to him by an old prairie hunter who told him to make himself seen if he ever found himself in front of stampeding buffalo, so he began jumping up and down waving his arms frantically. As the buffalo crossed back into the shallows nearest him they noticed and began to split into two living brown rivers of buffalo, one flowing around either side of him. They continued to come like the stars in the night sky it seemed.

Sharp-Knife broke free from his disbelief and took aim at the occasional buffalo that veered too near to him. He fired each arrow one after another, with a careful and steady hand. As the last of the buffalo came across the river and up the bank, he let loose the last of his arrows. The riverbank and ground all around him looked completely torn up. The place where he stood along the bank by his small camp appeared like an island of grass the only spot left undisturbed by the living brown river that came and went around him. He hadn't even noticed the little licks of flames that teased the tall grasses on the opposite bank as he turned and watched the last of the buffalo disappear out of sight.

Scattered at some distance all over the ground behind him were mounds of dark brown fur bleeding into the earth with deep crimson red blood pooling about them. He began to retrieve his arrows as he watched the Fire Spirit destroy the brush and grass on the other side of the river. At times, the slight breeze made the smoke thick and hard on his lungs, but at no time did the fire manage to cross the broad flats of the Great Spirit River. He watched the fires opposite him burn and eat up everything before dying down and leaving the earth stained black. When he felt satisfied that the fire would not cross, he began to run to catch up with his people.

Sharp-Knife caught up with his people before they made their new camp. With the news he carried, his people decided to turn around and head back to the river, they could camp there until their traditional land healed. By that evening all of the younger folks had arrived back at the scene of the buffalo massacre and there they went to work butchering the animals. Later the elders caught up and assisted with the last of the butchering as well. They held a great feast and hailed Sharp-Knife as a hero. As they went about cutting up the buffalo and collecting the hides and bones for tools, they returned the arrows they found buried deep in the animals' chests to Sharp-Knife. True to form, when everything lay butchered and taken care of, Sharp-Knife found only two arrows missing.

One thousand and eleven years later a young boy and his father sat on the banks of that same river in that same spot fishing. Not much had really changed over the years except perhaps that the river now went by another name and the bank where Sharp-Knife killed so many buffalo had eroded a bit more over time. The boy sat on the bank watching the tip of his fishing pole when he noticed a white pointy rock sticking out from the bank standing in sharp contrast to the wet brown sand surrounding it. The boy's fingers closed around his first arrowhead; and he immediately cherished it as much if not more than the original owner had. Somewhere up in the great hunting grounds of the next life Sharp-Knife smiled as the boy asked his father if he thought perhaps someone lost it hunting deer.

Chapter 7: Long Nose's Funeral

White Bear heard stories of Long Nose all his life. Some said Long Nose embodied both person and spirit in one. Grandfather spoke of him nearly every day, and more than once through the years they sent offerings to him with travelers who passed through on their way to Long Nose's grand village. Grandfather frequently reminded White Bear that without Long Nose's mercy and kindness he might not be alive. Long Nose conquered all the villages far and wide showing no mercy. He made slaves of entire villages, and in some he simply murdered the occupants.

When a messenger came to their village early one spring and spread word that Long Nose had died, it caused grandfather considerable heartache and grief. The messenger said that at least one person from their village, and more, if possible, should come to the great village to participate in Long Nose's funeral. The messenger said that offerings should be brought in his honor as well. The ceremony would begin with the arrival of the next new moon. The messenger scarcely left the small village before White Bear's grandfather suggested that White Bear should make the trip. Others dreamt of the great adventure as well, but the event came at a busy time of year for the small village, and most could not simply walk away for weeks at a time. White Bear, as his grandfather pointed out, remained young and without wife or children to worry about and thus made the perfect candidate.

His grandfather harbored a desire to go as well but simply felt too old and too slow to make the trip. Other important people in their small village agreed with White Bear's grandfather, and so they decided White Bear alone should make the trip and represent their village. Several people immediately brought White Bear small trinkets and offerings for him to take with him. To make it on time he would need to leave the next morning.

White Bear's grandfather stayed up with him late into the night talking about the route he must take. White Bear had never traveled farther than the Great Falls to the south and grandfather assured him this trip would take him much farther away than that. White Bear felt both excited as one might expect a young man in his position to feel, but also deeply worried about making such a long journey through strange lands. His grandfather had made the trip to the Great Village one time as just a young man, and now he relayed all that he knew about it and about Long Nose. His grandfather drew a map in the sand of the wigwam. It, and the landmarks depicted there, seemed at first familiar. White Bear felt confident in going as far as the falls, but grandfather explained his need to walk around the falls for some distance with his canoe and get back into the same river and follow it many more miles to the south and west.

"Eventually, about two days past the falls, you will come to another river, even bigger than our beloved Great Spirit River, and you will see it runs brown with mud."

White Bear watched as his grandfather expanded the map in the sand pointing to where the Great Spirit River intersected with the big muddy river he spoke of.

"Then you will have to canoe for three more days straight south in the muddy waters. Don't feel alarmed however for despite the poor looking water you will find it indeed filled with fish, turtles, frogs, ducks, and all sorts of other game so you should eat well on your trip."

White Bear now watched as his grandfather circled a spot along the east bank of the great muddy river, "Here you will find the village of Long Nose. It is here you will go. You will find many people there along the banks and more canoes than you can count. You cannot miss the place young White Bear," he said.

The next morning White Bear awoke to find grandfather already busy packing a canoe for his trip. They loaded it with food, a blanket, fishing nets, hunting gear, and in some other offerings for Long Nose. Grandfather again explained the route in great detail to White Bear who listened intently so he would not forget any of the landmarks along the way. Once White Bear sat in the canoe and felt ready to push off, grandfather handed him a heavy package wrapped in fine skins. White Bear peeled the skins back to look inside and found four long and beautifully made stone blades wrapped carefully. All four were made from the sacred stone of the north and were some of the finest blades White Bear had ever seen.

His grandfather smiled and winked one eye, "I've been saving those for a very long time, and I promise you they are sure to please Long Nose," he said before backing up and pushing the canoe off into the current of the river.

As White Bear began to paddle his canoe out to the main channel of the river his grandfather and a few others gathered on the shore to see him off and sang an ancient prayer for travelers.

The nervousness White Bear experienced started to fade slightly as he became immersed in the solitude of the river and his surroundings. He paddled lazily downstream all day and did not set up camp until darkness closed in. He chose a long narrow sand bar that formed during the spring floods and now offered a warm and dry place to sleep. After starting a fire with some driftwood and casting his nets out for the night he retrieved the fine stone blades his grandfather gave him.

He took them out and examined them by firelight one at a time. Each one seemed even finer than the one before it, and when he laid all four blades out in the sand by the fire, they made an impressive sight indeed. The firelight glinted off the sacred stone like a million tiny stars were trapped inside. Before falling asleep he carefully wrapped the blades back up again and stowed them once more in the canoe with the other offerings his grandfather gave him.

In the morning he felt surprised to find his net filled with many fish. He made a mental note to himself to fish in this place more often. He picked through the net, keeping his favorite fish to eat, and threw the others back. After eating a bit and extinguishing his fire, he again took off down the river. He traveled all of the next day in the same way as the first, but as he approached the place known as the Great Falls some rain clouds gathered. He spent that night under a sandstone overhang along the river to stay dry.

He felt much relieved to find the skies clear by the next morning. That day he spent mostly on land, carrying and dragging his canoe up and then down the steep trail through the rocks along the banks of the river. Once he found safety below the Great Falls he again loaded his canoe with his belongings and slipped it back into the river. Eventually White Bear made it to the place where the Great Spirit River intersected the muddy river his grandfather spoke of. He looked at the swirling brown waters and felt almost hesitant to canoe into them. The Mud River, as he now called it, seemed much larger, wider and deeper than the Great Spirit River he felt so accustomed to.

He traveled for three more days along the Mud River, fishing and camping along sand bars at night. He ran into more and more people as he continued south. He could tell by the way they made their canoes and by the fabric of their strange attire that they too traveled from distant lands strange to him.

White Bear knew that he approached very close to the Grand Village of Long Nose because in spite of the Mud River's great width it now felt crowded with so many canoes. Along the banks of the river he also started to see garden beds filled with squash, beans, corn and other crops. The closer to the Grand Village he came the larger the fields of crops became and the thinner the woods grew. All of the forest around the Grand Village for quite some distance appeared completely removed from the land, and to White Bear it seemed a strange site to see so many gardens and so few trees.

His neck started to hurt from turning his head and gaping, and he felt almost silly and child-like. Between the different people and the different landscape, he kept craning his neck around from side to side to see, wondering in amazement. He pulled his canoe up on shore where many others gathered in a flurry of activity. Everywhere people seemed busy going to and from somewhere important. He pulled his canoe up the riverbank and dropped it once he crested the top. Before him, stretched out nearly as far as he could see, lay the largest village he had ever seen.

He stood there motionless for a long time simply observing all that unfolded before him. Everywhere people camped by small fires and everywhere there stretched huge garden beds. In the distance he could see a wide flat avenue that led to a high mound. On top of the mound sat a hut flanked by two bonfires. He wondered to himself if maybe the home belonged to Long Nose himself but grew quickly distracted by people walking in front of him. He noticed that everywhere he looked he could see boys, perhaps 10 or 12 years old painted completely from head to toe in bright red paint.

Many of them seemed busy carrying firewood to the great mound in the distance and still others seemed to serve as guides to groups of people taking them to and from places. More than once he caught bits and pieces of conversations as people walked all around him but as often as not the conversations took place in strange languages White Bear did not understand.

After standing there for quite some time he decided to follow suit like the others and make a small camp for himself. He noted that more than a few people simply built fires in open areas and used their canoes for windbreaks and shade, so he followed their example. Off on the edge of a corn field, near one of the only trees in sight he built a small fire and unloaded his canoe. He roasted some fish that he brought with him from the river and thoroughly enjoyed himself. He entertained himself by watching all the commotion. He never imagined so many people inhabited all of the world, let alone one village. He thought as a child growing up that his grandfather greatly embellished his stories of Long Nose and the Great Village. Now he no longer doubted any of the old stories because he sat camped among it.

White Bear awoke the next morning, startled awake, by one of the boys from the prior day standing before him all painted in bright red. At first the boy seemed afraid when White Bear moved toward him suddenly, and he jumped back. But White Bear quickly made sense of his surroundings and motioned to the boy to come back. He tried to apologize and at the same time the boy in red started to say something; but after just a few moments they both realized that each spoke a language different from the other. Some of the words the boy uttered sounded vaguely familiar but altogether it made no sense to White Bear.

The boy motioned with his hands for White Bear to get up and follow him. White Bear looked all around and watched as other boys, also painted red, busily woke up the travelers and lead them toward the mound in the distance. White Bear gathered up his offerings as he saw others doing the same and followed the boy. Along the way the boy stopped to wake other travelers up as well and motioned for them to follow him too. Soon they all seemed headed toward the big hill, passing through field after field of garden beds. White Bear and his people also planted some of these same things but never on such a massive scale as what he now witnessed.

White Bear hadn't realized the incredible size of the big mound and other smaller mounds flanking it until they approached. They walked a long way and the entire time the mounds seemed to grow in size before his eyes. Even the smaller mounds on the sides appeared enormous, and White Bear decided that this Long Nose person must bear incredible power indeed to build such things.

As they drew closer their groups formed a line leading to the big mound, on top of it he could see people dressed in grand costumes, adorned with feathers, and also painted red. The people on top of the mounds looked small from where he stood. In the distance he began to hear the rhythmic beat of drums. Waiting in line started to take a toll as the sun rose higher in the sky and the cool morning air turned it into a warm and rather humid day. White Bear tried to make small talk with the people both in front of him and behind him but none of them spoke the same language. After a while the boys in red came around with water bladders and ears of corn. They offered a drink and something to eat to all of the travelers. Slowly but surely the line crept forward toward the mound.

By mid-day White Bear neared the bottom of the mound, and he could see much more clearly what happened around him. One by one, the boys ushered travelers up the mound where they then handed their offerings over to the men in the costumes. There they seemed to separate the offerings into different piles; and then the boys in red ushered people down the back side of the mound and back in the direction from which they came.

White Bear marveled at the men in costume, they all wore brightly colored feathers, many of which appeared to come from birds he had never seen before. One man wore a snow-white belt around his waist composed of thousands of shell beads, another man had a gorget around his neck that shined so brightly it looked as though he might be wearing a piece of the sun around his neck. All of the men wore fine purple earrings made from stone and all painted in reds, black and white paint to great effect. Two of the men wore axes hanging from their belts of the finest quality White Bear had ever seen. All in all, the men at the top of the mound impressed him greatly.

White Bear grew increasingly nervous as he neared the front of the line. He found himself looking down at his handful of offerings and hoping they would appease the occupants. As he followed the line up the center of the mound the trail grew steeper. When he reached the point where just two or three people separated him from the front of the line he could see the offerings from all these people heaped into different piles. To one side grew a mountain of food stuffs that included many meats, fish, berries, nuts, and tubers. Many of the food items rested in finely made baskets or clay bowls.

To the other side White Bear could see a heaping pile of skins, antlers, and bundles of feathers. He recognized a highly sought-after wolf skin near the top before his eyes shifted to a much smaller pile in the center of the mound directly behind the costumed man accepting the traveler's gifts one at a time. The smallest of the three piles held his attention longest, filled with the most beautiful assortment of stone blades, beads, polished pipes, and other fine items. Among the pile he saw a number of knives and other tools made from the same shiny material as the gorget adorning the man's neck.

Wide-eyed, White Bear suddenly found himself face to face with the man standing in the center of the mound. He did not realize it but his hands shook badly as he held out his leather bundle and trinkets. The man took the trinkets, looked at them, and tossed them on the pile with all of the skins and antlers. Then he took the leather packet from White Bear's trembling hands and unwrapped it.

The man's eyes looked pleased as he examined each of the four blades before turning to lay three of the four on the small pile of precious goods behind him. When the man turned around and again faced White Bear, he said something to the boy standing next to him that White Bear did not understand; and then he handed White Bear something in return. White Bear felt temporarily stunned because he had not witnessed this happening to any of the other travelers; but he quickly accepted it when the boy in red said, "Take it!" in White Bear's own language.

White Bear nodded his head in thanks, but the boy did not return the gesture. Then White Bear watched as the man took the fourth blade, the largest of them all, and placed it upon the alter where another costumed man quickly destroyed it with a blow from a heavy axe. The boy in red pulled at White Bears arm to escort him down the back side of the mound. White Bear turned and looked over his shoulder just before he started down the back of the mound and encountered a view, he wished he could stand and examine more closely. Far off in the distance he could see the Mud River and between where he stood and the river, he could see a thousand little tendrils of smoke arising from the vast fields of garden beds.

"You speak my language," White Bear said as they descended the back of the mound. "Yes, I speak your language," the boy said. White Bear looked down to see what the costumed man pressed into his hand and felt surprised to see a beautiful necklace made from the same shining material as the man's gorget.

"Your gifts pleased Long Nose," the boy said, "because he does not offer many gifts in return." White Bear clutched the beads even tighter in his hand afraid he might lose them. He couldn't wait to show this fine gift to his grandfather. Then the boy explained, "Those beads are made from the sun stone. But the sun stone can't be flaked into shape like an arrowhead; we instead shape it by beating it with hammers and heating it in fire."

Eventually the boy and White Bear made their way back to his little camp area, and the boy remained briefly to visit. The boy explained that he did speak the same language because he too came from far to the north, perhaps even from the same people as White Bear, but long ago. That the people of Long Nose took him as a slave while he was still a young boy so now, he spoke with a thick accent. "You should stay here a while White Bear; the ceremonies are sure to continue for days. If you stay you might even witness the return of Long Nose himself," he said as he nodded toward the huge mound they just came from. "I will return later and bring you some food if you wish to stay," the boy said.

White Bear agreed that he would, then the boy set off to escort still more travelers helping them make their way up the mound.

White Bear tried to sleep but the constant beat of the drums combined with the fascination he held for the beautiful necklace now around his own neck kept him awake deep into the night. Late the next morning White Bear awoke to the gentle prodding of the red painted boy. The boy brought him some food and water. The food embodied a type White Bear had never experienced before, but tasted sweet, and White Bear quickly ate it all.

"The offerings have all been made. Now we will wait to see if Long Nose will return like he promised he would. Most of my work, for now, is done; and so, if you don't mind, I will stay to visit here with you."

White Bear smiled at the news. "Yes, I would like the company! It is not fun to listen to strange tongues all day," White Bear pointed out.

"I know what you mean, I do not know what many people are saying just the same as you, I speak only our native tongue well, and that of Long Nose now."

White Bear spent the rest of the morning and a significant portion of the afternoon listening to stories about Long Nose and the Grand Village. The red painted boy indeed had a front row seat to many great things, building of mounds, the defeat of large numbers of enemies and harvests from fields that fed the entire Grand Village through the harshest of winters.

That afternoon one of the boy's stories was interrupted by a different red painted boy who came running from area-to-area yelling, "At sunset Long Nose will come back! He will come back atop the great mound for all to see! He comes as both God and man!" In other directions White Bear could see other boys yelling and spreading the message as well.

"We should go now to get a good spot," the boy said as he stood and motioned toward the mound. White Bear stood and thanked the boy again because without him he would not know what was going on still. They moved toward the mound along with a group of other people. People began to press against one another in a vain attempt to move closer. As the afternoon started to fade into evening White Bear noticed the drums begin to beat steadily faster and a huge fire set on top of the mound. On either side of the wide fire the costumed men who had accepted the gifts the day before now knelt down, heads lowered. As sunset approached and the western sky turned a brilliant orange color, the drumbeat reached a loud and fevered pitch. Tension and excitement transcended languages, and the crowd as a whole grew anxious.

Just when the sun completely dipped beyond the horizon the drums suddenly stopped beating and the resulting silence seemed deafening. Then, without warning or explanation, a brilliant shinning figure stepped straight out of the fire and onto the platform at the front and center of the mound. The man shone like the sun even in the dim light; and when he raised his arms the great mass of people at the base of the mound fell to their knees. White Bear also fell to his knees in disbelief. He covered his prized necklace with one hand when he realized Long Nose wore the same material from head to toe. His arms, his chest, and even his face as well as his unusually long nose shone with the material.

A great roar of excitement arose from the crowd when drums once again began to beat, and the mass of people stood up. White Bear stood in disbelief and consciously tried to soak up every detail so he might pass along the story of all that happened to his small village when he returned. When the roar of excitement started to calm down Long Nose lowered his hands and motioned for silence. The drums stopped again, and a silence fell across the gathered masses. Long Nose began to speak, but White Bear did not understand and waited patiently for him to finish so the boy might explain to him what he said. When Long Nose finished speaking, he stepped backward into the fire and disappeared from view. As the crowd started to disperse, the boy explained what Long Nose said.

"Long Nose just told us that he traveled to the afterlife and met with many Gods there all seated in the great hall of legend. There they approved of his rule and agreed to send him back to the Grand Village so he might continue to rule for many more years."

That night they held a great celebration like nothing White Bear had ever seen. All around great bonfires roared and people feasted. White Bear wanted the red painted boy to stay, but he could not because he needed to help pass food out. Together, the red painted boys brought large baskets of food out to all parts of the crowd scattered about the garden beds. The baskets overflowed with roasted corn, squash, meats, fish and many other items. The hosts encouraged everyone to eat their fill, and they did. White Bear joined with a group near-by and sang and danced around one of the fires. He noticed many others looking at and admiring his shining necklace as it glittered like the stars in the light of the fire. White Bear stayed up and danced with the others until the first hints of day started to appear in the sky.

When White Bear awoke the next day, he found many people already packed and leaving. He stayed by his fire and watched as many people again lugged their canoes across the dirt paths and fields toward the river. He also packed his and made it ready for the return trip, but he took his time in hopes the red painted boy might come by one more time. White Bear wished to thank the young man once again for all of his help, but as the morning turned to noon his hopes of seeing him faded, and he finally started to drag his own canoe back to the river. Just as he approached the riverbank a boy tapped him on the shoulder. White Bear did not recognize him at first because he no longer wore the red paint, but then did indeed see this as the boy who helped him.

"Thank you again, I would not have understood much had you not helped me," White Bear said.

"That is why Long Nose has us, to help him in these matters," the boy replied.

White Bear offered to break his fine necklace in half in order to share half of the beads as a means of thanks, but the boy refused.

"Long Nose does not permit us to take gifts; we are only servants," he said. Then the boy handed White Bear a leather pouch.

Inside he found a bright red powder. "This is the favorite color of Long Nose, if you ever need protection paint yourself, use this as it is strong medicine. Just add some water. Use it to bless the sick but remember to always spread the word of Long Nose when you use it."

White Bear nodded. "Thank you," he said simply before the boy turned and was off toward the Grand Village again.

The trip back up the river seemed much more familiar, but it also became more difficult. It took him two days longer to make the return trip going up stream than it took him to paddle downstream. When he camped on the sand bars of the rivers at night, he admired his shiny beads made from the strange material much as he had admired the beauty of the four blades he took with him on the way down. He closed his eyes at night and tried to remember all of the details of the costumed men and of Long Nose himself. White Bear felt consumed with preserving every moment of the memory for the benefit of others.

When White Bear rounded the last corner in the river his own village came into view. He could see his grandfather sitting on the river's edge mending fishing nets. When he pulled his canoe up on shore people already gathered there, and all demanded details and stories. White Bear sat by the village fire and told the story in every agonizing detail that he could recall. The entire village sat and listened with great interest, but perhaps none so much as his grandfather. Grandfather repeatedly stopped White Bear in mid-sentence and asked him to clarify some trivial detail.

White Bear never did return to the Grand Village of Long Nose, but he did spend the rest of his years speaking of Long Nose's greatness in much the same fashion his grandfather did. He proudly showed his shiny beads to all who expressed curiosity and found out over time that he needed to clean them by rubbing sand on them or they turned green. When the string that bound the beads together broke and he carefully constructed a new one. When White Bear approached old age himself, he felt surprise when a young man all painted in red from head to toe visited his village one day. He spoke of Long Nose's passing.

White Bear prepared his own grandson to make the trip to the Grand Village of Long Nose much like his own grandfather prepared him. White Bear did not have any fine blades to send with his grandson as an offering, but knowing how Long Nose loved the sun stone as he called it, he polished the beads with sand one last time to make them shine like the day he received them atop the great mound in the Grand Village. And he gave them to his grandson to take with him. White Bear did not know it, but the necklace fell two beads short of the original number present when he received it because when the string that held them together broke he lost two beads in the sand by the river.

Within just a few hundred years all memory of the Grand Village and of Long Nose got lost from the people of the land. A great sickness killed many, and migration of strange people from the east forced many of the survivors to move from their lands. The Earth reclaimed the Grand Village and trees grew there again. Five hundred miles to the north, in 1998, a man with a metal detector searched a popular fishing spot along the river. He hoped to find some lost change or perhaps even some lost fishing lures. As he searched a strong penny signal caused him to stop and dig. The bead no longer looked shiny but instead glowed with a thick green patina.

The man recognized the patina as that of a copper bead and detected the rest of the area with even more vigor hoping to find more beads, but when the day ended, he found only two. He placed the two beads in a display case with copper artifacts found in a different area years before. The person who found White Bear's two lost beads commented more than once how he wished his artifacts could talk and tell the story of their life. He had no idea what an incredible tale these two relatively unremarkable copper beads might tell, if only they could speak.

Chapter 8: The Mammoth Hunt

Sitting Bull worked to help pack up their temporary camp along with the rest of his tribe, but seriously resented the necessity to once again move out across the open plains. They had camped at the current location for only two days, but the local creek offered good fishing. Sitting Bull enjoyed those two days with not only the warmth of the temporary camp, but also a full belly; and he hated to leave. Even though spring felt not far off, the winds of late winter still stung as they trudged across the tundra.

It seemed pretty early in the year for his hunting party to travel this far north. But with every passing year the mammoth grew harder to find. So when they stumbled upon the tracks a few weeks earlier his group decided to start following the herd immediately. The older hunters occasionally stopped to examine the tracks in the frozen mud. They saw the tracks of one big bull, three females and a baby. Sitting Bull's father pointed out that this would not be an easy or safe hunt because when a herd had a baby in their midst, they fought with particular aggression eager to defend the young.

Sitting Bull's father also pointed out that if they continued on their present course they might head north, through the narrows in the place of rocks and water. Such a route would bring the hunting party into a perfect situation to ambush the herd. Sitting Bull said nothing, but secretly hoped the herd might veer off back out into the tundra and perhaps discourage his little hunting party so they might return home toward the south where he knew the sun already warmed the land.

Over the next few days the herd's tracks continued north to the place of rocks and water just as Sitting Bull's father hoped. The little band of hunters kept a watchful eye toward the north. They knew from experience the animals spooked easily. As they drew closer to the place of rocks and water they made a plan to veer around the animals as they slept one night so they might beat them to the place of rocks and water and set up an ambush.

The place of rocks and water consisted of a large bluff that carried on for many miles to the east and west. An ancient river cut its way through the rocks in just one place, and in so doing created a narrow valley. Tall bluffs flanked the riverbanks that offered the ideal place to ambush these large and dangerous animals. Sitting Bull's father twice experienced success hunting in the narrows of the place of rocks and water but represented Sitting Bull's first attempt. As the animals drew closer to the narrows their speed slowed. It almost seemed like the animals knew the river represented a perfect ambush site.

The hunters took great care moving far around to the west in the dark of night while the animals slept. Sitting Bull despised the long hike in the coldness of the night but trudged on hoping the end result might prove worth it. At 16 summers old this plan provided him with his first opportunity to hunt a mammoth. Many hunters already waited at the crest of the wind whipped bluffs when morning started to reveal the landscape to Sitting Bull and the others. They stood looking out toward the south over vast tundra. Behind them, to the north, stretched an enormous swamp filled with thick vegetation that the mammoths found difficult to ignore.

Sitting Bull's father pointed the marshlands out to his son, "The marsh on the back side of this bluff carries on for more days than you can walk. This is where the mammoth numbering in the hundreds used to spend their summers grazing all day." Then his father turned and pointed to what looked like a little dip in the bluffs up ahead, "There, that is where the river cuts through the bluffs. Those are the narrows, and that is where we will be successfully killing a mammoth if they keep on their current path," he said.

Sitting Bull and the other hunters did not need to wait long to find out if the mammoths might be coming or not. By mid-morning, when the winds eased up a bit and the sun again made itself known, several brown shaggy lumps appeared on the horizon toward the south. The oldest hunters in the group studied the beasts slow trudging movements with intensity for a few minutes before they felt satisfied that they indeed headed for the narrows. The hunters wasted no time and started to run just below the crest of the bluff toward the narrows.

When the group of hunters reached the narrows, Sitting Bull's father started to give instructions.

"Here," he said, pointing to the bluffs on either side of them. "We will climb up and take positions all along the bluff. I will be in the back, and I alone will start the hunt. Not one hunter shall move a bone until I throw my first dart. I will not attack until the last beast is in front of me so that when they start to scare and stampede, they will move farther down the narrows where the rest of you will wait. We should aim our darts at the youngest female because the herd is most likely to leave her behind if we kill her. If we kill the baby, the herd might stay behind and protect the body. When they come through make no movement. If they spook, they could turn around and head back out onto the plains where they are most difficult to get. Be careful and may the spirits smile upon us today." He barely finished his speech before several hunters started to climb up the bluffs.

Several others waded into the shallow river and started climbing the bluffs on the other side of the river. Sitting Bull picked out a place more or less at random along the bluff, and he too started to scale the steep walls looking for a place that might protect and hide him but still offer a good place from which he might launch his atl-atl.

Sitting Bull eventually found a wide shelf along the bluff that offered him enough room to wield his atl-atl. It sat a little lower on the bluff than most hunters perched themselves because it fell on the verge of being within reach of the old bull if he really wanted. But its closeness also offered a much better chance to deliver a death blow with one or more of his atl-atl darts as well. He considered it a calculated risk. Hunters who delivered the death blow on any mammoth instantly gained the respect of all members of the clan. Such an event bestowed great honor. Besides the honor, mammoths had become such a rare sight that Sitting Bull didn't know if this might be his only chance to see let alone kill one. A twisted and stunted pine tree stood rooted along the same stone shelf that Sitting Bull selected for his perch, and so he stripped it of its branches and made something of a cushion between him and the cold stone beneath to lie on.

Sitting Bull, like the other hunters, remained motionless as the bulky beasts started to come close into the narrows. Sitting Bull had seen a few at a distance once, and the bones of many still lay scattered around his home in the south, but this event provided his first opportunity to watch these animals up close. They seemed even larger flanked by the stone walls on either side. The bull led up front and took just a few calculated steps in the shallow waters of the river before raising his trunk into the air. Sitting Bull knew that the animals would smell for hints of danger, and his hesitation made Sitting Bull wonder if the old bull might recall a similar hunt or similar threat in this place. The older hunters claimed these beasts possessed a better memory than people even.

It seemed like it took an eternity for the animals to make their way up the little narrow valley, but as the old bull came closer Sitting Bull's heart started to beat faster, and he struggled to remain motionless. The old bull stopped directly below Sitting Bull's perch and slowly raised his trunk high into the air again. Sitting Bull suddenly regretted sitting so low on the bluff wall now, because from where he sat the old bull's trunk could reach higher into the air than level with him, and he knew if the old bull found him it might take precious little for the hulking beast to grab him with his trunk and throw him to the valley floor.

The old bull's trunk telescoped from side to side smelling the air like a third eye and then the animal pulled it back. The bull appeared old, and his once keen sense of smell no longer served him as well as it once did. In the generations before Sitting Bull, this old bull might have already been ousted by a younger bull, but mammoth had become so scarce that there were no longer any young bulls left to challenge him. Sitting Bull felt lucky in that way because a younger bull might have already discovered and killed him for his mistake of sitting so low on the bluff walls. Sitting Bull turned his gaze, without shifting his position up the valley and could see that while the old bull below stood almost in the open country of the marsh and through the narrows, the last female just now reached the place where his father sat.

Farther down the narrows Sitting Bull's father launched his first atl-atl dart at the youngest female. As the atl-atl made contact with her neck she trumpeted a loud warning call to the rest. The baby started to run with the other two females in a hurried panic, and the old bull who walked just past where Sitting Bull sat now turned himself around, lowered his massive tusks, and stomped his foot taunting his invisible aggressors.

The other hunters let their darts fly at the wounded female, and she continued to trumpet loudly. Her warning calls vibrated off the canyon walls and echoed out into the plains and marsh alike. Sitting Bull, now on his hands and knees looking over his rock shelf, watched as the baby and two females ran by him. The wounded female approached quickly, and he readied one of his darts.

Sitting Bull cocked his arm back and balanced the six-foot dart between his fingers, when the moment grew just right; he let it fly with a hard but graceful swing. His first dart found a soft spot between the ribs of the female, and it punctured deep into her lung. She started to slow down as she drew even with where Sitting Bull stood. He readied another dart and looked into the animals huge, wide eyes as the second dart also hit home between her ribs.

The other two females and the baby trotted by the old bull who now stood watching the murderous scene unfold. Some of the hunters who had perched themselves at the very top of the bluff now ran down closer to where the wounded female stood and launched their atl-atls. Still launching from high above where Sitting Bull stood, most of them failed to penetrate her thick hide from such a distance. Sitting Bull readied a third dart now as the massive beast stood there on the rocky gravel bar of the river staining the ice-cold river water bright red with her blood. Just before he launched his third dart however the mammoth knelt down on her front knee. She paused and then knelt down with the other.

Darts still rained down from above sticking in her thick hide and some bouncing off. Her giant eye rolled back into her head exposing the bloodshot white of her eye. In slow motion she slowly leaned over to one side and fell onto the gravel bar. She remained there with slow and labored breaths dying while the big bull watched. Sitting Bull watched as the old bull seemed to weigh his options looking at the dying female and then back toward the remainder of his herd that continued to run out into the open marsh in the distance. He paused and blew a loud trumpet before turning himself and following the others.

The hunters all came down from the valley walls and gathered at a safe distance from the dying female. They recounted the story of the hunt even before it drew to a close. The others instantly recognized Sitting Bull as the hunter who delivered the death blow before the animal even took its last breaths. They waited for nearly an hour for the animal to finally stop breathing and die. Once they felt safe, they approached and started butchering her. All of the hunters made some attempt to gather their atl-atl darts because they could not easily replace either the wood shafts or the stone points this far north.

Because Sitting Bull delivered the death blow, he got first choice of the meat; and they allowed him to gather all he wanted before anyone else did. He cut a large portion of back loin from her and a slab of liver as well. Some of the other hunters teased him about wanting to carry so much meat all the way home, but when they finished every hunter in the party stood just as laden down with meat as Sitting Bull. Sitting Bull's father did not like that the winds changed as they worked, nor did he like the look of the clouds in the sky that began to form. He encouraged his hunting party to hurry in their butchering so they might get moving south again before another late storm struck. A few flakes of snow started to fall upon the partially butchered animal as the hunters headed back south through the narrows and back out toward the open plains, crouched over under their loads of meat.

More than 10,000 years later a group of friends spent a warm summer day walking along the banks of the river in those same narrows looking for lost fishing lures when one of them found one of Sitting Bull's lost atl-atl tips that once lodged deep inside the lung of the last mammoth ever successfully hunted in Wisconsin. They young man showed the point to his uncle and later felt inspired by it enough to write this very book.

Chapter 9: Fishing Otter and the White Buffalo

The custom of his tribe dictated that a boy could change his name when he crossed over into manhood, if the name no longer seemed appropriate. This became the case with Fishing Otter. At his birth, his father named him Little Otter, but as the boy grew, he spent so much time on the Great Spirit River fishing that he eventually became known as Fishing Otter instead. The lands along the east bank of the river in those days held only a small population, and Fishing Otter and his small clan felt the world belonged to them alone.

Most of Fishing Otter's friends and family preferred to hunt elk and deer in the forest, or buffalo on the prairies, because a single kill provided so much food. Fishing Otter agreed, but he always returned to the river as soon as the opportunity arose. As he grew into a young man he developed fishing skills well beyond that of the others. He learned to make fish traps from the abundant willows along the banks, he knew the best places to dig clams, and he easily caught more turtles than anyone else.

He replaced hunting in the forests and prairies altogether eventually with these skills because so many people seemed willing to trade their extra meat taken from those places for his extra clams, fish and turtles. He knew the river in all its seasons and learned to exploit it in some fashion through them all. Sometimes, after setting his fishing nets and traps he simply waited. And while he waited, he sifted through the river cobbles to find good pieces of flint and quartz from which he made atl-atl points. He flintknapped so many fine points that he also traded them to his friends and family who quickly used them up hunting. He kept an ample supply of atl-atl darts with him all the time because sometimes animals came to drink at the river, especially in the summer. These animals provided a target too easy to pass up regardless of how many fish, turtles and clams he caught.

One of Fishing Otter's favorite places to fish lay along a stretch of prairie just south of their camp where the river cut a deep gash into the grasses and earth. The bank rose steeply, and the gravel bars below lay thick and difficult to cross, but he often found better fishing there than anywhere else. Fishing Otter went to this favorite place early one spring in hopes of catching a good haul of fish, but felt disappointed to find the waters still ran high. He would still spend the day fishing, but he knew his chances for success declined in proportion to the height of the water. He forced himself to stay and let his traps soak for several hours. Just when he felt prepared to call it quits, he thought he caught the earthy-musk scent of buffalo wafting through the air. Carefully and slowly, he grabbed his atl-atl, a handful of darts, and started up the steep bank of the river.

Fishing Otter removed his fox and eagle feather headdress as he neared the top. He slowly parted the tall grass at the lip of the bank with his two hands and peered out over the sea of grass. His nose didn't lie, before him stood hundreds of grazing buffalo, each lazily plodding along without the slightest hint they sensed his presence. He picked an atl-atl dart at random and carefully slid it into position; at the same time, he studied the herd to pick the best target. He could easily forget the poor day of fishing if he could get a good young buffalo for his family instead.

As he studied the herd something caught his eye, just a glimpse of something white. But then he lost sight of it with the shuffling by of more lumbering giants and rising dust. Then, a moment later he saw it again, this time for a split second longer. His heart instantly jumped to life in his chest, and his head began to buzz. He blinked his eyes hard on purpose expecting to lose sight of it again, but when he opened them again, the image remained. He had heard many legends about the sacred white buffalo, and he even had an uncle who regularly made offerings to the mythical beast, but now he crouched staring at the real thing grazing among the rest of the herd not 50 yards in front of him.

His uncle had always told him that one day he would slay a white buffal and asked him to please let him have a single bite. He said that those who ate from the sacred animal would be given not only good fortune, but all of eternity. There were other legends about the magical creature as well, but Fishing Otter had only listened to the hunter's legends half-heartedly, instead focusing his attention on the legends that revolved around water spirits.

Fishing Otter smiled at the thought of what his uncle's face might look like when he came walking into camp draped in a white buffalo skin. He tried to steady his now shaking hands with little luck. He slowly cocked his arm back and prepared to let his dart fly at the magical beast. He said, "Please let my aim be true." Holding his breath, he hurled the dart with all his might. He then watched in horror as the spear fell short and stuck in the ground between the animal's legs.

He ducked back down into the tall grass of the riverbank, stunned. The animal truly must possess strong magic he thought since he showed no fear of him at all. With fast calculated moves he prepared another atl-atl dart and again cocked his arm back before slowly rising from the grass. The beast stood so close now that he could see the animal had clouds in its eyes. This seemingly supernatural attribute made Fishing Otter tremble with fear as he loosed another atl-atl dart at tthe buffalo. The second dart found its mark and lodged itself deep inside the lungs of the animal.

He stood and yelped in celebration; he could tell by the hollow sounding "thunk" the spear made when it struck that he'd made a good shot. He watched as the buffalo trotted off to the east a short way before falling over lifeless. Fishing Otter went to work immediately butchering the buffalo, careful to skin it without damaging the hide. When he recovered the spear point that made the kill, he buried it in the ground on the very spot as an offering to the spirits.

Fishing Otter, least skilled hunter of the clan, wore the heavy white hide over him and pretended to be a buffalo as he entered his camp. A small child first noticed him and ran in the opposite direction screaming. The screaming child soon had everybody in earshot converging on Fishing Otter who then threw the hide off and let out a shrill yelp like hunters did when they returned from a good hunt.

Nobody seemed more surprised than Fishing Otter's uncle whom he chided by saying that he could have just one bite of the sacred animal. In the end, the legends came true because Fishing Otter continued to live a very good life and in fact lived to an advanced age when compared to most of his day. He did not pass on to the next life until the ripe old age of 68. Fishing Otter retold the story of how he killed the magical beast time and time again, often embellishing the story as the years wore on. He started life known as Little Otter but became known as Fishing Otter.

By the end of his life, he became known simply as White Buffalo. The story of him and his hunt carried on for generations after him. Eventually people said that White Buffalo fished the river as a man during the day but ran the prairies as the white buffalo at night.

The place along the river where he killed the buffalo eventually became known as Otter's Prairie and hundreds of years after that, when the Europeans arrived, they found the river in that place known as Otter Creek. And so it remains to this day. Now a large bean field lies in the area where Fishing Otter killed the white buffalo, and the farmer's son found the very point with which Fishing Otter killed the buffalo and then buried the stone point as an offering. The boy found quite a few stone points scattered about that particular area over the years. This one wasn't the nicest he ever found, but for reasons he could not explain, it became his favorite find. Maybe some of the luck and magic wore off of the white buffalo and onto the point because the boy who found it also went on to live a long and happy life.

Chapter 10: The Harvest Celebration

Boys became men early during Running Black Deer's life. Fathers taught their sons at a very early age how to throw an atl-atl and hunt. If something happened to the father, the closest male relative taught the boys. Running Black Deer's favorite way to practice with his atl-atl came playing a game called Chunk-Kay. Chunk-Kay consisted of a game played on a long narrow prepared court of compacted, smooth ground, on which a stone disk rolled. The game tested the hunter's skills by each one trying to knock the disk over as it rolled down the path. Those who came closest to the disk won. If Running Black Deer had time, he would play this game of skill from sunup to sundown each and every day. But life did not generally allow for such time. Most years Running Black Deer only found enough free time to play the game of Chunk-Kay during the Fall Harvest Celebration.

For most of the year Running Black Deer's people scattered widely across the land to make use of many different resources. Families spent all year gathering great quantities of various food stuffs to help them make it through the winter. Running Black Deer's father for instance liked to camp by a small lake in the bluffs to the east where he gathered huge quantities of dried blueberries and killed deer and smoked venison.

Other families spent their time gathering root crops or fish, still others focused on making fine skins and leather. In the fall, all of these widely scattered families converged at one place along the banks of the Great Spirit River for a

Fall Harvest Celebration. Here the families who enjoyed great success in gathering various resources could trade with others, so they did not have to eat the same thing all year round. Running Black Deer's father traded some of his dried blueberries and venison for dried fish, buffalo, elk, tubers, and other items. Elders encouraged children to trade and participate too. In between bouts of trading there were huge Chunk-Kay contests between individuals as well as families and even clans.

Young men found wives at the Harvest Celebration and at night the elders retold the ancient legends around huge bonfires. Everybody shared and feasted for a couple of weeks during the Harvest Celebration and for these reasons all of Running Black Deer's people looked forward to this yearly migration with great anticipation.

For the previous two summers Running Black Deer's family stayed in a bark house two days east of the Great Spirit River on a small crystal-clear lake. Running Black Deer's mother and father spent their days picking blueberries and hunting, leaving him to entertain himself. He taught himself to build fish traps in the lake by lashing sticks to one another. He found no stones in that sandy area and the sticks lay on the forest floor in abundance around the lake. He tied them together with grass lashings and spent days making his traps. He would place them out in shallow waters where they started off as a wide cone shape. He started far off and walked toward the open end of the cone splashing and making noise by hitting the water with a stick.

Far ahead of him the fish swam to get away. As they encountered the stick wall, he built they followed it into the cone and eventually through the tip of the cone where they suddenly found themselves inside a giant submerged basket. Running Black Deer made fish drives like this several times a day and sometimes caught so many fish in the basket that he thought it might break. He dried his fish on huge wooden racks that sat above a smoldering smoky fire. He and his family ate all of the fresh fish they could stuff themselves with nearly every day, but in addition to this Running Black Deer managed to smoke an impressive amount of fish then carefully stowed the fish away in woven bags high in the trees to keep bears from eating it.

In the weeks just prior to the Fall Harvest Celebration Running Black Deer intensified his fishing efforts. He sometimes worked all day catching, cleaning, and smoking fish. By the time his family got ready to pack up and head to the Harvest Celebration he'd stockpiled an impressive amount of fish. This year he needed to build a sled just to carry his dried and smoked fish. He knew many of the fish would remain with his family to make their winter less stressful, but he also knew his father would certainly allow him to trade at least some portion of them away for whatever he desired. So, he spent a considerable amount of time daydreaming about potential trades.

Custom dictated that no one trade goods on the first day of the Harvest Celebration. Instead, the people prepared multiple Chunk-Kay courts and played countless games. Running Black Deer loved to play and proved good at it. He beat several of the older and more skilled hunters each year, something that earned him status among the people. That first night everybody feasted and shared with each other as the elders and members of the Turtle Clan told stories around the fires. That night when Running Black Deer and his parents retreated to their temporary bark house for the night his mother spent a considerable amount of time trying to convince his father that he should trade some of his berries and venison for some of the new clay jars one clan from the south brought with them to the celebration this year. Running Black Deer's father however talked about trading for some good quality stone to make stone points and knives from. He also pointed out that perhaps he needed an elk skin shirt again. Running Black Deer's mother then pointed out they also needed a new buffalo blanket as theirs felt old and musty.

Back and forth late into the night the two tried to persuade each other but Running Black Deer could only focus on what he wanted to trade for, and nothing weighed more heavily on his mind that night than the sweet maple syrup he traded for the year before. His stockpile of fish only traded for two bladders of the sticky sweet syrup, and he drank that all in just a few days. He tried to control himself and failed, this year he decided he would ration it out better.

Running Black Deer awoke, like most of the others, after only a couple of hours of good sleep. When he awoke, he found many people already busy negotiating trades. As fun as Chunk-Kay seemed, so were the trades. They required a fair amount of skill and talking if you did not want others to take advantage. People skilled in negotiating could do very well at the Fall Harvest Celebration and others looked up to them just like a skilled hunter.

Before he left the bark house for a day of trading, he untied one large bundle of nice quality dried fish and handed the hefty bundle to his mother. "Here, take this mother, trade it for anything you like," he said.

His mother's eyes welled up with emotion at his kind gesture.

Running Black Deer wasted no time and headed straight for the camp of the family who brought the sweet maple syrup the year before. Even before approaching the man Running Black Deer could see he did not have anywhere near as many bags of the sweet stuff hanging around his house as he did most years. The man smiled as Running Black Deer approached as he remembered him from the year before.

"Bad news little boy," the man said as Running Black Deer pulled his sled full of fish up to the man's camp.

"What?" Running Black Deer inquired.

"The trees didn't want to give us much this year; I don't really have any extra syrup to trade you. What we did collect an old bear managed to get into one night," and the man paused to show the fresh bear claw necklace that he now wore around his neck. He gave a mostly toothless smile, "but the bear tasted sweet," he said.

Running Black Deer felt crushed. There were other things to trade for of course, but nothing as sweet as syrup.

Running Black Deer knew the man could see the look of extreme disappointment on his face and finally offered to trade him for a small amount. The man disappeared into his bark house momentarily then returned with a clay jar. "Here, how many fish do you think this is worth to you?" he asked as he handed it over to Running Black Deer.

Running Black Deer took the cool clay jar in his hands and looked inside; it was half full of syrup. He felt like telling the man to take all his fish the syrup made him so happy, but he offered only one bundle.

The man scoffed at the first offer, "Syrup and a fine clay jar like this for one bundle of fish?" The man acted disgusted. Running Black Deer offered a second bundle and the man reluctantly agreed. When Running Black Deer returned home his mother's eyes instantly lit up when she saw the fine clay jar, and then he remembered her conversation with his father the night before. "You can have the jar mother. It's one just like you wanted, but you must wait until I empty it," he said smiling.

Running Black Deer spent the next few days trading his remaining bundles of fish for a variety of items. He traded one bundle for a fine stone knife set into an antler handle, another bundle he traded for a bag of nuts of a type he did not know. The people he got the nuts from said they came from very special trees found only far to the south. Likewise, his father traded for a variety of things. Most of his smoked venison and dried blueberries went to get a new buffalo hide blanket, however. He traded for that with one of the families who spent the summers out in the open prairies hunting buffalo.

After 10 days of trading, Chunk-Kay, and feasting, it grew time to pack up. Each clan and each family again planned to make their own way in the world. They all made their final preparations for the winter now close at hand. In spring and summer, they would again work on stock piling whatever resources became available and most of them would not see each other again until the next Fall Harvest Celebration. Running Black Deer and his family planned to hike north for many days. It represented the longest walk of the year for his family. They would go to the place of the pines in the far north where the old growth white pine forests grew in a place so thick that not even the cold winds of winter could penetrate them. The trees grew so large and so close together that some years the snow laid like a blanket high up in the sky on the tops of the trees and the snow never even made it to the ground.

His parents preferred this place to spend the winter. Running Black Deer complained because he found it an intensely boring place to live. The lakes and streams simply grew too thick with ice to fish and other game became scarce during the cold months. Running Black Deer's father sometimes took stone with him to make stone spear points and knives to pass away the hours during long winter months. His mother worked most of the winter stitching together the previous year's skins into new clothing, and Running Black Deer spent a good deal of time splitting bones and making needles and fishhooks to entertain himself.

Running Black Deer and his family had barely settled in for the winter before his pot of maple syrup grew empty. His mother however seemed delighted and started to use the pot immediately. At the Fall Harvest Celebration, she learned that these new clay pots made great soup containers. After a few uses she agreed, it made cooking easier than using the bladder bag she normally hung over the fire and cooked with using stones. The family used the little clay jar daily for cooking but toward the end of the winter it cracked. Just a small crack near the rim at first, but it rapidly started to open up. Running Black Deer's father thought that he might fix it somehow but none of his ideas worked. Running Black Deer thought that he might fix it as well by filling the crack with clay. So, when they eventually abandoned the winter camp in favor of their summer camp by the little lake, they brought the cracked clay jar with them.

Once they'd taken care of all the chores associated with setting up their summer home Running Black Deer finally had an opportunity to try and fix his mother's clay pot. He dug some clay from the bank along the lake and pushed it into the crack of the jar. When the clay dried, however, it simply fell out and the crack remained. The next time he put clay in the crack and then put the jar in the fire, but again the new clay dried and fell out, not only that, but the crack worsened. Eventually they set it outside their bark house because it became completely unusable. Running Black Deer's mother so liked the pot, nobody dared take it and throw it in the place where they took their garbage. Instead, it stood outside their house by the base of a tree. Running Black Deer's father promised to trade for more than one of these pots the coming year, and Running Black Deer promised his mother he planned to trade all of his smoked fish to learn the secret of making these clay pots. Then he said he planned to make her more than she could ever use.

The days turned to weeks, and the weeks turned to months. When the first hints of color started to change the leaves on the trees from green to yellows and oranges the family again headed toward the Great Spirit River to the place of the Harvest Celebration. They again amassed a great deal of goods and felt eager to trade again. It seemed as though fewer people set up camp this year though. The loud shouts of kids and adults playing Chunk-Kay and feasting seemed less robust. Running Black Deer soon found out that people from Red Earth had killed or taken captive many of their people that year. Running Black Deer heard of the place before and knew that it existed far to the north and east, but he had never been there. He listened as the adults gathered and spoke in hushed tones. Rather than 10 days the people only stayed three. Trading happened as usual but at night the men did not sing and dance, instead they watched the forest for the people from the Red Earth. At the end of the third day, the group decided they should all move farther to the west, across the Great Spirit River, and try to distance themselves from these people who caused so many problems and heartache.

Running Black Deer and his family never returned to their little camp by that lake. In the years that followed they moved still farther west into strange lands. The little clay jar they left sitting by the tree endured hot summers and brutally cold winters and soon many cracks covered the jar. When nothing remained but a pile of shards lying there, the leaves of a hundred falls did their work to cover the shards up. A hundred years after that an oak tree grew in that same exact spot. The little sandy slope down to the small clear lake eventually became a county park where a lot of families went swimming in summer. On one such hot summer day a husband and wife took their young son there and put a blanket out in the shade of the old oak tree that grew there. As they enjoyed the beauty of the lake and the shade of the tree the boy spotted a piece of the clay jar that the work of a woodchuck brought to the surface. The boy showed it to his mother and father who explained people lived there for many years, long before Europeans arrived. Though no experts, the boy's parents suggested the shards from the pot might be hundreds, if not thousands, of years old. This made the boy glad.

Chapter 11: Runs-From-Skunk

Runs-From-Skunk lead a brutally hard and lonely life. He felt like an outcast from almost the beginning. His father died in war when he was just six, and his mother was taken captive that same year. No immediate family remained to take him in. Most children in his position eventually starved to death. Runs-From-Skunk however proved exceedingly tough. He survived the first couple of years by begging for meager handouts from other families. During that time, his people Of the Flowing Waters moved farther north due to war in their normal lands.

These new lands did not provide the game in as much abundance as their old lands. Because the land did not offer up as much food, times became hard for everybody. Runs-From-Skunk only barely managed to beg for enough food to survive. He often went to the trash heap to find bare bones to gnaw on. He slept in a poorly made bark house for a time because he never learned the proper way to make one. Above all else he felt lonely and angry. He would give anything to have his parents back and to have enough to eat just once so he could know what it felt like to sleep with a full stomach.

His harsh upbringing helped Runs-From-Skunk to survive the following winter. Many people in his tribe slowly starved to death that winter. But not Runs-From-Skunk. He grew accustomed to hunger, and he also learned to behave like the squirrel and put as much food away as he could without telling the others. They did not share with him as a young child, and now he decided he did not want to share with them either. What the other tribe members did not know was that Runs-From-Skunk had learned to hunt with great proficiency over the years.

Most of his people primarily worked as fishermen and depended on the river to provide for them through the winter. Runs-From-Skunk fished like the rest of his tribe, but he did not rely entirely upon fishing. He also hunted elk. When the winter grew so harsh the river froze over many of his people grew hungry because they had not put any extra food aside for the winter. Now he treated them just like they treated him when he once went hungry by sending them away with little or nothing. He told them to go dig through the garbage pile to look for bones to chew. As the long winter continued on and the river remained frozen, some people started to die from starvation. Around that same time Runs-From-Skunk killed a huge bull elk deep in the forest.

Runs-From-Skunk hung the quarters high in the tree above his bark home for all to see and feasted in front of them. Many came to beg, but he chased them away and taunted them just like they had chased him for years. He felt nothing in his heart for these people who once felt content to let him go hungry as a child and potentially die. Finally, some of the men from the tribe got together and decided to simply take the elk from Runs-From-Skunk since he would not share. Then they planned to ban him from the village forever. The next morning the group of men approached Runs-From-Skunk and told him they planned to ban him from the village forever.

"You must leave now," they told him simply.

"That's not possible in the midst of winter like this, you know that!" Runs-From-Skunk said. He argued with the men back and forth, but when one of the men took a lit torch and held it to Runs-From-Skunk's bark house he knocked the man down and started to beat the man with his fists. Then a second man tried to pull Runs-From-Skunk off the man, but he pulled a knife tucked in the man's belt and cut him. A third man lunged at Runs-From-Skunk, but he killed that man. The others ran to get their spears and by the time they returned Runs-From-Skunk had killed another man and cut the other so badly that he eventually died. Runs-From-Skunk was forced from his dilapidated bark house with nothing more than a stone knife and fishing net. The men and their families cut the hanging bull elk down and feasted upon it like a pack of ravenous wolves. They roasted bits of it over the flames from Runs-From-Skunk's bark house.

What was left of that winter became the hardest days Runs-From-Skunk ever faced. He confronted hunger and freezing winds for days before he found a deep ravine that cut into the sandstone close to the river. He found a wide, deep cave in the bottom of the ravine and there he took shelter in the comparative warmth of the earth. Later he managed to catch a few fish from the river with his net though he had to walk across dangerous river ice to do so. His modest fishing success wasn't enough to keep away hunger however, and he soon lost a lot of weight. By the time spring truly started to arrive and melt things Runs-From-Skunk found himself bordering on starvation for the second time in his life. Worse yet he felt consumed with depression. He wondered why the Great Spirit bothered to bring him into this world because it seemed he had no purpose other than to absorb the evilness of his fellow man. For the first time in his life, he prayed.

Spring brought much needed food for Runs-From-Skunk, but he still needed many other things. He left his spears behind, his clothing, and almost all of his stone tools. He'd re-sharpened his one remaining knife so many times that it looked short and almost useless. He needed so many things so badly and he'd become so lonely he decided he should follow the Great Spirit River to the south hoping to find somebody else to live by. He heard rumors of a fierce group who lived in the south that painted their faces white and fought fearlessly in battle. These people caused his own people to move farther north in the years before his birth, but he no longer felt afraid of them or anyone. He adopted a fatalistic attitude that whatever happened, happened. He had stared death in the face for so long already that he no longer felt afraid of it.

Runs-From-Skunk walked south along the banks of the river for many days and noted that even the plants looked different farther south. He entered a land he truly felt unfamiliar with and in the middle of one afternoon he stopped dead in his tracks when he noticed a large group of small smoke columns reaching up into the sky before blending together in a single gray haze. He'd found a village, and probably one filled with the White-Faced Ones. He dropped his ridiculously small and useless knife on the riverbank and tightened up his belt, cinching his ragged and smelly clothes tight against his thin body. He determined not to enter their village with any weapons; he planned to go to his new life or his death openly and without fear.

Runs-From-Skunk could sense he looked wretched because people either stared in wide-eyed disbelief or ran to hide as he entered the village. Children stopped playing and hid behind their mothers and the mothers in turn hid behind their bark houses afraid of Runs-From-Skunk. He continued down the path through the middle of the village unchallenged and walked up to a large fire pit surrounded by wooden benches. He surmised that this pit served as the village hearth. Next to it a woman lay sleeping.

Dogs started barking at the scent of the stranger, and the woman sleeping by the fire awoke. When she looked up and saw Runs-From-Skunk's figure she screamed and scrambled to get to her feet to run away. Moments later a number of men surrounded Runs-From-Skunk with war clubs and spears yelling and taunting him to make a move. Runs-From-Skunk simply opened up his hands and spread his arms as he looked up to the sky, expecting to feel the plunge of a spear in his chest at any moment. He did not recognize these people because they were wearing the white paint on their faces, but he did indeed stand in the midst of the White-Faced People now.

They spoke in a language that sounded vaguely familiar to him. He understood a few words, but for the most part their threats and harsh words meant nothing to Runs-From-Skunk. He remained emotionless as they attempted to interrogate him. He could tell they wanted to know why he came there and what he wanted. But the language barrier proved too great for him to explain his background in any detail. The men forced Runs-From-Skunk to sit on the ground and one of them tied his hands with rope while another man ran off. A short while later the man returned with an old woman. Runs-From-Skunk did not recognize the woman any more than she recognized him at first, but as soon as she began to speak in his native tongue, he looked in wide-eye disbelief. Her voice sounded as familiar as the leaves in fall, after so many years, he'd found his mother.

Runs-From-Skunk spoke quickly, trying to explain everything about his life, since the White Face took her captive. She began to cry, and the men of the tribe demanded she translate. She however, in order to protect her son, told him that she would explain that he came to them simply as a lone hunter, one of the last of his people. She explained to him that he should never reveal their true relationship.

She took a long time in talking to the men, and they repeatedly asked her seemingly scornful questions. She replied to each one in detail it seemed until the men asked
no more questions. When they finished with Runs-From-
Skunk they told him he could stay, but he must swear alle-
giance to them and learn their ways.

Over time Runs-From-Skunk learned the entire situation. The White-Faced People of this tribe raided the villages to the north to secure a larger hunting territory to
feed their ever-growing tribe. They viewed the tribes to the
north as vastly inferior and held them in great disdain.
Runs-From-Skunk found their perception true. These
people mastered many unfamiliar arts. They made much
better nets for fishing and set traps throughout the forests
which caught more game than he could believe. Over time
they taught him their ways of hunting, their language, and
they even allowed him to take a wife. Over the next few
years, he truly became one within their tribe and accepted
as one of them. These people did not poke fun at him, and
they did not try to steal from him.

In his fourth year with the White-Faced Ones talk grew
of a war party. Several hunters discovered a recently used
camp in the far north where the clan there caught many
fish. The White-Faced People seemed afraid that these
people of the north might eat all of the fish in the waters if
they did not make them leave. A war party formed; they
invited Runs-From-Skunk to come along. He learned they
burned a sacred stone in the south to make their white
paint. All of the men applied the paint to their faces and
chests, some of them even applied it to their war clubs before heading out.

After walking a few days to the north, they found
grounds that seemed familiar to Runs-From-Skunk. Eventually he took them to the camp where his tribe banished

him, but they found it abandoned. Runs-From-Skunk stopped and examined the earth where his house once stood and fought to keep the anger from welling up inside of him. The rest of the war party started to spread out to look for clues to see what direction these fishermen traveled but Runs-From-Skunk didn't need any clues to know.

Runs-From-Skunk lead the war party directly to their other camp just a few miles up the river. There they surrounded the camp on all sides at close range without discovery. Runs-From-Skunk examined the wretched looking bunch from a distance and recognized many familiar faces. He also noted that perhaps only half as many people remained in the tribe as when they kicked him out. He felt superior to these people now as well, and he and his war party made short work of dispatching the entire group. They left a single man behind alive to bury the dead so that ghosts would not follow them back home. After the cremation of all the bodies, the last member of the clan begged for his life. But they made him sit upon the heaping fire until he too died and burned. Runs-From-Skunk felt nothing for them and said nothing of their fate to his mother when they returned to their home village. That night the White-Faced Ones held a huge celebration because of the war party's success, and they sang, danced, and feasted well into the night.

Runs-From-Skunk's mother died a few years later without ever learning the fate of her people. Runs-From-Skunk went on to raise a family of his own in that village and carefully provided them with all the love and food he never knew as a child. Runs-From-Skunk died a very old man in that village, and some of his descendants still live in that same area to this very day. More than 5,000 years later a young man, a bit of a misfit himself, found the stubby little used up knife that Runs-From-Skunk dropped on the riverbank before entering the village of the White-

Faced Ones. The young man laughed at the site of the stubby and crude stone artifact. He wondered if anybody who made such a lousy knife could ever experience much success as a hunter.

Chapter 12: Two Oaks and the Fine Blade

Two Oaks and his people spent most of their time in the flat forest lands between the Mud River and the Spirit River leaving that part of the country only in spring when the fish began to make their spawning runs up the creeks. Then they would travel a few days walk to the southwest across the Spirit River into the land of hills and valleys to fish. In the winter the clan split up, each family going out on its own to hunt and trap and come spring all the families gathered at the valley they knew simply as Grass Valley.

When the spring fishing concluded, the clan would return to the flat forest lands between the two rivers until winter again arrived. The spring camp in Grass Valley was Two Oaks favorite place to make camp. It was always nice to see the other families after spending the winter apart; and for this reason, Two Oaks normally arrived first at the spring camp, sometimes even while snow still covered the ground.

Many of the other families enjoyed the spring camp in Grass Valley just as much as Two Oaks and his family. The bluffs that surrounded Grass Valley offered a wide array of medicinal plants early in spring that could not be found in many other places, and so Two Oaks and his family wasted no time picking many of them ahead of the rush sure to come. They did not need to wait long for others to arrive. Two days later Two Oaks' brother-in-law, Singing Hawk, arrived with his family. They needed to work hard to make the camp ready for the rest of the families. The spring floods had come fast and deep that year; and their fish dam in the creek sustained considerable damage. Even though some small bits of snow lingered in the shadows of the valley, the weather warmed quickly, and the two men didn't mind wading into the creek to fix the fish dam.

The fish dam consisted of little more than a rock wall that crossed the entire creek from one side to the other and which angled downstream in the middle to form a cone shape. They would place nets at the end of the cone to catch fish. But the flood waters toppled the stone walls in more than one place. Together they worked to pry large cobbles and small boulders from the surrounding landscape and placed them with careful hands, patching the holes in the wall one stone at a time. Yells from a distance one afternoon interrupted Two Oaks' and Singing Hawk's work. Both men froze and strained their ears for a moment to make sense of the noise over the sounds of the running water from the creek.

"Father! Father! Strange men are coming up the valley!" A boy's voice sounded in the distance. Two Oaks and Singing Hawk sprang from the creek and darted back toward their camp; but even before they arrived the men could see the new arrivals presented no threat. The hunters approaching came from the south.

The hunters from the south wore distinctive head dresses made from raccoon skins and eagle feathers that made them recognizable even at a distance. These southern hunters sometimes passed through Grass Valley on their way to the north to trade with other people. Or sometimes they passed when they hunted in the area. They never caused any trouble, and always behaved in friendly ways, but Two Oaks secretly never truly trusted them. In spite of the uneasy feeling these southern hunters gave him, Two Oaks offered them food and a seat by the fire as custom dictated. They did not speak the same language, but clearly each felt respect for the other. After eating the southern hunters prepared a place to sleep off away from the others down by the creek. Two Oaks and his brother-in-law returned to work on the fish dam.

When they walked out of ear shot from the hunters Two Oaks confided in Singing Hawk. "I've never really completely trusted those southern hunters," he said.

Singing Hawk paused and thought before responding, "They come through our valley here many times before and never caused us any problems."

"I know this Singing Hawk," Two Oaks explained. "But did you notice how young these two are? Did you notice all the scars on their bodies? Perhaps they are warriors more than hunters. Perhaps they know they can fool us; and tonight, when we sleep, they may kill us and take our wives and children for their own."

Singing Hawk again paused before replying, seemingly weighing his options. "We can take turns staying awake all through the night to watch them if it will make you sleep better," Singing Hawk said.

When the spring sky started to hint at the approach of darkness the women fixed some stew. The hunters shared some of their game and they had enough stew to fill every-one. Later, when darkness filled the valley Two Oaks stoked the fire and stayed to visit with the hunters. They could not speak each other's language, but they made some attempt to learn a few words of each other's tongue. Before long, one of the two hunters went off to his bed by the creek bank, but the other stayed up with Two Oaks.

Singing Hawk, fearing Two Oaks would wake him in the middle of the night to watch over the hunters decided it best if he went off to sleep as well. Two Oaks and the young hunter sat by the fire late into the night. They examined each other's clothes and decorations to see how they were made. They also examined each other's knives and atl-atls with great interest. Two Oaks looked upon the hunter's atl-atl with great envy because it appeared much better made than his own, and he made mental notes to change his design when he made another. After Two Oaks handed the hunter his atl-atl back the young man loosened a sheath from his belt. Two Oaks momentarily froze when he mistakenly thought the young man perhaps planned to attack him, but relaxed when he realized he just planned to show Two Oaks his knife.

The young hunter realized what happened, smiled, and then mockingly jabbed at Two Oaks. Two Oaks felt embarrassed but quickly forgot when the young man drew the knife from the sheath. The blade looked huge by comparison, made from a white stone Two Oaks had never seen before. It appeared to almost glow in the light of the fire. Two Oaks handled the fine blade with great admiration, examining it from every angle. The blade was not only large, but also very thin and well made. The handle was constructed from a thick section of deer antler, and a great deal of time went into carving the handle into the shape of a deer's head.

Two Oaks felt embarrassed when the hunter motioned toward the sheath that hung at Two Oaks' side, indicating that he wanted to look at his. Two Oaks felt ashamed of the small and rather crude knife he made from a creek cobble, but he handed it over to the traveler none the less. The hunter looked it over quickly and smiled again before handing it back.

Two Oaks then went to work trying to arrange a trade for the fine white knife, but the younger hunter refused all attempts at trading for the knife. Eventually Two Oaks gave up when he realized it didn't matter what he offered, the hunter simply would not trade his knife away. When the moon rose high above the bluff, ducking in and out of the clouds, both Two Oaks and the young hunter ventured off to sleep.

Some of Two Oaks' worries eased after the long and friendly visit with the one hunter. Though he looked young, and his many scars spoke of many fights, he seemed cordial and friendly. Two Oaks tried to sleep but tossed and turned. After some time passed, he imagined the hunter sneaking up on his wigwam in the dark. He knew he had no reason to think such things, but the thought persisted just the same. Finally, Two Oaks decided to sneak out in the darkness and check on the hunters. If he found them both to be sleeping soundly, he might be able to better fall asleep himself.

He crept from his house and headed off in the direction where the hunters made their beds, by the creek. Two Oaks stayed in the shadows of the basswood trees that lined the creek so the hunters would not see him if they woke. As he moved closer still his movements became more careful and planned, he moved quietly through the shadows as if stalking game. When he finally reached the place where the hunters prepared their beds he found both sound asleep. He briefly studied each man sleeping and felt both foolish and relieved.

He turned to sneak back to his house the same way, but just as he turned the moon again peeked out from behind a cloud and something caught Two Oaks' attention. Hanging on a branch by the creek's edge he saw the hunter's belt with the sheath and knife tied to it.

Rather suddenly and without very much thought, Two Oaks found himself slipping quietly into the waters of the creek where the sound of running water might better hide his approach. He inched his way down the creek to the area where the hunter's belt and knife hung on the branch. He found that it hung directly above a deep hole that he and Singing Hawk dug the summer before in hopes that it might help hold more fish. Without thought to what he did he made his way along the edge between the deep hole and the creek bank. He reached up slowly and barely managed to grab the springy young branch with the tips of his fingers. Slowly and carefully, he pulled the flexible branch down to his level and removed the knife. Again he found himself admiring it. It almost glowed a blue-white, in the light of the moon.

He tucked the knife in his own belt and then removed the sheath from the belt and let it go in the water. He hoped the hunter would find the sheath in the water in the morning and figure the knife had simply fallen into the water during the night. Without any more hesitation, he turned and carefully made his way back up the creek the same way that he had come. When he arrived at a good and safe distance, he searched for a small rock that he deemed the right size. He threw it far down the creek as close to the place where the two hunters slept as possible. The loud splash sounded like an explosion of noise to Two Oaks who had just spent the last hour moving as quiet as he could. But it failed to even wake the two hunters. He hoped the splashing noise would wake the hunters and convince them the knife had fallen into the water in the dark, but he felt just as content that they remained sleeping.

Two Oaks crept back to his wigwam and in the still of the night dug a hole in the dirt floor to hide his new prized knife. The next morning, he awoke to the sounds of birds chirping in the trees. He found the two hunters already by the community fire; the one who lost his knife clearly seemed upset. He motioned Two Oaks to come over and in spite of the language barrier it grew quite clear that the hunter wanted to know where his knife was and that he felt suspicious. Two Oaks pretended that the questions confused him, and he tried to say so to the hunter. As the hunter motioned, Two Oaks followed him back to the place where he slept the night before. He pointed to his belt hanging on the branch by the water. Two Oaks made a cutting motion with his hand and the hunter nodded angrily.

Two Oaks responded by pretending to search the tall grass along the bank for the knife. Then he paused and looked at the belt and then the deep-water hole beneath it. Simultaneously the scowl lifted from the hunter's face as he began to realize the knife may have slipped from the belt and into the water. Soon, both the hunters and Two Oaks busily searched the deep-water hole for the knife. Even as they searched a sense of guilt started to slowly creep into Two Oaks' heart. After a long while the hunters gave up and seemed content that the knife had simply fallen out into the water. It seemed even more obvious to the hunters when one of them later found the sheath in the water much farther down-stream.

After the hunters continued on their way, and the days passed, the feeling of guilt welling up inside of Two Oaks became unbearable. His family sensed something wrong and even Singing Hawk asked him if he felt ok. Two Oaks lied to everyone and said he felt fine. Two Oaks began to feel stupid for stealing the knife. He could not ever use it as somebody would either recognize it as the knife the hunter lost or at the least, inquire as to where he obtained such a fine piece. Soon other families arrived in the valley and people seemed less keen on what bothered Two Oaks, but the guilt continued to gnaw at him just the same. He decided he needed to rid himself of the knife so that he could move on with his life. He told his wife he planned to go on a deer hunt in the bluffs early the next morning. It was a little late for deer hunting, but his wife didn't complain because she welcomed the possibility of fresh venison.

Early the next morning, before anybody woke up, Two Oaks dug the fine knife up from the floor of his house and tucked it into his belt. When he traveled a safe distance away from their camp he slung his bow over his shoulder and pulled the knife from his belt. Though he still felt very much consumed with guilt, he again admired the quality of the blade and handle as he walked.

By mid-morning Two Oaks walked miles from his camp and came to a beautiful place where rock formations rose up from the ground in towering formations. It was along one of these rock formations where he found a deep crevice and slid the knife deep in it. He didn't think anybody would ever come to such a remote place and find the knife, but he stuffed the crevice with some moss and pine needles just in case. Later that day he tracked down and took a deer. On his walk back to camp he swore to himself that he would never take something from another person like that again. When he finally arrived home his wife could see that some of the tension and sadness had lifted from his face, and he looked better. His wife joked with Two Oaks saying, "If fresh venison makes you so happy perhaps, we should eat it more often."

It wasn't until many thousands of years later, when two young boys explored the rock formations in that area that they found the knife. At first the boy walked right by it but just a glimpse of something white caught just enough of his attention that his youthful curiosity forced him to stop and back up. When he peered back into the crevice, he could hardly believe his eyes. He broke a stick off of a nearby tree and pulled the blade out from inside the deep recess.

Both he and his friend had found arrowheads in the area before, but neither of them had ever seen such a large and perfect blade like this. The boys stopped to show their find to people and friends all over town. People presented a lot of theories, but the most commonly held belief was that the knife served as some sort of ceremonial offering. The boys spent the rest of the summer searching the bluffs in the area for other artifacts like that knife, but never did find anything else like it.

Chapter 13: Yellow Thunder's Love

Yellow Thunder grew up on the banks of the Great Spirit River. To the east of his village lay vast forests and prairies. Because the forests and prairies contained many small creeks, springs and lakes it became a favorite hunting ground of his people. To the north lay vast pine forests. There the hunting thinned, but the fish and beaver remained plentiful. To the south great prairies stretched out filled with buffalo, but warrior tribes also filled these areas. To the west lay the Great Spirit River, and on the other side of the river rested swamp lands for several days travel and then a mixture of forest and prairie inhabited by other tribes.

Yellow Thunder and his people mostly stayed to themselves, completely content to hunt and fish the lands near their village and to harvest the fish and clams that filled the Spirit River. Fortune smiled upon Yellow Thunder's village for many years and the number of houses in their village grew dramatically. Elders even spoke of splitting the village in two and settling a new village in a slightly different area, but so far, the idea remained undecided. The elders claimed remaining as one village provided additional safety. In this large village Yellow Thunder came of age; and in this village he fell in love.

Yellow Thunder reached his 15th summer the year he fell in love. And the girl who won his affection reached her 14th summer that same year. Summer Moon was the daughter of White Eagle, the Eagle Clan leader and elder. Custom dictated that a man could take a woman as a wife only when the father of the girl agreed, and only after the elders voted to approve the marriage. Since Summer Moon was the daughter of such an important member of the village it would not be easy to convince her father that Yellow Thunder proved the best choice for his daughter. Yellow Thunder knew a difficult path lay ahead because all the young men of the tribe took notice of Summer Moon and her beautiful looks. So many young braves came to court his daughter that White Eagle seldom let her venture far beyond the outer limits of their village. Therefore, it came as no surprise to White Eagle when Yellow Thunder finally worked up the courage to ask for his daughter in marriage.

Since so many young men bothered White Eagle seeking his daughter's hand in marriage, he came up with an idea that might at least slow some of them down. He decided that starting with the very next would-be suitor, he would accept the marriage offer for his daughter only if the man could complete three tasks. This he planned to tell them, would provide proof he needed to ensure they possessed enough bravery to win his daughter's hand. White Eagle was always a shrewd thinker however, and he designed a set of tests for the suitors that would also help make him wealthy. When Yellow Thunder showed up at White Eagle's house that day White Eagle told him the first of three tasks would be to bring back tools made of the sun stone.

Yellow Thunder had only seen things made from the sun stone one time when a hunter and trader from the north came down the river in a canoe with some of this material to trade for buffalo hides. The stone was not like the stone they usually made their tools from, but rather a shiny and soft material that glittered as brightly as the sun when polished. The trader told Yellow Thunder and his village about a place in the far north where the trader's people dug this sun stone up from the earth and then fashioned tools from it in hot fires by pounding it. The things the trader brought with him that day were well received by the village and many of the women in particular put a high value on the beads, awls, bracelets and other items. Yellow Thunder also remembered that White Eagle carried with him an axe made from this material for several years before losing it in a spring flood.

Yellow Thunder told his parents and brother about his desire to marry Summer Moon and about the three tasks he needed to complete. Yellow Thunder's father immediately recognized what White Eagle was likely doing and tried to discourage his son from traveling so far from home into unknown territory. But nothing could discourage Yellow Thunder. Because Yellow Thunder's brother and father experienced great good luck in fishing and hunting that year, they decided to allow him to go for a few weeks if he must. They wouldn't need him at home to help until berries started to ripen up and the ducks began to migrate.

Yellow Thunder managed to convince his brother to donate two fine buffalo hides to his cause. He also traded all of his feathers and two deer hides to his friend for two other buffalo hides, since he knew the trader from the north sought buffalo hides in the past. He hoped that the trader would still find them valuable now as well. That evening he loaded the four large hides into his family's biggest canoe along with a bag full of venison jerky, some dried fish, some dried berries, some acorn mush, his atl-atl, and his fishing net.

Yellow Thunder left early the next morning before the birds awoke. By the time the sun started to turn the sky colors on the horizon he had already paddled up the river out of view. As a child he spent a lot of time on the river, and now he made good time in his canoe. By the time evening settled the first day he was already nearing an area his people called the White Rocks. They normally did not travel any farther north than this because they found it difficult to carry the canoes around this area and because other peoples lived to the north.

It took him almost half of the second day just to get around the white rocks. He had to carry the heavy buffalo hides one at a time and all of his supplies plus his canoe. By the end of that second night, he officially passed out of his home range. Nothing looked familiar anymore, and he did not sleep quite as easily in this strange place. The thought of Summer Moon filled his mind when he finally drifted off to sleep.

By mid-morning of the third day he could see some slender smoke trails ascending into the sky in the distance. As he paddled closer, he could see a small fishing village. When he came close several men walked to the shore. Though they did not look mean, they did carry their war clubs at their sides. He made a sign of peace to them, and they returned it so he made his way to shore. He felt much relieved to find they spoke a language so close to his own that he could speak with them without difficulty.

These people found him interesting and asked him many questions. He patiently answered them all one by one, and in turn they brought him some turtle soup and tea to drink. When they finished asking him questions, and he finished explaining where he planned to go, he inquired about the sun stone and if any of them had ever seen it or knew where to find it. They said they were indeed familiar with it, but its source lay far to the north and was not easy to find. There was only one person among the village who claimed to know the way there, but he was an old man.

The people of the fishing village took Yellow Thunder
to the hut of the old man who once traveled to the place of
the sun stone as a young man. Yellow Thunder felt happy
to find this man perhaps not so old as what the villagers
made him sound; but he did possess a severe limp, the result of an old war injury to his hip. They called the old
man Otter Rock and said they called him this because he
ate more clams as a young man than even an otter did.
Otter Rock went on to describe how he traveled to the
place of the sun stone as a youth, and how he managed to
trade for a great number of tools made from it by bringing
the locals some of the gray stone from the far south as well
as a buffalo hide. Otter Stone said this place lay so far
north that not even buffalo went there. He said the place
became very cold in the winter, and people of the village
their prized buffalo hides for their thick hair and warmth
in the cold.

Yellow Thunder listened intently as Otter Rock described how to get to the place, but Yellow Thunder did
not recognize the landmarks Otter Rock used to tell the
story, and he quickly became confused. Finally, Otter Rock
offered to serve as his guide if he would in turn share
some of the sun stone tools with him. Yellow Thunder
agreed, and the next morning the two set off from the fishing village. The canoe now sat lower in the water with the
weight of another person, and it slowed the time it took to
cover the miles, but Yellow Thunder felt quite happy to
have some company for the rest of the long journey.

It took more than a week, but finally Otter Rock pointed
out a creek running into the Spirit River and said they
must travel up this little creek. They followed that for
several miles before making a small portage to another
stream and continued north. Three weeks later they finally
arrived at the place of the sun stone. The locals welcomed
them in a friendly manner much like Otter Rock's village

welcomed Yellow Thunder; but this time they did not understand their hosts. None of their words seemed to make any sense or sound familiar, but it didn't take long to communicate what they had come for and what they brought to trade.

At first these people of the sun stone only wanted to give Yellow Thunder a small amount of tools for all his buffalo hides, but by the afternoon they smoked several pipes and agreed to a more equitable trade. Yellow Thunder would leave with a pouch full of sun stone tools, beads, and bracelets. He also traded for fine spear tips, several knives, 100 awls or more perhaps, and two axes like White Eagle once used.

The trip back to Otter Rock's village passed quickly as it now all flowed down-stream, no more fighting the current for every mile. It took only half the time to return as it did to get there. Yellow Thunder thanked Otter Rock many times when he stopped to let him out of the canoe. Yellow Thunder felt anxious to go home, but Otter Rock made him wait on the bank until he returned with some dried fish for him to take along. Yellow Thunder thanked him again and cast off. When he finally came around the corner and could see his village in the distance downstream his eyes momentarily filled with tears. He had never before felt so happy to return home; and he hoped he would never have to travel so far away to strange lands like that again. The tears were also tears of pride. Surely White Eagle never expected Yellow Thunder to actually find the place of the sun stone, never mind do it so quickly and come back with so many fine tools!

A group gathered on the shore by the time Yellow Thunder landed his canoe there. Most smiled and even waved, glad to see Yellow Thunder again. Some of the other braves had by this time learned of White Eagle's task and eyed Yellow Thunder suspiciously as he came ashore. Yellow Thunder however ignored them all and first went home. There he gave his parents and brother gifts of some of the sun stone things. He even kept a knife for himself. Everything else he put back in the bag though and went to White Eagle's house. There, without saying a word he handed the bag to White Eagle. White Eagle untied the bag, and his eyes grew wide, there on top lay two fine axes made from the sun stone. Then his eyes drifted past the axes, and he could make out all the other wonderfully shiny pieces. While distracted, Yellow Thunder peered past White Eagle into his house. After his eyes adjusted for a minute, he could make out the outline of Summer Moon sitting by the fire stirring some stew. A smile came to Yellow Thunder's face, and his heart started to flutter about like a butterfly.

White Eagle then looked at Yellow Thunder and said something, but Yellow Thunder was so taken by the beauty of Summer Moon he did not hear him. White Eagle stepped slightly to one side thus breaking Yellow Thunder's view of Summer Moon and his trance.

White Eagle told Yellow Thunder that he had indeed done very well, but that this represented an easy test. Now he needed to prove his bravery in the second task. Yellow Thunder's smile vanished and suddenly the butterflies from a moment before now formed a hard ball in his throat. White Eagle said his second task must be to bring him three scalps from the Black-Faced Ones on the prairie. Yellow Thunder felt crushed. The Black-Faced Ones who lived on the prairie were almost legendary in their fighting skill. Tribes on all sides gave them a great deal of room so as to not cross paths with these fierce warriors. To make matters worse, Yellow Thunder was not a particularly strong fighter; he shied away from fighting whenever given the option. Glancing one more time at Summer

Moon sitting in her father's house though gave him more confidence.

That night he told his family of White Eagle's second task. This time his mother begged him not to go, and his father refused to eat in protest. His brother teased him saying that maybe he would get lucky and find three of them recently dead and take the scalps from corpses. Yellow Thunder had difficulty falling asleep at the thought of fighting not one, but three Black-Faced Ones to the death. When he finally did drift off though, his only dreams were of Summer Moon sitting by his side in his own house someday. Though his parents protested, and others teased him, he gathered his atl-atl, his war club, and some provisions before heading off down the river toward the south.

Yellow Thunder traveled to the very edge of his people's territory. There he spent the night on an island in the river. From that point on he traveled at night because he didn't feel safe in this land. He ventured on for five days after leaving his people's territory before figuring he traveled far enough into the prairie region to find the Black-Faced Ones. He found a small creek feeding into the river at one point and hid his canoe at this place. From here he traveled on foot across the prairies in search of a Black Faced village. He considered his only chance might be to wait for a hunting party to leave, or for some member to stray out just a little too far where he might ambush them. In spite of playing many scenarios out in his head time and time again he found no one. No signs of the Black-Faced Ones or anybody else for that matter. He always heard the prairies in the south loomed large, but he never imagined anything like this. After a week of walking, he finally found a huge valley with a swiftly running river at the bottom. He even saw trees growing along the banks, the first trees he'd spotted since leaving the river.

Because he walked in a strange land, he did not want to venture too far out away from the only water he knew about and decided to follow the river upstream in his search for the Black-Faced Ones. On the third day, of walking the river he came to a place with very fast running water and many large white rocks. The place looked dangerous, and it reminded him a little bit of the other locations with white rocks he saw far to the north of his village. That all seemed like another world now though. Here he crept through the underbrush and willow trees trying to proceed with quiet and not leave too many signs he passed this way. Suddenly he heard a noise though, and he froze in his tracks. His heart beat heavy in his chest, and his palms began to sweat instantly. Slowly and carefully, he worked his way to the thicket's edge. There, out by the white rocks he could see a group of children cleaning clothes, beating them against the large boulders that surrounded them. He watched them for a couple of hours before deciding they did not belong to the Black-Faced Ones he sought. He did not know who they were, but he thought more than once he had heard words familiar to him.

In the early afternoon some women came to the river and joined the children cleaning. He had started to get a headache and began to peel some bark from a willow when he heard a sudden scream. He looked up just in time to see one of the women slip from a large boulder into the rushing waters. It took almost a minute, but he soon realized that the current would take her right by his hiding place there on the bank. Again, his heart started to beat hard, he didn't even have time to think anything through before the woman came straight at him screaming and flailing her arms. Clearly, she might drown.

He dropped his weapons and threw his shirt off before jumping in. He held firm to a fist full of willow branches with one hand while extending his other arm out to grab the woman. As soon as he pulled her from the water, and she regained her breath her eyes grew wide. She knew he did not belong to her people, and she looked afraid. She screamed crazily and would not stop in spite of Yellow Thunder trying to motion to her that he offered her no threat. Before Yellow Thunder knew what happened he found himself surrounded by warriors. One of them grabbed the woman and pulled her away to safety. The rest formed a circle around Yellow Thunder and slowly closed in with war clubs in hand. Yellow Thunder thought that now he might die and began to pray out loud.

Then he heard words familiar to him, though pronounced in almost a slur, they sounded like words he knew. One of the warriors asked him if he belonged to the Black-Faced Ones. Yellow Thunder started to laugh, these people seemed afraid that he might be a member of a Black Faced raiding party or something. When he started to speak and try to explain the warriors suddenly started to murmur to one another and some stepped back a bit.

After a couple more minutes of frantic explanation and some miscommunication, Yellow Thunder managed to convey that he was not a Black Faced One, he considered them his enemy. This seemed to please the people around him; and they invited him back to their village which sat just above the place of the white rocks on the high ground.

That afternoon he learned that he had stumbled into the Thundering Buffalo tribe's village. While they were not really friendly to outsiders, they accepted Yellow Thunder because he too hated their enemy the Black-Faced Ones. The husband of the woman he saved came to see him as well. He did not say much but wanted to know what he could give Yellow Thunder as a gift to show his appreciation. Yellow Thunder politely declined because he still needed to travel far and didn't want to carry any additional things with him. Then he went on to explain his whole task, why he came there, how beautiful Summer Moon seemed to him, and all of his life's details. Some of the Thundering Buffalo's people seemed amused at his ordeal, and others remained indifferent.

Before lying down, for the night the husband of the woman he saved came again to Yellow Thunder. Darkness surrounded him, but Yellow Thunder could see he carried something with him, a war club. Yellow Thunder at first felt alarmed, but then realized the man wanted to give it to Yellow Thunder as a gift of appreciation. Yellow Thunder noted how well made it was and the beautiful quill work on the handle. Tied to the bottom of the handle he found three scalps, all of the style of hair that the Black-Faced Ones wore. He handed the club with the scalps to Yellow Thunder and told him the story of how he and his three sons ambushed a Black Faced hunting party just a week before and took the three scalps. He explained why they felt so jumpy and fearful that he might be a Black Faced One looking for revenge when they first found him by the river. Yellow Thunder thanked the man more than once. His second task was now complete, albeit, in an unexpected way.

The Thundering Buffalo tribe sent two young braves with Yellow Thunder so that he could find his way back across the prairie to the river where he hoped to find his canoe. Along the way he decided he could not and would not ever reveal just how he came to possess the three scalps. Besides, White Eagle never specifically said that he must *kill* three Black-Faced Ones, only bring back three Black-Faced Ones scalps. Eventually he made his way back to his canoe and paddled his way back up the river. Unlike coming home from his first task, this time going home took much longer. He stopped more often while paddling up stream to fish and rest. Like before though, a crowd of people formed along the bank of his village long before he came ashore.

His friends and family seemed legitimately surprised at his return. Later he found out that his mother even cut her hair in mourning as custom dictated when someone died. He scanned the faces on the shore hoping to find Summer Moon waiting too but did not see her. After pulling his canoe up on shore he found himself overwhelmed with questions. When they saw he carried a club with three scalps some of the young braves started giving off shrill victory war cries. This in turn caused more people to come out of their houses and the woods.

Yellow Thunder had difficulty moving through the crowd that gathered. Then out of the crowd came White Eagle; he bore a look of disbelief. White Eagle took the club from Yellow Thunder and closely examined the scalps, they appeared fresh, and they certainly did look like Black Faced scalps. With White Eagle's approval villagers started a community fire and people started singing, dancing, and beating drums as custom dictated after a successful fight. When people pressed him for details, he only said that he felt fearless and would do anything to earn the hand of Summer Moon in marriage.

That night as most of the village danced and sang around the fire White Eagle found he could not sleep. He couldn't believe that Yellow Thunder could complete two difficult tasks like these. When Summer Moon whispered in her father's ear, he knew that he must reconsider the situation. Summer Moon now asked to go to the village fire to dance with the others, and he let her. When she came into the light by the fire the music suddenly stopped, and Yellow Thunder, along with everyone else, locked eyes on the beautiful young maiden. When Summer Moon walked over and embraced Yellow Thunder in the fire light the entire village erupted in shrill calls and singing. Even White Eagle heard from the confines of his home what happened at the fire. White Eagle's wife touched his arm and smiled. He knew it was time to let go.

When the fire died down and people started to wander off to sleep Yellow Thunder reassured Summer Moon that no matter what third task her father assigned, he would surely complete it just as he had the first two. White Eagle snuck out to check on his daughter and overheard the conversation. The next morning Yellow Thunder, with a small group of people following along, went to White Eagle's house to find out about the final task. White Eagle already expected Yellow Thunder and stood outside his door waiting. Yellow Thunder started to speak but White Eagle motioned for him to come inside, something he had not done before. He pulled the door shut behind them. Inside Yellow Thunder found a small fire lit and a pot of soup simmering over the fire. Off to one side sat Summer Moon and her mother. White Eagle motioned for Yellow Thunder to sit next to Summer Moon. After sharing a pipe with him, White Eagle offered his daughter in marriage to Yellow Thunder and the next day they married in the village center.

Yellow Thunder and Summer Moon lived a long life together, eventually having four children who survived to adulthood. In time Yellow Thunder's adventures became legendary among the people who lived along the Great Spirit River. Some of the stories passed down and are still told today though they became somewhat exaggerated over time.

Last year, along the banks of what once was known as the Great Spirit River, a man with a metal detector looked for a long-lost property stake on the corner of his lot.

When he got a loud signal, he dug for what he thought
might be the marker, but instead found a copper knife
thick with green patina. The knife once belonged to Yellow
Thunder who gave it to White Eagle to gain his acceptance
more than 4,000 years earlier.

Chapter 14: The Great Hunt

Every year the buffalo passed through the small prairies just east of the Great Spirit River around the same time. And each year the Wa-Shu-Shay people waited in anxious anticipation of this event. The buffalo provided all of their blankets, clothing, tools, many of their medicines, and of course most of their meat for the year. Hunting buffalo was dangerous, however. So elders required the boys of the tribe to wait until their 13th summer before they participated. On this particular year, Spotted Deer and Red Hawk participated for the first time. The two boys, both close friends since their youth, looked forward to their first hunt. In many ways it represented a rite of passage.

When the days started to grow shorter the men of the tribe prepared their atl-atl darts and other hunting gear. Spotted Deer and Red Hawk made their atl-atls and darts ready weeks early. They troubled their fathers and other hunters more with their constant questions and unrealistic expectations than their lack of preparation. Eventually their fathers suggested the boys go to spirit rock and perch themselves up high to watch for the first signs of buffalo. The hunters of the tribe quietly snickered and smiled as the boys headed off knowing full well the buffalo would likely not appear for more than a week more.

The boys didn't mind going to the rock to watch. The hunters made someone go watch each year and announce the presence of the buffalo when they arrived. The boys would get to signal the start of their first hunt, even if it came a bit early. Together they climbed the side of the sandstone rock until they reached the summit. Though the rock also served as a holy place, the boys had climbed it many times over the years as they searched for small game. This great rock rose high over the flat plains of the prairie, and from the south knoll they could look out on the prairies for great distances. It was on this little knoll that the boys sat for the next few days more or less continuously discussing their hunting tactics and who would be bravest in the hunt.

On the fifth day on the rock Red Hawk nudged Spotted Deer awake from his nap. Red Hawk smiled and pointed off to the south. As the sleep slowly cleared from his eyes Spotted Deer could see a dozen or more black dots milling about to the southwest of their knoll. The boys didn't waste any time climbing down the steep rock and running back to their village. Their short, loud, and shrill calls raised all the people in the village, and soon the village came alive. Men and women scrambled from their houses and threw wood on the community fire. Before long most of the village danced about the fire, singing, and replicating the boy's loud hunting calls. The village spent the remainder of the night making last minute preparations for the buffalo hunt.

Spotted Deer and Red Hawk, like many of the hunters, did not sleep at all that night because the hunting party left well before daylight. Altogether nearly 100 hunters set out that year to hunt, a good number. The hunters left in the dark carrying their heavy hunting packs and gear all silent and in single file. As they filed out of camp the medicine man chanted an ancient prayer.

Spotted Deer and Red Hawk, though still excited, now started to feel the gravity of the situation. Both grew up in the same village, and both had heard many of the horrible stories about hunters being gored or trampled to death in years prior. They also felt the tremendous weight of their father's hunting packs on their back fulfilling the custom for the younger members to carry the older hunter's gear in addition to their own.

After what seemed like more than double the walk needed to close in on the buffalo, the group of hunters stopped in a shallow ravine in the prairie. Even in the dark Spotted Deer recognized the place because the ravine, if followed far enough to the west, eventually entered into the Great Spirit River. He and Red Hawk had taken its path many times over the years. Now they unloaded their heavy hunting packs with sighs of relief.

Both Spotted Deer and Red Hawk remarked how light of foot they felt without the packs, but the others quickly reprimanded them for their loud comments. The elders split the hunters into two groups. Most of the experienced hunters along with the youngest hunters made up one group while most of the older hunters or those with old in- juries made up the other, smaller group. The larger younger group would consist of the Shi-te-to-da Nok-ta- donton or "buffalo walkers" while the smaller older group of hunters would consist of the Nok-ta-donton Jib-woa or "buffalo sleepers."

The buffalo walkers split into teams of two, each one put on a full buffalo hide carefully prepared for this pur- pose. Inside each skin a scaffolding of sticks gave the skin a life-like appearance and offered a surprising amount of room. Red Hawk and Spotted Deer both lifted their hide over the top of them and placed their atl-atls and dart points inside on the scaffolding. More than 30 other pairs of hunters did the same thing as the boys. When the morn- ing light showed itself the teams of hidden hunters slowly came up out of the ravine in a line and blended in with the herd. While the buffalo walkers prepared themselves, the buffalo sleepers went the other direction and hid them-selves at pre-arranged points along the prairie so that when the drive started, they could force the herd, at least part of it, over the edge of a steep ledge.

Spotted Deer and Red Hawk found their place in the middle of the line where they knew they would encounter the middle of the herd, one of the most dangerous places for a hunter when the hunt started. The boys hardly no-ticed the first of the morning light coming up on the hori-zon before other hunters nudged them from behind and told them to follow the team in front of them. It didn't take long for the boys to hear the sounds of the herd all around them. Spotted Deer strained to see through the small eye holes to follow the team in front of them. To get lost now would not only ruin the hunt for the day, but it could also cost people their lives. Eventually the team they followed stopped as did all the teams in the line. From there they spaced themselves out to make the distance between them more even.

The boys waited for the signal, and it seemed to take longer than it should. While they waited, they carefully and quietly made their atl-atls ready. Then quite suddenly a shout arose, starting at one end of the line and quickly following along, both boys joined in the shouting as soon as they heard and so it carried on down the line. At the same time, they threw off their skins and jumped up and down waving their arms. Like a giant unseen hand, the ac-tivity swept over the herd splitting it in two divided by the long line of now exposed hunters.

The herd began to panic and run from the hunters in both directions. The portion of the herd that split to the west would run over the edge of the steep ravine and the portion of the herd that ran to the east would run until their panic subsided, free to go on about their grazing. The entire line of hunters immediately began to work to push the one part of the herd to the west toward the edge of the cliff. Before the herd managed to put much distance between them and the hunters Spotted Deer had already launched his first of many atl-atl darts. It stuck high in the back of a big bull but seemed to make no difference to the beast.

The bull stopped and turned to face his tormentor. By the time Spotted Deer readied another dart and started to throw it the bull had already cut the distance between them in half. He didn't realize it at first, but Spotted Deer started to shake so badly that his second dart missed by a great distance. Red Hawk quickly grasped the seriousness of the situation and changed aim from the large calf he bore down on to the now charging bull. Spotted Deer froze, motionless.

The buffalo approached threatening to trample him, but his friend Red Hawk let loose his dart and it found its mark between the ribs of the bull, piercing both lungs just in time. The bull crashed to the ground with blood pouring from its nose literally only inches from Spotted Deer's feet, but they had no time to celebrate. The hunt continued to unfold around them in full swing. Both boys readied new darts and again chased after the herd killing or wounding two more buffalo before driving the last of them over the steep ravine.

The real success of that year's hunt didn't become fully apparent until both boys stood on the lip of the ravine and looked down at the carnage there. More than 200 buffalo took the plunge over the edge; their bodies now lay crushed and trampled on the rocks below. The wiser, more experienced hunters speared the survivors to death. Over the open prairie behind them lay another bloody scene as they could see the bodies of dead and dying buffalo stretching out for a great distance across the grass. The hunt barely ended before the women of the village appeared with baskets and knives ready to start the butchering process.

The boys and other hunters generally helped out with the butchering task as well; but many took time to start fires on the prairie and in the ravine first so they could roast some of the more delicate cuts as soon as possible. From all over the prairie and ravine shrill shouts of joy and celebration unfolded. Spotted Deer and Red Hawk made their way back to the big bull they killed already recounting the harrowing story to each other. Spotted Deer started a fire there while Red Hawk cut the still warm heart from the bull to cook on the fire. Before they completed the butchering that day the story of the boys' close call and exceptional heroism spread throughout the village. Others forced them to tell the story time and time again for many years afterward.

In 2011 a father walked with his seven-year-old daughter down a long dirt road that ran through the woods along the edge of a steep ravine. As they walked, they talked about all sorts of things including the people who once live there thousands of years before. Spotting a large flake of flint in the sand of the road the father pointed out that it probably belonged to the natives who made stone tools long ago. Just a short distance farther down the trail the little girl picked up another stone and asked if it came from the Indians too. The father couldn't believe his eyes; she held a beautiful little stone projectile, and he told her that indeed belonged to an ancient Indian. She held the stone point that Spotted Deer threw at the charging bull but missed.

In all the excitement the boys forgot to even look for it, and so it laid there for more than 3,000 years. The prairies

lost its battle with the forests during that time; and now,
this little dirt path that cut through the woods got used
just enough to allow the old atl-atl point to make its way to
the surface again where the little girl found it.

Chapter 15: The Black-Faced Ones

Falling Rain and her family held a well-earned reputation as the best mat and basket makers of their people. The skill developed out of necessity though because Falling Rain's father, Returns From War, did not possess keen hunting skills; and the mats, baskets, and other items Falling Rain and the family made they needed to trade for food. The family used local oak and basswood for many of their projects, but some products required specific materials. Fish traps, for instance, worked best when made from exceptionally flexible material like willow. Willow however didn't grow very well where they lived and so once a year they needed to all travel to the lowlands in the east to harvest willow from some of the vast stands that dotted the area there.

This willow harvesting trip brought a certain degree of peril with it because just beyond the lowlands on the open oak savannahs lived the Black-Faced Ones. Falling Rain grew up hearing horrific stories of wars not long past in which the Black-Faced Ones committed terrible acts. They killed her uncle before her birth. The story said her uncle formed part of a war party that the Black-Faced Ones overtook. When they found him, they skinned him and tied him high on a lodge pole. The Black-Faced Ones also took women and children captive and spared no one.

These thoughts pressed heavily on their minds as Falling Rain, her mother, and two younger sisters set off in mid-summer. Falling Rain's father made excuses to stay behind and simply warned Falling Rain to stay mindful of leaving too many travel signs lest the Black-Faced Ones find their trail and follow them. The four women set off with a good supply of food, enough to last them for the entire walk both to and back from the lowlands, a trip normally taking about a week total. In spite of stopping to take advantage of a large patch of wild strawberries, they made good time. By the afternoon of the third day, they entered the lowlands where they found their first big willow tree. Harvesting was simply a matter of pulling down the long strands of willow and cutting them off with a stone knife. Once cut, they formed the choicest pieces into bundles for transport.

Since they did not want to spend any more time close to the Black-Faced Ones than absolutely necessary, they decided to start harvesting right away in spite of the sun rapidly closing in on the horizon. Falling Rain worked on one large willow by herself while her mother and two younger sisters went to work on another only a short distance away. Falling Rain never heard a single noise when the Black-Faced Ones killed her mother and two sisters. She never noticed the Black-Faced Ones following them during the day, and she didn't notice the dark eyes now as they focused on her from the cattails behind her.

Falling Rain always harbored a terrible fear of snakes so when a blade of grass barely brushed upon the back of her leg, she suddenly spun around. The sudden turn around caused the man in the cattails to duck down instinctively so she could not see him. The movement he created in doing so however now caught Falling Rain's attention. Her heart started to beat wildly immediately as her fight or flight instincts kicked in. She stood motionless for a moment before the man in the cattails again raised up his head to check on his quarry. Then Falling Rain saw his charcoal blackened face staring at her with cold-blooded eyes. Both Falling Rain and the Black Faced One launched into the chase at exactly the same time. Falling Rain ran straight to where her mother and sisters worked only moments before with the man right behind her, his breaths audible over her own.

When she came within sight of the tree where she remembered them working, she saw their three bodies sprawled out in the grass and two Black-Faced Ones, arms covered in blood, kneeling over them cutting their long hair from their lifeless bodies. She screamed out in terrified agony and spun around to meet her pursuer head on. With the knife she used to cut willow raised in one hand she lunged at him trying to kill the man, but he simply grabbed her arm and overpowered her. The knife fell to the grass and the Black-Faced Ones tortured Falling Rain under that tree for most of the night before finally killing her at dawn.

In the years that followed the Black-Faced Ones, under increasing pressure from the east, moved farther and farther into Falling Rain's tribal grounds. Eventually the Black-Faced Ones killed or ran off all of her people; and their names are now lost upon the winds of time.

Thousands of years later farmers dug ditches to drain the lowlands in that place of their perpetual dampness so they could farm on a massive scale. A group of friends frequently fished for trout in the ditches in the area. On one such trip a young man found a crude stone knife in the dirt dredged out to form the drainage ditch. He found the knife that Falling Rain used to cut willows so many years before.

Chapter 16: Better Hunting Grounds

Raining Oaks had moved many times. When he was just six he and his family left their first hunting grounds south of the place where they lived now and moved twice more afterward. They lived in a time when few people roamed the area, and they only moved when game grew scarce. Now, in his 17th summer, Raining Oaks moved again. The last winter proved particularly harsh and had a surplus of rabbits and fish not come his way some of their small band would have starved. All of the leaders in their group, men and women alike, agreed they needed to find a place with plentiful herds of deer. So that spring they made plans to move again, this time to the west, past the Great Spirit River and into the forests beyond. Before all the families could pack up and move, however, scouts needed to go and find a suitable place for a village in the forest.

Elders selected Raining Oaks, because of his youth and bravery, and because he had no wife or children, to go along with his cousin, Stinging Winds. Together they scouted the forests beyond the Great Spirit River, a land neither of them ever visited prior to this trip. They traveled down-stream along the river for three days looking for a place to cross. Eventually they came to a shallow but fast flowing section of the river where they crossed. From that point on they found themselves in a strange land. They ventured out by following the river north again so they could line themselves up with their current camp across the river on the opposite bank.

As they headed north, they crossed mostly lowlands damp from flooding, all of which proved completely unsuitable for a camp. On the morning of the fourth day, they found themselves across the river from their small band, and from there they moved into the forests to the west. It took one full day just to get out of the flood plain created by the river. Early on the second day they finally found the high ground above the flood plain, but they also found something they hadn't expected, a single small rabbit snare set up under a fallen tree. Now realizing someone else hunted the area, they paused for discussion.

They couldn't know for sure who set the snare. Perhaps a lone hunter set it to feed his family, or maybe a hunter from a large village. The hunter's people might befriend them and let them pass, or they could show hostility to outsiders. They could not tell without moving on. Both men were young and neither one of them wanted to pass on a chance to build their reputation, and so they decided to continue to move farther inland and look for the person, or people who put the rabbit snare down. They wouldn't need to travel far. After only an hour of walking they came to a large creek the bank of which featured a well-worn path along its high ground.

The two men didn't need to speak, they both knew by looking at the width and depth of the trail that many feet passed this way, and likely it led to a large village. After following the path for a few minutes up a gentle slope they suddenly found themselves coming up over a hill covered in a stand of giant pine trees. Just beyond the stand of trees they saw smoke trails rising into the sky from a great many hearths.

They had only just commented on the number of smoke trails when they heard a warning yelp emitted from somewhere in the tall grass off to their side. Within just a minute they heard many yelps and calls coming their way from the village. Raining Oaks and Stinging Winds both silently wanted to run for their lives, but neither man made a move. They knew the safest plan required them to stay at a distance and wait. They didn't need to wait long, in just a few minutes they found themselves surrounded by more than 50 warriors. These people did not look like any they'd ever seen. They wore ornaments in their ears, painted their chests with white paint, and wore a great many adornments in general. They also wore their hair shaved except for a single ponytail in back; the combined look resulted in a fierce appearance. They tried to introduce themselves, but it immediately became obvious that they did not speak the same language. Suddenly Raining Oaks found himself wishing he could trade them something as custom dictated to make an offering in trade when meeting with strangers.

The strangers took Raining Oaks and Stinging Winds rather forcefully to the village. There the two could see that not only did these people dress and talk differently, they also built their houses much differently. Both men grew absorbed in their surroundings, but then suddenly the strangers shoved them to the ground from behind and took their weapons from them. At the command of the chief, male villagers tied the two young men to a single post in the middle of the village. Both men now started to fear the worst. While their people typically treated strangers with some kindness and would let them pass through their lands, they had heard of people not so kind. They now feared what these less than generous people might do. When some of the younger warriors started to dance around the pole sneering at them and making war calls, they knew it meant trouble.

Things did not get better for Raining Oaks and his cousin. Both men lay stripped naked, and the women came out to look at them, laughing and throwing stones. The villagers encouraged the young boys to throw things at the two as well, stones, sticks and dog feces. By the time the sun sank near the horizon both men lay bleeding, beaten and filled with agonizing terror. They both agreed to have any chance at all they must break free from the pole and run as far and as fast as they could. Both men agreed that if one of them broke free that he should not wait for the other, that one escaping was better than none.

At sunset the villagers built a great fire at some distance from the pole, and the entire village seemed thoroughly pleased with the day's events as they danced and sang about the fire. From time-to-time small groups or a single person came over to where they lay tied and hit them or threw stones at them. At one point a young warrior, even younger than Raining Oaks and his cousin, came over carrying Raining Oaks bow and arrows, from a long distance away the young warrior shot two arrows. The first one stuck for a moment in Stinging Winds' side before falling to the ground. The second arrow missed completely. The young warrior looked at Raining Oaks' bow and arrows with disgust before breaking them over his knee and throwing them at the two. As the night went on some of the people thinned out going off to sleep. In between rounds of abuse the two men now went to work trying to free themselves. Stinging Winds managed to pick up one of the broken arrows with his toes and lift it backward to a point where Raining Oaks could grasp it with his tied hands. Raining Oaks then used the stone point to cut his restraints.

When he finished cutting them enough to know he could get free when he wanted, he handed the arrowhead to Stinging Winds so that he might also cut himself free. But they missed the connection and the broken arrow fell to the ground. Raining Oaks shifted his eyes from the broken arrow laying at his feet upward to see the wide-eyed look of another young warrior who figured out what the two were doing. The young warrior immediately yelled, causing a great stir. Without any more hesitation Raining Oaks freed himself and whispered a blessing to Stinging Winds who remained firmly tied to the poll.

Raining Oaks ran until he believed his heart might explode from his chest. He ran until he could no longer find enough air in his lungs to stay conscious. On a slight rise in the terrain he paused, hunched over with his hands on his knees, he turned and could see two of his tormentors at some distance, also at a loss for air. After just a few moments he started running again, his head felt light and he worried he might pass out but ran on anyway.

He tried to slow his pace slightly to make it something he could sustain but did not stop to take a break again for many hours. When he finally did stop again, he saw no trace of his tormentors. He refused to sleep and instead walked through the night. When the night started to give way to the day, he again picked up the pace and started running. By the time Raining Oaks returned to his people he appeared almost unrecognizable to them. Filth covered his body from top to bottom an his face and body bore bruises and he looked gaunt.

His tribe quickly took him in, gave him clean clothes and food. Finally, safe at last and with a full stomach, Raining Oaks fell into a deep sleep for a long time. When he awoke, the elders sat nearby waiting to hear what happened. Raining Oaks recounted their route in every small detail and told them about their terrorizing experience with the strange tribe to the west.

Calls of mourning went up throughout the village once word spread that Stinging Winds would not return. The loss of a young man like him was a serious matter for the tribe. In time, Raining Oaks' people moved their village farther to the north and east, away from the violent neighbors.

In 1955 a man weeding his garden behind his house felt the hoe dislodge something. Reaching down he picked up a small arrowhead from the ground and examined it closely. He had seen that type of stone in the area before but marveled at how well made the piece was. As he slid it into his pocket, he wondered what type of game the hunter used the point to kill. He envisioned an ancient hunt that resulted in the death of a huge whitetail buck. The arrowhead he found actually belonged to one of young warriors who shot it at Raining Oaks and Stinging Winds more than 800 years before he built his house there.

Chapter 17: The Eagle Clan

For Charging Bull and his people, the clan who inducted you could make all the difference in the world. Each clan received an assigned primary task. All the clans worked together to take advantage of the season and take advantage of certain resources as opportunities presented themselves. But when the situation came and went, they again returned to their primary task. In this way the people of the village split their duties and specialized their skills.

The Deer Clan worked primarily as hunters, they made deer traps, deer drives, and made good use of deep snow to harvest many deer. They became such good hunters villagers rarely went hungry.

The Otter Clan spent their time working the Great Spirit River collecting its resources, making fishing traps and fishing, trapping beaver, making fish nets to gather fish, harvesting clams, and gathering other aquatic resources.

The Beaver Clan gathered materials and built things. They gathered all the firewood for the village fires, gathered stone for making tools, helped people build their houses, and made the finest reed mats used both to lay on and as roofing material.

The Turtle Clan was the smallest of the clans, and they gathered things. They filled their days with digging roots, picking berries, and most importantly, keeping good stocks of medicine.

Last but not least came the Eagle Clan who served first and foremost as warriors and protectors of the village. They spent most of their free time practicing games of skill and agility. Virtually every young man in the village wanted to belong to the Eagle Clan. In times of war, men from every clan fought if needed, but that wasn't the same as serving as a full-time member of the Eagle Clan.

Now that Charging Bull entered his 10th summer it became time for the elders to place him in a clan. He could first request a clan. He did this by taking a seat in the sweat lodge with the elders and clan committee. Here, like all the young men, he pleaded to belong to the Eagle Clan. To impress the elders, he told them how much faster and stronger he was than all his peers. Charging Bull's people however currently enjoyed a time of peace. They did not need to fight with the Ojib-nak-en-daton to the south or the Black-Faced Ones to the east. Because of this they felt reluctant to place him in the Eagle Clan. Other clans needed his help more. So they decided to give Charging Bull the same slim chance given to the last several candidates. They would allow him to join the Eagle Clan only if he could find and kill a bald eagle within three days. If he could not capture or kill an eagle in three days, they planned to assign him to the Beaver Clan. His three days began at dawn the next day.

Charging Bull spent the rest of the day trying to solicit advice from his family and friends on the best way to catch an eagle. His father laughed and suggested he'd spend his time better by gathering firewood because he most assuredly would be a member of the Beaver Clan in three days. Some of his peers offered only slightly better advice. One suggested he catch the biggest fish he could and then crawl inside of it and wait for an eagle to come and have lunch, then grab it. His little brother thought it best to find a nest and wait until the dead of night to climb the tree where the nest rested, and simply pick the bird up and carry him down while he slept.

Charging Bull rose with the light of day as it first showed itself as a dim glow against the night sky. After eating he gathered his atl-atl, best darts, and best knife. He slung a bag over his shoulder containing a blanket and some dried venison before he headed up the river. He knew from experience that the rocky sandstone bluffs farther upriver provided a favorite hangout for eagles. They nested high atop the giant white pine trees that thrived there. By noon he found himself at the site of the bluffs and wasn't disappointed. High in the trees there he could see a large nest; and across the river he noticed an eagle perched on a dead limb hanging out over the water.

Charging Bull planned to try climbing the tree with the nest in it at night; and in the meantime, he decided to fish for bait for the eagles if the night raid didn't work. The day grew warm and humid, so wading out into the river with spear in hand felt refreshing. By evening he speared two large fish; one he prepared for dinner, and the other he planned to use for bait if he needed it. Charging Bull waited to climb the tree until long after dark, planning to let the birds settle in for the night. When the sliver of moon started to climb high into the night sky, he extinguished his little fire and let his eyes grow accustomed to the dark. In only minutes he climbed halfway up the giant tree. He climbed slowly and carefully to avoid making noise. His pace slowed even more as he neared the nest. When he approached within an arm's length of the nest, the bird suddenly spread its wings and took off from the nest flying away into the darkness. The eagle either saw movement or sensed danger. The bird's sudden flight startled Charging Bull but did not surprise him. He knew none of his plans allowed for an easy outcome.

Bright and early the second day Charging Bull carried out his next plan. He placed the large dead bait fish on an open stretch of sandy beach near the water's edge. A freshly dead fish laying at the water's edge was irresistible for an eagle. Meanwhile, on the riverbank directly above the fish he built a low but solid blind that hid him from the sky. When the eagle came to get the fish, Charging Bull planned to stand and use his atl-atl to launch a dart at it. By mid-morning the atmosphere became humid and the air inside the blind stifling. With time, sweat started trickling down his face and neck; eventually one curious bird finally gave in to the temptation. As the bird swooped in, however, Charging Bull suddenly remembered with wide-eyed disappointment that he forgot to weight the dead fish down. The eagle did not land as Charging Bull envisioned, but instead swooped in, grabbed the fish, and carried it off in a flash. With no time to plan, Charging Bull stood up and launched a dart at the giant bird as it started to fly away with the fish but the dart went over the birds back and landed in the water. Now out of bait, Charging Bull spent the rest of the day fishing to get more.

That night he made yet another plan, knowing that the next day would be his last chance to join the Eagle Clan. He noticed earlier in the day a large section of hollow log partially buried in the sand along the river. He decided to place all the fish he caught at the end of the log and then crawl inside and cover the end of the log with some pine boughs. When the eagles came for the fish, he planned to grab and kill it. He couldn't sleep that night, and instead went to work collecting some pine boughs. Before the early morning light started to filter down into the river bottom Charging Bull crawled into place. The log felt a little bit tight, but he tried to get comfortable. He could see perfectly unless the bird came from behind. All he could do was hope.

He didn't have to wait long. This time the bird eagerly took the bait. He heard the eagle swoop in, but at first he saw only the shadow. The bird landed on the lip of the log above where he lay hidden, its talons clasping the log just inches from his face. Charging Bull's heartbeat intensely fast. He slowly moved one hand to the edge of the log while with his other hand he reached for the knife in his belt. In one quick movement Charging Bull reached up and grabbed both of the eagle's legs in one hand while partially pushing himself free of the log. The huge bird beat its wings, hitting both sides of Charging Bull's head and body with what seemed like claps of thunder. While he squirmed his way free of the log and into the open, the eagle freed one of its legs and in an instant used its talons to swipe three bloody grooves down Charging Bull's arm. In the next moment Charging Bull caught the bird's neck with his other hand and broke it.

Charging Bull lay there for several minutes trying to take stock of what just happened. Though he did no running, he lay panting, completely out of breath. All around him he saw signs of a great struggle; small feathers blew out over the river. Around him lay scattered pine boughs and fish. Though the year before he saw an eagle another hunter killed, he didn't recall that hunter's eagle being as large as this monster that now lay in front of him. It took a couple more minutes before the pain in his arm finally grabbed his attention.

The first person to see Charging Bull returning to camp that evening was his father; and his eyes told the story. He, as well as the rest of the village, seemed surprised and delighted. He knew the clan would hold an eagle dance that night to welcome the clan's newest member. That night however became his last happy night because by early the next morning his arm felt swollen and looked red and Charging Bull came down with a high fever. The talon wounds on his arm grew infected. His mother summoned the medicine man, and she took care of him the best she could, but within three days Charging Bull died.

A young man and his father fished on the same river more than 3,000 years later. As they fished the young man spied a stone projectile partially buried in the sand. He found the same point that Charging Bull lost when he launched his atl-atl at the eagle on the beach but missed, sending it sailing over the bird's back out into the water.

Chapter 18: Whispering Pines

Whispering Pines got his name from the camp where he was born. During that time, people often died young. Any child who made it to their 10th summer was not only celebrated, but also utilized for the good of the entire group. Even as a youngster he received tips and training on tracking game and making stone points and darts. He also learned how to throw the atl-atl and many other useful bits of information. When Whispering Pines turned 10, his father started intensive training. Every day his father made him practice with his atl-atl, and encouraged him to stalk all sorts of game in the forests to improve his stealth. It didn't take long before his father invited him on his first hunt.

Two days before they planned to leave on the hunt they started to fast. The tribe believed only a hungry hunter could remain quiet enough and focused enough in the forest to properly hunt. It was late fall, and not the most ideal time to hunt. Whispering Pines' people preferred to hunt in the deep snow during winter that made tracking and killing the deer easier. But the coming wedding celebration meant many people in their group might run low on food, so they decided to go on an early hunt. Whispering Pines' father told him not to worry about the lack of snow because past experience taught him that when the leaves started to fall from the trees the big bucks lost their minds with love. Whispering Pines wanted to get a big buck beyond all else. Hunters who killed big bucks always earned respect. With buck antlers he could make many useful tools. His father often spent large portions of the winter close to the fire scoring, breaking, and shaping antler needles, harpoons, and a great many other tools from the antlers of the deer he killed earlier in the year.

After the group of hunters reached their destination, they drew up plans. Using a stick to draw in the sand Whispering Pines sat on the edge of a peninsula which ended abruptly in a cliff that fell off into steep ravine. Below that flowed the river. Hunters said that by driving the deer over the cliff they could take many deer at once. The area contained one small, narrow but long, hill running to the southeast that deer sometimes used to escape. They decided to post a hunter there to block off the escape route. Because Whispering Pines did not share familiarity of the area with the other hunters, they decided they would post him on the narrow ridge to prevent any deer from escaping. Without further delay Whispering Pines' father took him to the place and found a suitable tree big enough to hide him. His father told him if one or more deer came that way he should make sure not to step out from behind the tree until the deer drew very close and he needed his atl-atl loaded and ready to throw.

For Whispering Pines, it seemed like an exceptionally long wait by that tree. His mind kept wandering off in daydreams. After several hours passed Whispering Pines suddenly found himself startled by the sounds of many shouts in the far distance. He now knew the hunt had begun, and he readied a dart in his atl-atl. He moved closer to the tree than before and purposely quieted his breathing to concentrate on the sounds in the forest that might indicate a deer coming his way. With all the fall leaves on the ground, hearing the deer should not prove too difficult.

Over the next half hour, he listened to the shouts and could tell where the line of hunters moved in the distance. They would soon pass his post, and the likelihood of him seeing, much less killing, any deer greatly diminished with the passage of time. Another half hour passed and now Whispering Pines felt sure the others had probably already passed his location. He slowly relaxed and even started to daydream a bit again knowing that the chances of any deer getting through the line of hunters and coming his way greatly decreased with every passing minute.

Just as Whispering Pines' mind wandered to the sweet taste of honey, he had found the summer before, he heard a rustle far off in the woods. He immediately snapped back to attention and again hugged the giant pine tree. After another moment he heard more, he could tell no squirrel, or human made that sound, but a deer, and he could hear it coming his direction. Fumbling for his bag of dart tips he grabbed one and placed it in the socket at the front of the atl-atl loading the dart. Then he steadied himself and concentrated on the sounds.

After a few more moments, he could tell a single deer still headed right in his direction. He carefully avoided exposing himself too soon and waited for the sound of the feet to approach as close as he dared. Just as he planned to step aside from the tree and shoot, the sounds of the hooves stopped.

He froze momentarily. Did the deer smell him? Did he make a sound? The deer lingered so close he could actually hear him breathing on the other side of the tree. Then, as carefully as he could, he inched out from behind the tree with his dart at the ready. His heart almost stopped. There in front of him stood a magnificent buck, looking back in the direction of the other hunters. Without wasting a single second of this perfect opportunity, he launched his dart point. It hit solid and severed a major artery in the buck's neck. The deer only ran a short distance before collapsing to the ground.

Whispering Pines stood there above the buck trembling, he'd never felt happier. The buck he downed was one of the biggest his people had seen in several years. His massive set of antlers would provide enough material for his family for more than a year of tool making. By the time his father came back to get him, he already had the deer field dressed. He wasted little, his bag grew stuffed with all the organs they found useful, his mother would make a water bag from the bladder, stew with the heart and liver, and his grandfather would relish the freshly roasted tongue. The other hunters also experienced great success; one of them killed a buck but a smaller one than what Whispering Pines took. The group took six deer in total, a great hunt by everyone's standards.

Whispering Pine never even noticed that as the buck approached and he fumbled for a dart point to load, he accidentally dropped a point at the base of that big white pine.

More than 6,000 years later a boy found that same point while walking out in a farmer's field looking for arrowheads. The boy noted the nice shape of the point, and that it appeared unused. He quietly wondered if perhaps some ancient hunter missed his quarry with it and simply never found it.

Chapter 19: Ghost Trader

Spotted Bear heard rumors from the returning war party that the dark water people of the north spotted a pale faced trader wandering about their lands. He traded many magical things that defied all attempts at description for only the skin of the beaver. Spotted Bear continued to hear the occasional rumor from time to time. Most often he did not hear of the visits until long after the Ghost Trader, as he people grew to know him, left the area. Finally Spotted Bear heard that the Ghost Trader soon planned to build his wigwam on the lake known to his people as Otter Lake.

Because Spotted Bear held a great deal of interest in trading, and because all the stories he heard fascinated him, he decided to spend his free time that winter catching and skinning as many beaver as he could find. Some of his people warned him that the Ghost Trader dealt out bad spirits and sickness at times and they thought they should avoid him. In the end, all the stories of magical items out-weighed Spotted Bear's concerns. Over the course of the winter Spotted Bear managed to catch and skin nine beaver. By spring the skins finished curing and he pos-sessed sufficient stock to trade.

When a hunter returned late that spring bearing news of a strange pale-faced man building a home on Otter Lake, he wasted no time. He packed a small travel bag, grabbed his bow and arrow, his nine beaver pelts, and started off. The walk unfolded uneventfully to Otter Lake and took the better part of three days. When he arrived at the lake toward evening of the third day he bedded down on the far side so he could observe this strange magical man for a while. He saw right away that others shared the area with him, and that some already traded with the man. The next morning Spotted Bear rose early and walked to the Ghost Trader's camp before anyone else awakened.

The Ghost Trader appeared startled when he opened his eyes and found Spotted Bear standing close by him, but quickly relaxed when he noted the fine beaver skins he carried under his arm. Spotted Bear started to introduce himself, but one of the other partially sleeping people lying about the camp told him not to bother because the trader did not speak their native tongue. So started the long process of getting to know each other. They first shared a bowl of tobacco while they re-kindled the fire. When they finished the Ghost Trader opened up one of several large boxes. From the box he retrieved some strange food stuffs he then prepared over the fire and shared with Spotted Bear. The food did not taste like anything Spotted Bear recognized, and the cooking device he used did not look like any wood or stone device he'd ever seen either.

After their breakfast and another round of smoking the Ghost Trader looked over the beaver hides. Spotted Bear had never seen anybody look at a beaver skin with such obvious curiosity and affection. He looked at each and every skin like this, setting the two biggest hides in one pile, and the other seven in a second pile. Then he motioned for Spotted Bear to hand him his arrows. He did so and the Ghost Trader carefully examined his stone arrowheads. After looking them over he handed them back to Spotted Bear.

The Ghost Trader then went again to a large box and opened it; from it he took out a handful of items and returned to the fire. First, he pointed to the two large beaver pelts and then pointed to his other hand which held arrow points. These arrow points looked different though, and Spotted Bear motioned to examine them. He noted that they felt cold, super thin, and razor sharp. They all looked perfectly uniform, and he thought them the finest arrowheads he'd ever seen in his life.

Again, the Ghost trader pointed to the two fine beaver pelts and then to the handful of fine arrowheads, Spotted Bear nodded in agreement; he made a good trade. The Ghost Trader then pointed to the other seven hides and again went into the large box of magical items. This time he came back with a fine blanket and a braided plug of sweet-smelling tobacco. When the trader offered the brightly colored blanket and the plug of sweet tobacco for the seven smaller beaver hides Spotted Bear couldn't believe his good luck. When they completed the trade the two men again shared a bowl of tobacco. Spotted Bear thought this Ghost Trader must possess a limitless supply of the sweet smoke because he liked to smoke it in such profusion. By noon Spotted Bear headed home.

It took a long time to walk home, but the trip seemed to go by quickly because he started an almost endless cycle of looking at his newfound wealth. He repeatedly pulled the blanket out and wrapped it around his shoulders. He knew his wife would be so pleased with it. Then he would smell the plug of sweet tobacco. He'd left his own pipe at home but couldn't wait to enjoy the fine tobacco and so he began to chew on small bits of it as he walked. Finally, he pulled out the handful of arrowheads and again felt pleased by their quality. As he walked, he removed what now seemed like clunky and useless stones from the tip of each of his arrows and replaced them with these fine points. When he returned to camp, he planned to tie them in tight, for now thick pine sap held them in sufficiently.

The foot traffic on the trail that led away from Otter Lake to Spotted Bear's village increased over time as more and more of his people went to see the Ghost Trader with each passing year. By the time Spotted Bear's children grew up nobody used stone points anymore. People simply threw them away at the end. As the years passed the trader and Spotted Bear's village came and went. Others came in their place however, and the trail never completely faded.

Over almost 400 years the old trail became a country dirt road. One man who lived on that road walked his dog down it each day; and one time, after a rain, he found one of Spotted Bear's discarded arrowheads laying there in the dirt. As many do, he wondered about the previous owner and how he lost it, not realizing Spotted Bear simply threw it away.

Chapter 20: The Thieves

Stands-With-Fist spotted them first. He awoke early one morning with a stomachache. Unable to sleep he decided to walk down to the river to check his fish traps. He caught a glimpse of a white canoe going around the bend in the river far downstream and did not realize what had happened until he reached the water's edge.

There, where he spent all of the previous day setting up six large willow fish traps, he found not a single one remained. Looking at the footprints on the riverbank sand and in the shallow water there it quickly grew obvious that two or more people helped themselves to five of his fish traps and all their contents. Stand-With-Fist found this irritating and wanted to take action. But when he told his people, most villagers believed the case amounted to an instance of some travelers passing through the area and helping themselves to a free meal. They did not feel action was required.

Three days later a different hunter returned to the village reporting several of his beaver traps and rabbit snares missing from the woods along the river. Again, someone mentioned those taken from Stands-With-Fist, but in the end the elders again chose to do nothing. Things remained quiet for nearly a week until one of the village children, a young girl, went missing one evening. Once someone took the child, the elders and people could no longer ignore this new problem, nor blame it upon traveler passing through the area. They must avenge the child's kidnapping for the sake of the village and for the sake of the girl's family.

Twenty-two warriors in all, including Stands-With-Fist, volunteered to seek out these new people and take revenge. The girl's family insisted that if they did not find the girl; they should bring back any child to make their family whole again. Some of the men took their atl-atls but most, like Stands-With-Fist, preferred to take their war clubs on the war path.

Stands-With-Fist's war club was made from a heavy, knotted, and solid piece of black oak. His father made it and gave it to him, and over the years he used the club to take many lives. He took only this club and a stone knife. Before leaving he shaved all of his head except for a single tuft on top to which he tied a single eagle feather split down the middle signifying that he had taken the life of the enemy before. He also mixed bear grease with charcoal from the fire and painted all of his face and upper body black except for the outline of a hand positioned over his chest. The other warriors in the war party adorned and painted themselves in similar fashion. When they finished all gathered together in one spot for a blessing. They looked particularly fearsome. One by one, the clan elder and the clan medicine man walked up to each warrior and laid their hands upon their heads and recited the ancient war song. After all of the warriors received this blessing, they headed off to the south along the banks of the river.

Much to their surprise, they found a small camp not even a day's walk from their own village. Though empty now, they counted 10 different beds among the tall grass there. The place looked like a one-night camp, and people likely stayed there on the night before they took the girl. Knowing they were close they now moved more cautiously. Stands-With-Fist scouted out ahead of the others searching for any sign of these thieves as they referred to them. Around noon the next day the war party finally found their camp. It lay spread out in an open grassy area above the river and surrounded at a distance by forest. Stands-With-Fist stayed hidden in the forest at a distance to watch these people. They counted 18 houses, altogether; and their camp appeared to consist of more women and children than warriors. Stands-With-Fist and the others decided they could enter the camp at night, take a child, and have their revenge. But just before dark they watched as 10 warriors got in canoes and headed downstream. Now they outnumbered the enemy warriors by more than two to one, and so they changed their plan. They would not simply steal a child; they would conduct a full raid and kill many of them so they would want to leave this land.

When the last hints of light faded from the horizon the war party spread out in a semi-circle around the camp. Once in place they all began to sneak in toward the thief's camp. When they reached the outskirts and the first of the 18 houses they let out war calls and ran into the camp. Stands-With-Fist ran up to the entrance of one of the homes just as a warrior emerged.

As he stood up from the doorway he met Stands-With-Fist's war club. The man spun around with teeth and blood spraying out in a wide arc. As the man fell to the ground Stands-With-Fist saw his fish traps, all stacked one on top of the other, lying in a neat pile right beside this house. Enraged he entered the house but found it empty inside. He took a burning log from the fire and set the house on fire. When he stepped out of the burning house he paused and kneeled down by the warrior he killed with his war club. From his belt he pulled his knife and began to cut the scalp from the dead man, it became Stands-With-Fist's last act though, because one of the few enemy warriors left ran up behind him as he cut and swung at his head with a heavy, stone topped war club of his own.

The man who killed Stands-With-Fist only lived another minute before someone killed him too. When Stands-With-Fist's war party finished, out of the entire village only the child taken from them in the beginning remained alive. All around the camp lay the bodies of the enemy, men and women alike. Stands-With-Fist became the only member of the war party to die that day.

For weeks afterward they celebrated the victory as one of the most lopsided every experienced. The thieves from the south never returned. The village assumed they ran away in fear. But what they did not realize was they had killed the last person on the run. The warriors that left in canoes that evening before they attacked never returned either because a larger tribe down south ambushed them and stole their food. Nobody ever returned to the place where all the bodies lay among the burned-out homes. The bleached bones of all the dead dotted that open grassy area for many years to come. Eventually of course they too rotted away, along with all the evidence of the camp's existence.

Almost 7,000 years later the course of the river changed so that the river no longer flowed close to the grassy area. The grassy area became little more than a knoll covered with large trees a half mile away from the river. In 1985 a man walked through the woods in that very spot during deer hunting season. Because the wind blew hard, he grew chilled and looked for a place to escape the wind while he waited for a deer. He finally found a giant tree recently tipped over, uprooting a large area and exposing the subsoil. As he sat there with his back against the roots of the toppled tree he spotted a stone just barely sticking out of the sand at his side, curious and bored he poked at it until he freed it from the frozen ground. There he found Stands-With-Fist's knife that he used to cut the scalp from the enemy warrior right before another warrior killed him.

Chapter 21: Deep Snow

Sleeping Bear loved hunting above all else. Many people hunted with proficiency out of necessity, but Sleeping Bear possessed more than proficient skill. He hunted with a passion. Even when his own drying racks sat filled with meat, as he preserved the meat with smoke, he hunted on, making sure no one in his clan went hungry. His ability to stalk game became almost legendary over time. He read the signs of the woods like no one before him or since. His sense of smell and hearing became second to none. His ability to work stone into fine atl-atl points and knives developed a reputation far and wide.

Sleeping Bear hunted all year round, but early winter became, by far, his favorite season to hunt because the snow made tracking much easier. That time of year produced the best quality animal hides as well. Also, at that time of year most animals possessed heavy fat layers from a long summer of feasting making their meat more delicious. The early winter of Sleeping Bear's 28th year came early though, and the snow kept falling. The snow fell much deeper than anybody alive could remember. Soon Sleeping Bear found himself needing snowshoes to hunt. By the middle of winter many people experienced difficulty with day-to-day activities like gathering firewood because the snow drifted deeply making travel difficult. Sleeping Bear started experiencing problems as well. The big animals like deer and elk started to gather in groups where the combined working of their hooves packed the snow making trails difficult to follow. One day Sleeping Bear found a group of white-tailed deer in a small corral of snow. He saw nine of them altogether, all of them confined to a round area only 20 or so feet across, surrounded by a six-foot-tall wall of snow. If the snow persisted too long Sleeping Bear knew all of these animals would eventually die of starvation.

Every other day or so Sleeping Bear went to the deer yard and took a single animal. While he felt bad about killing animals who had no means to escape, these deer remained the only source of food available for his clan. They alone stood between the clan and starvation. In a couple of weeks, he killed all nine deer. He continued to walk the woods in his snowshoes hoping to find another deer yard or perhaps a lone elk, but the deep snow and harsh winter made finding any animals very difficult. Rather than enjoying many weeks of easy hunting and feasting like he had grown accustomed to over past winters, he now found himself trying to quiet a rumbling belly. Each day he went farther from his home to hunt. He followed the frozen river for many miles in both directions but found no signs of anything either way. He also ventured into the forest for many miles with no luck. As days turned into weeks, he found himself walking farther than he had ever traveled in winter before.

Beginning to feel hopeless, Sleeping Bear's luck finally changed late one chilly day. Deep in a thicket of pines and cedar trees he found a wide area completely beaten down by the hooves of many elk. It was not as small as the deer yard, but the deep snow surrounding this pine and cedar thicket effectively trapped the animals there just the same. He had grown weaker though and needed to proceed with care to take an elk. Taking an elk was more dangerous than taking a deer, even more so when the elk became trapped like this. The first animal he took was a large female. He butchered her and hid most of the meat in a deep snowbank because he could only carry one quarter of the meat at a time. This large front shoulder of elk was most welcome back home and many families came to share a portion. When Sleeping Bear again saw the condition of many of his friends and family he decided not to wait but returned at once to retrieve another quarter. The following day he retrieved the other two quarters as well so that all of his people could eat good hearty meals.

Better rested, his strength returning, Sleeping Bear headed back to the elk thicket just a couple of days later to take another animal. As he approached the thicket he slowed down and readied his atl-atl. Bedded down at the edge of the thicket he found another large female elk. Sleeping Bear cocked the dart back, took careful aim and flung the dart at the animal. As usual, it hit the mark. the elk stood up only briefly before collapsing back to the ground, both lungs punctured by his dart. Sleeping Bear wasted no time butchering this animal as butchering in winter went smoother while the flesh remained warm.

He had just removed the skin when a sound behind him startled him. He didn't need to even look to know the bull elk of the thicket was approaching him from behind. He grasped his bloody knife tightly and spun around just in time to see the elk charge from less than 10 feet away. Sleeping Bear slashed wildly at the bull's underbelly and neck, but a hoof to the side of his head knocked him unconscious. Unable to defend himself, the now badly wounded bull proceeded to protect his territory and stomped and gored Sleeping Bear to death.

Sleeping Bear's family didn't find him until mid-spring that following year and by then they found little left of the female elk or Sleeping Bear. The old bull elk managed to live until the snow receded but eventually died from his wounds. Sleeping Bear's people carried what they found left of him back to their camp, cleaned and wrapped him in a fresh hide and buried him. In the same hide they put some venison and some stone tools alongside him before burying him in the ancient cemetery.

Four thousand eight hundred and thirty years later a man cutting a trench for some new electrical lines uncovered Sleeping Bear's knife that he used in his desperate attempt to protect himself from the bull elk in the last seconds of his life.

Chapter 22: The Spring Fish Run

Standing Otter always liked the annual spring fish run. As a little boy his family always made good use of the time by putting away as much dried fish as they could carry. He remembered fish runs fondly as days spent wading in the cool waters of the Great Spirit River digging for clams, baiting a variety of animals with the surplus of fish guts. But best of all, it was the time of year when no one went hungry. During some parts of the year, death by starvation presented a very real threat; and when opportunity arose to gather any type of food in large quantities people took full advantage and celebrated.

Standing Otter and his family now camped at the same spot along the same creek as his father and his father's father camped. The ground ran flat above a feeder creek of the Great Spirit River just 100 yards in from the river. There soft grass grew shaded by giant oak trees but more importantly the creek contained a narrow, shallow, gravel bar right below it. They used rocks from the river and sharpened sticks pounded into the creek bottom to construct a large funnel. Because they camped here every year they more or less only had to patch up and fix the fish trap at this place from the year before and make it better. As the fish rushed over the shallow gravel bar looking for the deeper spawning water beyond, a good portion of them would get caught in the funnel.

As they continued the funnel narrowed to a small hole. As they swam through the small hole they swam straight into a waiting basket. They all took turns simply scooping the fish out as they swam into the basket and then tossed them on shore where others picked them up and started the cleaning process. Still others tended the fire by the drying and smoking racks making sure the meat was preserved properly. Depending upon how long they camped there, they would see many different species come up to spawn. Some years worked out better than others, but everybody managed to gorge themselves for weeks at a time even in the worst of years.

Standing Otter and his people fished during other parts of the year in the Great Spirit River as well. There they used mostly nets and willow fish traps to catch fish, but the numbers never compared to the spring run. Standing Otter's people also dug many clams from the shallow flats along the river bottom, but they spent an equal amount of time hunting deer and other game in the forests that stretched up and down the river. Though his people numbered almost 100, they rarely needed to leave this small stretch of forest along the river. The spring run also brought others to this area though they never really experienced problems with these people. The spring run offered so many fish that no one group needed to worry. They generally found enough to go around. When the run ended the Chok-not-pa-na or "silent ones from the north" typically left to go back to their ancient hunting grounds much farther to the north and east. Likewise, when the run ended each spring, the Ba-gush-na-tok-na or "prairie people" made their way back to their traditional hunting grounds in the plains far to the south.

This year unfolded typical of most, as the spring run of fish up the creeks wore on and started to thin out, more and more of the young and old alike found excuses about why they could not help on any given day. The young men again grew hungry for venison and headed off, the old people with bellies full, took long naps during the day. By the time the spawning run ended everybody felt more or less full, but after a while they grew sick of eating fish. Standing Otter really felt no different. As much as he looked forward to the spring run, he never felt overly sad to see it go away again either. He wrapped up his share of fish in tight bundles inside hides and buried them deep in the ground for storage until fall when he again would find the fish appetizing.

Standing Otter took an early morning walk in hopes of finding some unsuspecting game that might have come to get a drink of water. Sometimes he would get lucky and sneak up on a deer or raccoon that did not go to bed on time. Today he found something else though, on the next feeder stream up from the one where they camped, he found the Chok-not-pa-na still lingering at their spring camp in spite of the fish run ending many days earlier. He silently hoped they did not plan to stay much longer. While his people never experienced any problems with them and traded with them for many years, he felt no desire for neighbors this close. The land there remained rich to some degree, but not enough game existed there to feed two villages. When he returned to camp that afternoon he mentioned it to the others, but found they showed little interest or worry.

As spring turned into summer Standing Otter and his people decided to move camp. They planned to stay on the same creek but move to its source where fresh springs bubbled ice-cold water out even in the worst drought years. The area also held vast swamps to the east of it which normally provided excellent hunting and trapping. They set up at the new camp, and a day or two later some of the younger hunters started to complain they found signs of others in the woods taking game. One hunter returned with two bags of guts showing how he found the remains of two deer taken from his favorite ambush site. A day later another hunter returned with the explanation, the Chok-not-pa-na followed them moving farther up their stream and setting up camp parallel with their own. Now it became obvious that the Chok-not-pa-na did not plan to leave this land. Standing Otter and the other elders gathered together around a council fire to discuss it.

His people did not go to war quickly, and generally did not go to war at all because with so few people the land usually provided enough for all most of the time. Standing Otter and most of the others believed that the Chok-not-pa-na would certainly understand if they simply went to speak with them. Over the course of much discussion, they finally decided that Standing Otter should go to their camp to ask them to move. Standing Otter did not really take to the idea because he always felt a bit leery of other groups. But he had no choice except to listen to the council. He would set out for the camp of the neighboring tribe the next day, and he would take Flowing Hair with him to translate. One of Standing Otter's friends traded for Flowing Hair with the neighboring tribe several years before, and she still spoke their language.

Standing Otter felt surprised to discover just how close the neighbor's village set to theirs. They came upon it less than one days walk from his own, and elders at the neighboring village gave him a seat at their council fire before the sun set. Once he found himself seated, they offered him a bowl of soup filled with meat and wild rice. Only after he finished eating and shared a bowl of tobacco with their chief did the chief inquire about the reason for his visit. Standing Otter explained the situation just as he and his people viewed it, he explained that he and his father and his father's father had camped, hunted, and fished this land for as long as anybody could remember. He explained that they did not mind sharing the spring fish run with the Chok-not-pa-na but preferred they stick to the original arrangement, moving on once the fish run ended.

He told the chief through Flowing Hair that the land spread out wide before them and the people numbered few. The Chok-not-pa-na Chief did not say anything for a long time; instead, he filled another pipe with tobacco and offered it to Standing Otter. As Standing Otter started to draw from the pipe the chief spoke. He explained to Standing Otter that everything he said was true, except that things had changed for the Chok-not-pa-na. Their traditional summer camps far to the north and east no longer felt safe, and they could not return to them because a new people from the east he referred to as Black Devils waged a war against his people. He explained that the Black Devils outnumbered his people by more than 100 to one. He told Standing Otter that the Black Devils set upon the land like a sickness, catching every deer, rabbit, fish, and other type of animal from the land to feed their huge numbers. When the Black Devils came to a land, they left it empty. He said that if his people returned the Black Devils would kill them or make slaves of them, and so in the end Standing Otter's people would need to share this land with them.

Standing Otter's father always taught him to think out every word he said and never to speak from emotion alone, so Standing Otter sat there a long time before saying anything. Finally, he started to explain that the good section of forest along the river may be big enough for two villages but they could not exist this close together. One of the two villages needed to move much farther to the south, and Standing Otter explained that the land there closely resembled where they sat now, just as rich in all the same resources. He suggested that the Chok-not-pa-na should move farther to the south because Standing Otter's people always lived here. The Chok-not-pa-na Chief again took a long time before speaking. When he spoke, he pointed out that the spirit star already sat high in the heavens and the night grew late. He said they should both sleep on it and resume talking in the morning. Standing Otter agreed.

When Standing Otter awoke the next morning the Chok-not-pa-na offered him a large plate of fish fried in bear grease and covered with honey. After eating the chief again came to speak with Standing Otter through his translator. The chief said he saw a vision in his sleep the night before that offered a fair way to decide who should stay in this land and who should move. He suggested a duel to the death. One man's bravery and sacrifice could save both villages from fighting and unnecessary violence. The offer took Standing Bear by surprise at first as he'd never heard of such a thing, but the more he thought about it the more sense it made to him. He sat in silence for a long time thinking. He thought that even if his side lost the worst outcome meant they moved a few more miles to the south. He knew all the land and knew it would provide for his people. Finally Standing Otter nodded in agreement and the chief of the Chok-not-pa-na smiled. Standing Otter stood in preparation to leave, and as he did the chief said that Standing Otter and his nephew Follows-The-Bear looked an even match.

Standing Otter did not really consider himself material for a fight to the death as much as somebody else. Now a man of middle age, he thought a young warrior from his group might happily step forward for such an honor, so the chief's suggestion caught him off guard. However, after only a moment's reflection, he decided he would fight on behalf of his people. He didn't want others to be-lieve him a coward. Nothing could be worse. So, he stood for a short while, and then simply nodded in agreement. The chief and Standing Otter agreed they would solve the situation by a fight to the death in seven days at a place between the two villages along the Great Spirit River. They both agreed they would let their war clubs at home; each man would fight with only his hunting knife. Standing Otter and Flowing Hair headed for home.

All of Standing Otter's people waited anxiously to hear his news, and many surrounded him even before he made it back to the council fire. After most of the women and children had again wandered off out of hearing range, Standing Otter explained everything that transpired to the council and all the men. Some of them complained that Standing Otter overstepped his authority when negotiating the possible relocation of their village. Their village, one pointed out, served as a home for more generations than anybody knew. In the end the people seemed upset but eventually fell silent because to back out of the deal now would label them all as cowards.

Standing Otter spent most of the next seven days in quiet reflection and meditation. He instructed his oldest son on how to best care for his mother and other brothers and sister if he should not return. On the evening before the fight, he asked his wife to sharpen a piece of flint to cut off all his long hair and singe what remained with fire. He did that so that the Chok-not-pa-na could not grab his long hair during the fight and use it to his advantage. When night gave way to day he used some grease and a special burnt stone to paint part of his face white. Over the top of that he painted black war marks, when he finished even his own children found him dangerous and strong looking.

Standing Otter lead the way down the riverbank where they agreed to meet. Behind him all his village followed except his own family. On the way his people sang old war songs to give him strength and inspiration. When they arrived at the spot, they found the Chok-not-pa-na following a similar tradition, singing their songs, and encouraging their warrior. Standing Otter felt somewhat relieved to see his opponent who was similar in age and size. He secretly feared having to fight, and lose, to somebody younger than himself. When both sides quieted down the chief of the Chok-not-pa-na drew a large circle in the sand by the river with a stick. Both men stepped into the circle.

Standing Otter took off his shirt and tossed aside his shoes as did the Chok-not-pa-na warrior Follows-The-Bear. Standing Otter then took out his hunting knife and threw the sheath to the side as well; Follows-The-Bear copied him. The chief said something he did not understand, and the fight began. Suddenly both villages screamed and let out war cries but neither warrior heard any of it. Both men started a careful dance around the circle, staring into each other's eyes. Standing Otter noted the warrior's long braid of hair and decided he might win this fight if he could grasp it. Before he finished the thought the Chok-not-pa-na warrior lunged at him and lightly brushed his arm with his knife. Now Standing Otter bled from the arm, and he briefly noticed the increase in noise coming from the enemy's ranks. Though only a minute passed Standing Otter felt as though the fight had gone on for many hours already.

Suddenly the Chok-not-pa-na warrior Follows-The-Bear lunged again, but Standing Otter moved faster this time and, as his enemy passed, he spun around in time to cut him deeply across the back. This time the Chok-not-pa-na warrior did not hesitate and lunged again knocking Standing Otter to the ground. Standing Otter received a cut across the side of his head as the two men wrestled for control of each other's knives. Standing Otter bled badly from his head, and the other warrior bled badly from the cut across his back. As they wrestled, the blood and war paint melted together to form a truly horrific sight.

When Follows-The-Bear managed to temporarily get one hand free he grabbed a handful of sand and tried to throw it into Standing Otter's eyes but succeeded in only getting it in one eye. Standing Otter felt as though he grew weaker by the minute, and now could only partially see. He could hear the spirits of his father and grandfather whispering to him. The blood running down his arm made his arm slippery so when Follows-The-Bear gave one last try he pulled his knife-hand free for just long enough to swipe it across his attacker. Perhaps luck more than intention guided the knife which caught Follows-The-Bear across the throat just below his jaw. Standing Otter did not at first realize the knife connected because blood did not immediately pour from the wound. Instead, he felt Follows-The-Bear's grip start to ease a little at a time and then completely eased all at once. Only when the Chok-not-pa-na warrior slumped over to one side in the sand did Standing Otter see the blood start to pour from his neck wound.

Standing Otter's village celebrated the victory well into the night singing and dancing as the Chok-not-pa-na villagers passed through their land in silence to the forests in the south. After the Chok-not-pa-na people moved away, time seemed to again stand still in that stretch of forest by the river. But it did not last. Just two years later the Black Devils who the Chok-not-pa-na spoken of arrived in Standing Otter's village killing most of them, including Standing Otter. A few of his people escaped across the Great Spirit River, but their people never really recovered. The Black Devils took all that they could and moved on.

The stones used to build the fish trap in the creek still remain partly visible to this day when the water recedes, and you know what to look for. Just up the river from that place sits the sandy beach where Standing Otter and Follows-The-Bear fought. After the fight the Chok-not-pa-na people took their fallen warrior to a funeral pyre where they sent him to the next world as part of their tradition. Nobody noticed or bothered to pick his knife up from the sand. Almost 900 years later a man found Follows-The-Bear's knife lying in the sand as he prepared to cook his catch of catfish caught at the same river.

Chapter 23: The Water Spirits

Legend said the Pur-uhna people felt abandoned by a water spirit who had an affair with an Earth spirit. It said neither spirit could take custody of the child because the water spirit would be banished from the water if the other spirits found out. And the Earth spirit would be banished from the Earth should the other Earth spirits find out. So, in the end the Pur-uhna people remained abandoned on the banks of the Great Spirit River between the realm of the Earth spirits and the water spirits.

Legend passed down from generation to generation said if any member of their people traveled too far into the earth or too far into the water the spirits who lived there would take them with a vengeance. Because of this they became masters of the shore, of the riverbanks, and of the tributaries. They found that game from the forests and plains came to the water and to the Pur-uhna people; so, they did not need to go in search of them. They also found the shallow waters of the Great Spirit River offered up an endless supply of fish, clams, turtles, snakes, frogs, and other things the water spirits left there on purpose for them.

The women of the Pur-uhna found some sections of riverbank filled with the finest clay for making pottery. The boys collected vast piles of driftwood that washed down the river with every spring flood. In short, the Pur-uhna found the narrow slice of land between earth and water provided everything they needed and more.

The Pur-uhna lived like this for so long that they believed they had always lived in that same spot—always. Sometimes others came up and down the river from other lands. Sometimes those people traded with the Pur-uhna, and sometimes they stayed away along the other shore of the river and simply passed by without word. They seldom experienced problems with travelers on the river until two canoes came upriver one day piled with things to trade. These traders called themselves Ma-na-dok or "People of the Rising Sun." With them they brought many new things that the Pur-uhna had never seen before including exotic stones for making tools, foods they never tasted, paints they never saw, and many seeds from plants they never knew. They in turn traded some of their finest stone from a place far up the river and many large elk antlers, the Ma-na-dok said these creatures did not live near their villages, and that the antlers would be worth a lot to their friends. Before leaving, they instructed those who traded for some of the strange seeds on how to grow them to make more.

Most of the Pur-uhna people were well set in their ways, however, so all the seeds they traded for ended up in pots of stew and soup in the weeks that followed, except for one pouch. Lives-With-Turtle kept his pouch dry all through that fall and winter. Many of his people remarked how tasty the seeds were when boiled in soup, but Lives-With-Turtle resisted all temptation. He did however use the colorful new stone he traded for to make himself some new spear tips and a digging tool. Lives-With-Turtle was not particularly well known for his flintknapping ability but felt pleased to find this new colorful material worked easily and that it made his points look far above average.

When spring came Lives-With-Turtle pulled all the grass, trees, bushes and plants from a section of land, and there he mounded up the dirt into a pile like the Ma-na-dok instructed him. In the mounds he planted each of the three different types of seeds he traded for, things that would later become known as corn, squash, and beans, though that year they had no names for such things among his tribe. The Ma-na-dok told him he must keep the ground moist but not wet when the rains did not do it for him, and so he made the mounds on the bank of the river where water ran close by. Some of his friends among the Pur-uhna teased him and said that rather than wasting his time he should eat the seeds; still others called him stupid for burying such good food in the ground.

Days passed before some of the plants started to sprout and grow. Lives-With-Turtle felt quite pleased once all the teasing died down, replaced with curiosity by many. As spring turned to summer and some of these new and different looking plants produced fruits, some people grew jealous. Lives-With-Turtle kept watering and caring for his little garden just as instructed until the seasons began to change and the plants began to wither.

That fall he finally managed to taste some of the seeds that the others raved about and found them very pleasing indeed. What surprised him even more was how good the fresh squash tasted! The beans, the corn, the squash were all good, but he found them to taste best when fresh. When he completed the harvest, he filled two large jars with seeds for the next year. Now people asked him to share, but he would not, instead he chided many of them for having been so short sighted. Others demanded he share his seeds with all the Pur-uhna, but he insisted it was no fault of his own that they did not have any. The fighting between Lives-With-Turtle and some of the other clan members grew into a serious problem with some of them even planning bad things for him behind his back. Eventually word of everybody's jealousy and Lives-With-Turtle's staunch selfishness reached the ears of several of the elders who then called a meeting.

The council met in private. As custom dictated, the conversation unfolded without hurry, and they considered all points. One of the elders who had himself tasted the seeds the prior year suggested that growing this new food might very well be something that all Pur-uhna should try. Another council member pointed out how much distress and trouble Lives-With-Turtle's planting and seeds caused, he suggested the seeds themselves might contain evil spirits that caused men to harbor hate for their brothers and friends. Another council member waited his turn to speak and suggested the growing plants, up until that point, remained the sole job of the earth spirits alone. Others then openly wondered if growing plants like this might in fact anger the earth spirits. The eldest member spoke last; he said that taking the earth spirits' job of growing things might destroy the life of the Pur-uhna.

He pointed out that they lived there on that land between earth and water for more generations than they knew. He said that they all lived long and prosperous lives in that place by accepting what the earth and water spirits provided them there. Changing tradition could not, and should not, be allowed.

The next morning the youngest council member, who happened to be Lives-With-Turtle's uncle, went to his house to tell him the news. The council had decided that if he wanted to grow seeds of jealousy and hate that he would have to take them across the Great Spirit River to lands beyond their own and promise to never come any closer than the opposite shore. His uncle also told him that if he would throw all his seeds in the community soup pot that night, that all would be forgiven, and life could continue on as before.

After his uncle left Lives-With-Turtle sat quietly a long time and thought to himself. While he certainly loved his people, he did not have any ties so close as to bind him. His mother and father had both passed on, and he wondered if a life on the other bank would really be so bad. All of his life had been governed by the decisions of the elders and the council. Most of the time he knew that it was for the better, but he still resented being ruled over in matters like this. It was a real risk for Lives-With-Turtle to leave his own people. He would be putting himself at great risk living alone, but on the other hand he would be free to do what he pleased. Even if his new plants and seeds failed him, he was more than able to go back to the old ways if he needed.

That afternoon several of those who had insisted he share his seeds watched with disgust and disdain as Lives-With-Turtle carefully dug up his jars of seeds and loaded them along with all of his belongings into a large canoe that his uncle provided him. Lives-With-Turtle asked a young maiden he held a flirtation with to go with him, but her father strictly forbade it. Lives-With-Turtle shoved off in his canoe with no fanfare. Many pretended not to care but watched from the corner of their eyes as Lives-With-Turtle cut through the shallow waters of the river and approached the main channel.

Lives-With-Turtle became more and more nervous as the sight of the river bottom started to give way to the blackness of the main channel. He grew up with too many stories about evil water spirits coming up from this very channel and snatching people to put the thoughts out of his mind. While he, and most of his people grew up on and in the river, they all avoided the main channel because of the river spirits. Now as he found himself carried farther downstream by the current, he also realized his canoe was dangerously overloaded. When his canoe got caught up in a strong river eddy Lives-With-Turtle panicked and the canoe tipped over. The canoe and all of his belongings quickly dispersed in the water with most of them sinking to the bottom before being rolled along it. A thousand Water Spirit legends burst through Lives-With-Turtle's head all at once, and he instantly panicked and drowned.

The Pur-uhna never learned of Lives-With-Turtle's fate because he drifted down river and out of sight before tipping. In a few years most of them no longer even remembered his name. In time the traders came again bringing seeds and other exotic goods, and eventually the Pur-uhna thought it prudent to learn this new planting lifestyle because the traders assured them that they would have far more food than ever before if they planted seeds. After Lives-With-Turtle was all but forgotten the Pur-uhna became well-adjusted farmers and even gave up their heavy reliance on hunting and fishing after just a couple of generations.

Three thousand years later a husband and wife pulled their canoe up onto a large gravel bar in the middle of the river to enjoy their lunch. When they got out the husband spotted some pottery shards scattered around the sand bar and recognized them as ancient shards. He spent some more time looking over the gravel before finding Lives-With-Turtle's stone knife made from the exotic material he traded for. When they left, his wife put the pottery and stone knife in their cooler and paddled on talking about what ancient life must have been like.

Chapter 24: Angry Bear and the Slave Traders

Angry Bear got his name when he was just 15 because he constantly got involved in fights. It wasn't that Angry Bear went looking for it, but trouble always seemed to find him just the same. Through the years he beat a fair number of his fellow clansmen and made more than a few enemies. Angry Bear and his people started out as a rough bunch. They lived on the northern fringes of the Oui-sha Shopka-na-da-bok or "People of the Southern Winds" territory. As such, they frequently received visits from Oui-sha Shopka-na-da-bok warriors and traders who demanded tribute.

The group held far too much power to even consider fighting because they owned all the land from where Angry Bear's people lived to the south where the world ended, and an even greater distance to the east and to the west. So, it came as no surprise when one year a delegation of Oui-sha Shopka-na-da-bok arrived and demanded that their small group hand over one of their own as a slave for tribute. In return the Oui-sha Shopka-na-da-bok would leave them alone for a period of time and their sun god Sha would bring them blessings they said.

The decision to send Angry Bear became easy for several of them had been badly beaten by him over the past few years when they accidentally angered him one way or another. Besides that, he had no wife or children. Angry Bear saw the Oui-sha Shopka-na-da-bok canoes pulled up on shore before the warriors saw him. Angry Bear knew this might result in trouble for many reasons and, sensing such, took his knife from the sheath at his side and instead tucked it inside his loin cloth. When he approached his house he saw an elder point to him, but before he realized what was happening, he found himself assaulted by several Oui-sha Shopka-na-da-bok warriors. He managed to knock one of them unconscious before a warrior knocked him out with a stout oak club.

When Angry Bear woke up from his sleep, he found himself tightly bound to a tree sitting in the dark. A short way off to the side he could see the embers of a campfire beginning to die. He faded in and out of consciousness through the night and when morning finally came someone picked him up and loaded him into a canoe like a piece of cargo. Two warriors paddled the canoe and guarded Angry Bear, one in front, and one in the back of the canoe. Angry Bear's legs as well as his hands were bound tightly behind him; and now, on his back in the bottom of the canoe the sun started to beat down on him. He pleaded with the Oui-sha Shopka-na-da-bok to give him a drink of water, but the warrior only laughed and spit on him. As the morning turned into afternoon Angry Bear kept moving from time to time, pretending to feel exceptionally uncomfortable. The truth was that each time he moved he kept inching the knife he had hidden in his loin cloth a little bit closer to his hands.

Before the day ended, he'd freed his hands from behind his back without getting caught. Still, he lay there, looking as though he remained tightly bound and complaining all the while. One of the warriors told Angry Bear that before the sunset his troubles would be over because they were approaching their home camp. Angry Bear looked toward the sun and decided it rested too close to the horizon to wait, he decided to act even though his feet remained tied.

With lightning speed, he sat up and plunged his knife into the eye of the warrior who had spit on him. Before the warrior in front even realized what happened Angry Bear dumped the canoe off to one side. While the other warrior busily swam trying to save himself Angry Bear cut the rope that tied his feet together. They quickly realized the river rose only chest deep where they swam, and they closed in on one another. The Oui-sha Shopka-na-da-bok warrior did not realize Angry Bear had a knife, however, and soon fell victim to the blade as well. The warriors in the other canoes saw what happened but could not catch up with them. Angry Bear managed a good head start on foot before the other canoes made it to the spot where he came ashore. Two of the young warriors pleaded with the leader in charge to let them pursue Angry Bear, but the man refused. They all carried loads of goods and several other slaves; they decided to let him run all the way home.

Angry Bear assumed that the Oui-sha Shopka-na-da-bok would follow right behind him wanting revenge, so he ran as fast as he could for as long as he could. He covered more than 10 miles before he even slowed down enough to look back. When a deer crashed through the woods at some distance from him, his mind could only imagine many warriors coming after him and he ran again. He started to run away from the river inland to parts he did not know. As he came over the top of a tall bank that marked the high ground above the river bottom, he spotted a large fallen tree. He decided to take just a quick break and hide behind the log. From there he could see a lot of the river bottom spread out in front of him; and if the warriors followed him, he'd see them before they could see him.

He flung himself down in the leaves behind the log and then he felt it. Before he could react, he felt the sharp bite again. He tried to jerk his leg away, but the snake sunk its fangs so deep into him on the second bite that it came flying up to his chest when he pulled away. Without thought

he grabbed the snake by the head and cut it off clean with
the knife in his other hand. The snake twisted and con-
torted on the ground by his feet as he slowly opened up
his hand with the snake's head. The sight confirmed his
worse fears; there on top of the head he saw the mark of
the spirit snake. Then he looked at the twisting rope of
snake and saw that it too had the red belly of the spirit
snake. He immediately started to look around for the
snake root plant.

The spirit snake once bit Angry Bear's cousin as just a
young kid. He remembered the medicine man coming and
giving the boy snake root. The root seemed to make the
boy better for a little while but in the end he died a slow,
terrible death. Now he walked rather than ran, he no
longer thought about his would-be captors, but only about
finding the snake root plant. Within a few minutes he
started to feel sharp pains spread up and down his leg.
Twice he stopped to rub the bite but that only seemed to
make it worse.

Soon the sun set, the forest already grew so dark that he
could not properly identify the plants. He realized with a
subdued panic that he could not possibly find the snake
root before dark. With his last minutes of light fading, he
looked for a place to die. He found a giant pine tree and
lay down on the soft needles under its massive branches.
His head started to pound with sharp pains as the forest finally went completely dark. Before morning Angry Bear
died.

The place where Angry Bear died was eventually
cleared of all the trees that grew there and men planted
crops. In 1973 a farmer's tractor broke down in the field at
that place and when he came down off of it to troubleshoot
the problem, he noticed the stone knife laying there in the
dirt. He picked it up and put it in his pocket before getting

back to work on the tractor. Later that night he showed his young son the "arrowhead" he found back by the river-bank.

Chapter 25: The Chief's Burial

Winding Spirit's people numbered in the thousands and their hunting grounds stretched from the edges of the prairies in the west and south all the way to Frozen Lake in the north and Angry Lake in the east. His people called themselves the People of the Lakes but really, they consisted of almost a dozen tribes. Each of these tribes owned territory, and each had its own council. But if a dispute developed between the various factions, they turned the matter over to the chief to decide. The chief had the final say in all matters; they could not challenge his word. When one chief passed into the next world, they elected another chief. Each of the tribes sent a single elder to the grand council fire where they spoke with one another, fasted, and prayed before voting for one of them to become the next chief.

The passing of one chief and the election of another tended to garner a great deal of excitement from everyone. Each tribe hoped their elder might be the one elected because it wasn't uncommon for the chief to rule in his tribe's favor, thus giving them more clout when disputes arose between the various tribes of their alliance.

Winding Spirit's tribe sent Red Clouds to the grand council this time. He went during the last grand council meeting as well when Stands-In-The-Sky became chief. Though Red Clouds grew old and slow, his wisdom remained unmatched by anybody else among them. Red Clouds joked with his people that he hoped he might last longer than Stands-In-The-Sky if they elected him because he served as chief for just over one year before passing away. Once Winding Spirit's tribe elected to send Red Clouds to the grand council, they started to organize a party to go with him. They planned to send boys and young men to carry the lodge poles and ceremonial regalia. A large number of warriors planned to go to show their support. And even a great number of young women would go in hopes of finding a husband. The election provided a rare opportunity to meet with people of their own tongue from far-flung places.

Some of the tribes traveled a week or more on foot to reach the sacred grounds, but for Winding Spirit's people, the sacred meeting grounds lay only a day's walk away and, in fact, it rested in part of their own hunting territory. The sacred meeting ground consisted of a single large plateau surrounded on two sides by a massive bluff and on the other side by the Lost River. The People of the Lakes gathered there to elect their chiefs for generations. Red Clouds, Winding Spirit, and all the other members of his tribe who tagged along set up camp right on the banks of the Lost River. When all the tribes gathered, they began work on Stands-In-The-Sky's burial. In honor of his name, they decided to bury him in an eagle mound, and they drew one out on the plateau. They built a hot fire of oak in the place that would become the eagle's chest and there they burned the former chief's remains.

As the remains burned the women wailed in anguish and the men danced around the fire, some beating drums. When the flames started to die down his family members came one at a time to make offerings. The chief's only remaining son lay down two fine stone knives and a large bundle of tobacco. His granddaughter added a large handful of brightly colored bird feathers to the coals. His wife covered it all with a thick buffalo hide blanket. Still others added trinkets. When that finished and everything burned, they began to add baskets of dirt. Everyone from each of the tribes worked on it so that it did not take long. One team worked on digging the dirt and filling baskets, another carried the baskets from the pit to the place on the plateau, and a small number stayed there to make sure they added the baskets in the right place.

In three days, they built a three-foot-high eagle made from basket-loads of dirt, the wing of the bird stretched to the east and west symbolizing the wandering nature of birds. The small, burned pile of bones and offerings in the middle of the bird became the spirit. Sixty similar mounds surrounded the bird that they built here, each with one or more former chiefs inside. Some chiefs lay buried in bears, some as birds like this one, and many simply lay buried in conical mounds that represented the connection between this world and the next. Only after they sent off the former chief in this fashion could they ordain the next one.

While Red Clouds and all the other elders from the other tribes attended the great council fire in private, everyone else remained free to pursue their own interests. They played many large games of Lacrosse and Chunkey in that place and formed many dance circles. Some, like Winding Spirit, simply went down to the river to fish and hunt as they saw fit. Most of the young men and women occupied their time around grand fires dancing and flirting. The grand council never took less than three days, and sometimes it lasted as long as a week. By the third day Winding Spirit grew impatient with fishing on the river. Hunting did not offer a diversion since the large numbers of people seemed to have scared off all the game. He no longer harbored a desire to search for love either. He had already taken two wives, but both women died, one during childbirth and the other from fever. Eventually he just found a place in the shade where he could watch a large Lacrosse game starting.

On the morning of the fifth day the grand council still sent no word. For many of the young people this came as exceptionally good news because it meant another day of dancing and flirting. But it annoyed Winding Spirit. All he could think about were the things he needed to do back at home before winter came. To ease his mind, he decided to go for a walk up on the bluff. Legend said the bluffs once served as part of the nest made by thunder spirits in the first days.

He took with him his bow and arrows in case he got lucky enough to see a deer or even an elk. He picked out a high rocky outcropping along the bluff as his goal and set off. It didn't take long before the trail veered off to the south and east where he found a large dip in the bluff. Winding Spirit instead headed into the tall grass of the prairie straight south. There he got the strange feeling someone was watching him. Several times he turned around suddenly expecting to find somebody there, but his gaze met with only the grasses waiving in the breeze. Going off trail in the prairie always bothered Winding Spirit a little. It offered a great way to sneak up on somebody because the grass there waved taller than the average person's head. But it also provided a great way for someone to sneak up on you.

As he neared the base of the bluff he crossed a small spring-fed creek and filled his water bladder. He turned and looked back one more time into the sea of prairie grass before he started his climb up the bluff.

The bluff proved to be a little more difficult to climb in this section than he anticipated. More than once Winding Spirit found himself forced to zigzag back and forth on the bluff to gain just a few feet in height. In spite of climbing out of the prairie grass he still got the feeling that someone was watching him. Twice he stopped and sat patiently looking down at the way he'd come, but he saw nothing. Winding Spirit finally arrived at the rocky outcrop he spotted from the prairie below. Taking in the fantastic view seemingly renewed Winding Spirit's energy. He sat there for a moment looking down upon the plain; in the distance he could easily see all of those mounds with all those former chiefs inside them. That's when the thought suddenly dawned on him; what if the uneasy feeling he had on the way up here came from the restless spirits. His people considered that whole section of prairie below the bluff sacred, a land of the dead among the living some said.

Suddenly the spectacular view took on less importance, and Winding Spirit wanted to head back to camp more than anything. Being followed by a spirit in a place like this seemed seriously dangerous in his mind. So, after spending only a few minutes on the rocky outcrop he started the long trip back down the bluff. Winding Spirit wanted to go fast because he could feel the fear beating in his chest. But he also knew that going fast could cause him to be careless in his decent and could easily cost him his life or cause a severe injury. So he did his best to balance the two. He again approached the bottom of the bluff where it met the prairie. Once he got a little too careless and slipped on a large boulder he crawled over. He didn't fall far, but it hurt. The fall also caused his quiver of arrows to scatter about the area. Convinced that some invisible spirit pushed him, he quickly gathered his arrows before again hurrying on.

Winding Spirit eventually made it back to camp without any further mishaps and once there found out that an elder from another tribe had been elected chief. The next morning Winding Spirit, Red Clouds, and the rest of his people returned to their village. A couple of the warriors returned with new wives. Winding Spirit also noticed that a few of the young women who came with them now were missing on the return trip. No doubt they became wives of somebody he knew. What he didn't know on that long walk home was that many years down the road he would eventually be elected chief of his people, and that he would serve as chief for many years before his people also buried him in a mound in that sacred place.

Today all the mounds are gone except one that is in a small park. The rest of the mounds were leveled over the years as people settled the land. All of the ancient burial ground now rests under a small Midwestern town. The area near the river where Winding Spirit fished and hunted contains business and fastfood outlets. The flat prairie where the mounds stood provide locations for schools, houses, and various public buildings. The rocky outcrop along the bluff where Winding Spirit briefly rested remains there, of course, but a mansion now stands there, a retired doctor's house. In fact, many nice houses line the bluff, and in a few places extended driveways and cement patios cause considerable run-off and erosion.

Near the base of the bluff the run-off from one paved driveway caused a small ravine to form during a summer rainstorm. When the owner stepped down into the gully to inspect the damage and try to calculate how much gravel he needed fix it he spotted a perfect little arrowhead laying there in the dirt. It came from an arrow that fell from Winding Spirit's quiver as he hurried back to the camp that day more than 800 years before.

Chapter 26: Dream Quest

Running Fox's people moved with the seasons. The spring thaw marked the beginning of each new year, and with it came a migration to the fishing camps in the north. The fishing camps were then given up for new camps farther west where the forest provided abundant berries and tubers. As summer started turning into fall, they moved to the land of many lakes to the south and east, there they trapped a great deal of beaver, muskrat, and other species. In addition, the land provided great quantities of acorns, mushrooms, and medicinal plants.

When the plants and animals started to show the first hints of the coming winter, the tribe elders and shaman would read the signs. Armed with the predictions of what type of winter might come, each family group would then decide where they would make their winter camps. When the winter gave way to spring, all the families then converged on the spring fishing camps to start the cycle over. Over the course of the year, from camp to camp, Running Fox and his people walked more than 300 miles.

Most of the people accepted the routine without question. Few, if any, complained because it was the only lifestyle they had ever known. Running Fox felt a little different though. He had been born with a mild hip deformity which caused him to suffer considerable pain when walking long distances. The medicine men and shaman of the tribe had both tried more than once to help Running Fox by driving the evil spirits from his body. And he tried a variety of strong medicines. When very young his father often times carried him for long stretches. When he grew too large to carry, he simply had to endure the walk. Over time, with each seasonal migration, Running Fox started to resent the moving more and more. Sometimes he commented about how nice it might feel to just stay in one place for a whole year, but the idea always fell on deaf ears. Running Fox knew what the others did as well, there just weren't enough resources in any one place to keep a family well fed and well clothed year around.

When Running Fox grew of age, he started looking for a wife, but he could find none who would have him. Some poked fun at his limp and others thought him unable to provide for them because of it. His uncle suggested he learn the ways of a medicine man because that way the tribe would provide for his needs and make him secure in his old age. This seemed a good solution to his aging hip problem. But Running Fox would have none of it. The inability of the medicine men to do any good left a sour taste in his mouth. Unable to find a wife, and with growing pain in his hip each year, he became more distant from most of his people and his family. When he did engage in conversation with someone it was only to complain of his own misfortune and his desire to live his life in one place. Quietly he considered suicide. After making the long journey from his winter camp to the spring fishing camp one year the shaman came to him and suggested he take a dream quest to look for advice and guidance. Though Running Fox felt skeptical, he decided he had nothing to lose by trying.

Running Fox waited for two days while the shaman gathered the proper medicines for the ritual. With everything prepared, Running Fox began a three day long fasting period. At the end of the fast, he met with the shaman who spoke for many hours about the ancient legends, of how to act in the presence of spirits, and of the journey he must undertake. He spoke for so long and in such detail about what might happen that Running Fox found himself becoming somewhat absorbed in the stories. Finally, the shaman handed Running Fox a small pouch and told him to find a place of solitude deep in the forest. When the sun started to come up he should eat the contents of the pouch and visit the spirit world for guidance. When the sun came up the next morning he would return to this world, refreshed, and with a vision to guide him. When Running Fox left the shaman's house, he quickly put all the stories and legends out of his head and adopted a more practical approach. The medicine men and shamans who tried to help him as a child had all told long and impressive stories as well, but in the end, they proved powerless. He assumed this attempt would be no different.

Running Fox went straight home from the Shaman's house and packed a small bag. In it he took a warm blanket, a bit of dried fish, a water bladder, and a spear just because he knew wolves lived in the area. With his bags packed, he immediately set out to find a place of solitude. He walked for some distance along the Great Spirit River to the south before picking some random small feeder stream to follow inland. As he followed the stream he came to a place where some large rock formations sprang from the ground high above the trees. That place looked as good as any, he thought, and he camped there at the base of it that night.

He awoke early when only a hint of light broke through the trees. He washed his face briefly in the stream before climbing the rock formation. As the sun broke over the horizon, he spread out his blanket on a flat spot high above the trees and sat down to open the shaman's pouch. In it he found a half-dozen dried and deformed looking mushrooms unlike any he knew. Mixed in with the mushrooms was a small handful of white berries, again unlike anything he recognized. He glanced at the horizon about to burst with the first rays of sun and shoved the whole contents of the bag into his mouth. He tried to chew the mix of mushrooms and berries, but it tasted foul and bitter. The taste forced him to take a drink from his bladder bag to wash it all down. He then slid his blanket over a little way so that when the morning gave way to the hot sun of the mid-day he sat in the shade of a tree growing up from a crack in the rocks there.

After perhaps half an hour Running Fox found himself feeling somewhat ill to the stomach and suddenly filled with the fear that the shaman might have poisoned him. Then, only a few minutes later, he caught glimpses of spirits dashing through the woods all around the rock he sat on. Everywhere he looked down into the woods he saw them darting to and fro. Now, as he watched, hundreds of spirits dashed about the forest floor under him. The sight scared him. He now wished more than anything that he had taken the shaman and his stories a little more se-riously. He struggled to remember what the shaman told him about how to act in this spirit world. Running Fox lost all track of time as the morning progressed. Many spirit visits occupied him, both good and bad. A beetle came to where he sat and drew him into a long conver-sation.

When the beetle left, the tree in the shade of which he now sat whispered an ancient song to him. Even as the day turned to night the spirits came and spoke with him. He felt so consumed with these visits that he did not even bother to light a fire. After day had turned completely to night, he grew aware of some more sinister spirits lurking in the forest below. Because the rock on which he sat har-bored a good and powerful spirit, the evil ones below could not bother him though.

Eventually, the spirit that occupied the rock he sat on spoke to him. The spirit pointed out that he lived a very fine life here in this area and then suggested that Running Fox could also live a fine life without moving in spite of what the others might think. When it seemed that all the spirits had finally left him, he carefully moved over to the edge of the rock and again looked down into the darkness of the forest. He didn't see as many evil spirits roaming about, but a few remained. A single dark spirit sat at the base of the rock and stared up at Running Fox refusing to leave. Running Fox yelled out loud at it and told it that he had no power here, but still the thing refused to move. It appeared to be waiting for Running Fox to come down. Running Fox eventually picked up loose rocks and started throwing them at the beast until he considered this might offend the good spirit. Then he took his spear and hurled that at the beast; still, it did not move. Finally, he lay down on his blanket and fell asleep.

When Running Fox woke up, he found the sun already far across the sky. His whole body ached, and he felt tired. He crawled over to the edge of the rock and looked down into the forest there but found nothing out of the ordinary. Looking around he realized that he'd lost his water blad-der and his spear, so with little more than his blanket he crawled back down off the rock. Before leaving he took a bath in the stream.

The shaman greeted him first when he returned to camp and insisted, he come and tell him everything he saw and heard from the spirits. With a newfound respect for the shaman, Running Fox went over every detail for him. After talking with the shaman, Running Fox made it known that he would stay at the fish camp that year and would remain there like a rock. He said he would remain there to greet them in the spring.

The first year that he stayed in that camp after the others left was by far the worst. The amount of pain he suffered in his hip and leg dramatically reduced, but intense loneliness replaced the leg pain after the others left for the next camp. It also took him a long time to scout out enough resources in the area to live comfortably. He ate a lot more fish over the course of the year than the others, and he became very good at catching them not just during the spring runs, but all year long. In time he found some wild berry patches not too far from where he lived, and he learned to like roasted clams he could dig from the river bottom with ease. After he had lived this way a couple of years, he finally had some company. One of the elders who had become very old also chose to stay there with Running Fox throughout the year rather than move constantly. The following year a woman who had lost her husband the year prior stayed on as well. Running Fox and the woman soon married.

In 1974 a young man and his brothers were given the task of cutting blocks from a sandstone rock formation so that their father could use the blocks to build a basement and foundation for a house on the land they had settled. While sitting in the shade of some trees at the base of the rock one of the young men found a beautiful spear tip, the same one Running Fox launched at the dark spirit while on his vision quest all those years ago.

Chapter 27: The Red Earth People

Many Elk and the people of his village first heard about the Red Earth People from their friendly neighbors, the Kanoktakott who lived in the east. They spoke of the Red Earth People in no uncertain terms; they said they were like living devils and a curse upon the land. Many Kanoktakott had been taken prisoner and killed by the Red Earth People that first year. In the second year Many Elk and his people heard similar reports from the Sau-nee tribe to the south.

By the third year it had become very clear to all the inhabitants of the land that the Red Earth People were waging war on all of them and trying to carve out a larger portion of the land for themselves. The Sau-nee, Oshkosh-notton, Kanoktakott, Many Elk's people, and several other tribes were forced to join into a single large village for their own security. They were not alone. Up and down the Great Spirit River grand villages were built, most composed of many smaller tribes.

Those were hard days for all the people of the land. The grand villages offered protection in numbers but made feeding everyone more difficult. The men could not hunt enough to feed everybody with only meat, so the women and children also tended small gardens and berry bushes to supplement their diet. None of the tribes who grouped up in these grand villages felt terribly happy with the conditions there. Food grew scarce, and sanitation became a problem with so many people living in one spot. Sometimes tempers flared between the various factions; but fear of the Red Earth People meant nobody became angry enough to set out on their own again either.

Many Elk and his people had lived in the grand village of the Fis-nu-nek for more than a year when a messenger suddenly interrupted their lives one afternoon. The messenger came from the grand village of the rocks some miles south of their village. He came and described how Red Earth Warriors encircled their village. Some of the young braves who heard this messenger started to give shrill war calls immediately, and so the news spread through the village like wildfire. Many of the warriors including Many Elk made themselves ready for war even before the meeting of the elders concluded. When all of the warriors gathered by the gate of the village, they numbered nearly 300. Nearly all of them wore painted designs on their faces and chests that both protected them and instilled fear in their enemies. Some of the children cried as the warrior fathers and brothers slipped from the gate one by one into the early evening sun.

The best trackers scouted ahead of the main body of warriors and the eldest and youngest warriors followed behind. Within a few hours of leaving their village they crept within sight of the fires burning all around the grand village of the rocks. The Red Earth People indeed surrounded them. Many of the warriors, old and young alike, whispered guesses about the numbers of Red Earth People who might surround the village. It proved difficult work to make an accurate estimation at such a distance, however, because sometimes they lit fewer fires than needed to make the defenders believe fewer attackers waited. In still other instances groups sometimes lit many more fires than needed in order to make their opponents believe they numbered more. Because of these tricky tactics Many Elk's group decided to wait until first light so they could more accurately determine the number of Red Earth Warriors.

Many of the warriors tried to catch some sleep in those early morning hours. Less than a handful had any luck. Several went off to pray and meditate, but most strained their eyes more and more with every passing minute to make out the shapes around the fires surrounding their friend's village. When daylight came even the older warriors could clearly see a formidable force of more than 400, perhaps even 500 surrounded the village. Chasing that many hardened warriors off on their own seemed a formidable task. They only hoped that the warriors inside the grand village would see them attack and come to their aid to help route these Red Earth People from the land once and for all.

Many Elk positioned himself in the middle of the warriors. Together they planned to move silently forward toward the village until the Red Earth People spotted them. Then they planned to rush forward and split roughly into two groups that would sweep to the right and to the left around the village. Many Elk nervously felt his belt again and again to confirm his knife was in place, and over his shoulder to make sure his quiver was full. As a group, they slowly emerged from the forest out into the grassland that surrounded the village. Quietly they closed the distance farther than what they originally anticipated. Eventually, war calls rang out from the Red Earth People's camp. Without hesitation, and as a single body, the group rushed forward. Just as they planned, they split into two groups. Many Elk, like many of the warriors, felt oblivious to the deafening scream of so many war calls at once. He heard only his heart pounding in his chest and his gaze scanned the grassy field for a target.

The villagers trapped inside the grand village of the rocks immediately noticed their neighbors coming to their rescue. And their warriors, as Many Elk's group hoped, quickly readied themselves to join the fight. What Many

Elk and the others did not know was that this village had fought these Red Earth People on open ground the evening before and lost many of their warriors. Now they had less than 100 warriors healthy enough to join the fight. Many of Many Elk's warriors locked in combat with Red Earth warriors, but Many Elk's eyes caught sight of the gate opening along the village wall, from it he watched as a mere trickle of the force they expected came out to join the fight. He did not have time to worry about numbers, the fight was on, and the fate of his people as well as people all along the Great Spirit River would likely be decided before the sun set that day.

A moment later Many Elk caught a glimpse of a Red Earth warrior running hunched over low in the grass. He rapidly closed in on two warriors locked in a life-or-death struggle with each other. Without a thought, he drew his bow back and steadied himself. It was a longer shot than he liked but he adjusted his lead accordingly and let the arrow fly. He lost sight of the arrow as it flew but could clearly see the warrior running hunched over suddenly stop and stand up in surprise. Many Elk watched as the warrior tried to dislodge his arrow from his shoulder, but Many Elk did not give him time. Before the warrior took another step, Many Elk hit his mark with a second arrow, this one lodging in the man's neck; moments later he toppled over.

Many Elk then closed in on the two men fighting; when he was almost there, he drew his knife and lunged for the Red Earth One wrestling on the ground with one of his own clan. Just as Many Elk plunged the knife deep into the man's ribs, he felt a stinging bite in his back. He narrowly missed being hit a second time as he spun to locate his attacker. What he saw horrified him, not one, but three men closing in on him running with their bows drawn. Many Elk was as brave as any, but he wasn't foolish. He turned and ran, trying to stay low in the tall grass where he could. He looked to his right and left as he ran and could see his people being chased from the field of battle in many places; they had attacked a number too large. He had barely realized this when another arrow hit him, this one also sticking in his back close to the first. He could feel the blood flowing harder as he ran, and knew little time remained.

He decided that if he was destined to die in that place, he would do it facing his enemy rather than running from them. Just as he reached the forest line on the far side of the village he stopped and turned, but rather than finding his attackers advancing, he watched as they ran back away from him. At first he couldn't understand what happened until his eyes focused on the village that now stood at some distance. He watched in horror as the Red Earth Warriors closed in on the many women, children, and elderly taking the opportunity of the distraction to try and escape. Rather than chase down the handful of wounded warriors, the Red Earth ones turned back to wipe out this village entirely. Many Elk cried as he watched many of his neighboring peoples cut down like animals in the fields.

Many Elk and less than 100 others of his warriors returned to their own village realizing Red Earth Warriors would surround them next, and they needed to prepare. Leaders decided what groups who had fortified themselves in this village for the past year would now pack in haste and leave. Each would now make their own path into the future. The Red Earth People fought fiercely and outnumbered them, but they could not track down all the various groups. Many Elk and his group left immediately heading to the north farther up the Great Spirit River. However, the injuries Many Elk and two other warriors sustained during the fighting slowed them considerably. Eventually, Many Elk made the others press on while he stayed back to rest along with Black Deer Moon who grew up with Many Elk.

Black Deer Moon had been hit in the face with a war club, and now his jaw hung loose in the skin. The club popped one of his eyes from its socket, and Many Elk barely recognized the man in spite of knowing him all his life. As night came Black Deer Moon worked to remove the arrows from Many Elk's back but could only dislodge one. Many Elk examined the arrowhead with the last of the day's fading light; he found it made of a sparkling silver colored stone he had never seen before.

When Many Elk awoke with the next morning's light, he found himself almost unable to move and in great pain. He rolled over to find his long-time friend Black Deer Moon dead. Many Elk spent several days in that place along the river and eventually, in spite of great pain, managed to bury his friend. In the days and weeks that followed he healed somewhat and caught up with the remainder of his people, but they held no joyous celebration or war cries as they once held when warriors came home. Over the next months and years all of the various groups formed a larger and more powerful coalition to hunt down and remove the Red Earth People from their lands.

In May of 1998 heavy rains softened the ground so much that a giant old oak tree along the bank of the river gave way and tipped over into the water. When its roots pulled up, they exposed a small triangular arrowhead to the sun for the first time in over a thousand years. The arrowhead was the same one Black Deer Moon pulled from Many Elk's back. A few days later some local fishermen happened to notice it as they walked to their favorite fishing hole.

Chapter 28: Out in the Cold

Rising Thunder was originally born on the plains to a tribe of buffalo hunters, but as an infant a raiding party from the Great Muddy River captured him and his mother. They never treated him as a captive, however. They instead raised him as though he was one of the Chaka-Na Won-ge, or "people of the forest." He grew up as the others hunting deer in the valleys during the winter and fishing along the Great Spirit River during the summer. He reached adulthood at a time when few people roamed the area and therefore never really experienced war or fighting other than the occasional long-distance raid to find new wives.

Though most of his life unfolded peacefully, life was not easy. Hunting and fishing could be exceptionally good some years and nobody would go hungry, but in other years people would sometimes starve. In his 15th summer, he took his first wife, but she died during childbirth just a year later. He married again when he turned 18 and started his family. Rising Thunder proved his skill not only as a good hunter and fishermen, but also as a wise planner. When others killed many deer or caught many fish, they gorged themselves and then lay around for days doing nothing. When Rising Thunder found a bounty of food he ate well, but he also worked hard to preserve as much food as he could. On more than one occasion this constant preparation for the future saved his life. His hard work also paid off in other ways. His wife seldom went hungry and repaid Rising Thunder by giving birth to nine children. Six of the nine lived to raise families of their own.

By the time Rising Thunder reached his 46th summer all of his children moved out to start families of their own. In his 50th summer his wife passed away with a fever. Rising Thunder preferred to stay in the lands he knew all his life and so built a solid house in the sandy flats along the Great Spirit River, but after two summers he grew lonely.

Seeing his father slow down in his older years and growing depressed, his youngest son, Dark Clouds, invited Rising Thunder to come and live with his family. Rising Thunder rejected the idea at first insisting that he felt just fine. But after thinking about it for a few days he changed his mind and moved a few miles south to the place where Dark Clouds now raised his own children.

Rising Thunder never anticipated it, but these years with his son and grandchildren proved the best years of his life. He spent countless hours teaching Dark Clouds' two sons how to make stone points, the best ways to set traps, and good tricks for catching more fish. As the years rolled by, Rising Thunder slowed more and more, however, and soon grew dependent upon Dark Clouds' generosity to supply him with enough food to make it through the winters. For the most part Dark Clouds, his wife, and their children didn't mind having the wise Rising Thunder living with them in the same camp. He often guided them through the seasons with his deep knowledge of the land. It seemed he could sense when the turkeys might lay their eggs or when the fish would spawn. He made sure that no opportunity to obtain food slipped by and also instilled the same work ethic he had followed his whole life in his children and grandchildren.

Rising Thunder lived considerably longer than most in those days. Dark Clouds' family held a great feast in honor of Rising Thunder when he reached his 70th summer. Those summer days soon gave way to the turning of the leaves though. As always, Rising Thunder first sensed the shortening days and smelled autumn in the air. The winter that year started much earlier than normal and the snows got deep fast. Dark Clouds, approaching middle age himself, did not have as many good hunts as he normally did. Because Dark Clouds had two more children late in life, he had many mouths to feed but not enough in the pot to go around. Rising Thunder at first simply ate less or sometimes passed on a meal here and there insisting that he felt full from the last meal even though a hard pain tightened in his stomach. He knew that if the winter did not break early, he would sing his own death song soon.

The winter refused to help the old Rising Thunder though, rather than breaking it worsened adding two more feet of snow. Eventually Rising Thunder told Dark Clouds that he planned to follow with the tradition of their people and give his life so the children might live to see spring. Dark Clouds objected at first, but soon realized his father had already made up his mind and would not change it. Rising Thunder asked Dark Clouds not to tell the children the truth, but instead tell them their grandfather went for a walk.

The next afternoon Rising Thunder spent his time bathing with water heated on the fire and grooming his hair. After he had cleaned himself, he put on his finest clothes and tucked his best knife into his belt. He threw his fishing net over his shoulder and brought his walking stick. For anyone who did not know better, he appeared a man about to go out for a day of fishing on the Great Spirit River. Before leaving he stopped by each of Dark Clouds' children and whispered an ancient prayer before kissing each one. The eldest children asked where he planned to fish and why when so much snow still surrounded them. When he had finished with the children, he embraced his son Dark Clouds. He thanked him for all his generosity and kindness over the years and promised to save a seat at the sacred fire in the next life. He then embraced Dark Clouds' wife and thanked her in the same way.

Without another word he stepped out into the late afternoon sun and trudged his way through the deep snow as well as he could. He realized he no longer possessed the strength he once held, yet he felt happy to go in this way now still under his own power and free will. In spite of his great age and deep snow, Rising Thunder traveled several miles on before the sun started to set and the light faded. Deep in the forest by a small lake where he had often fished as a young man, he found a small opening along the shoreline. There, with the last rays of sun, he sat and sang his death song, very quietly at first and gradually louder. As the sun set the temperature plummeted below freezing, but he kept up the song until he grew so cold that his tongue and voice refused to work correctly. At the end he no longer sang out loud but only in his spirit. He stared out into the frozen lake reflecting upon his rich life and many happy times. As Rising Thunder took his last breaths he watched as his wife of many years came walking across the lake to take him to the other side.

Six thousand years later two friends walked through a freshly plowed field along that same lake looking for arrowheads and came upon Rising Thunder's finest knife.

Chapter 29: Twelve Arrows

Two Elk, like his father, grandfather, and many generations before, was born in the quiet valley just south of the sacred hill. The valley had not one but two large springs that ran from the base of the bluff all the way down the valley to a point where they connected with Beaver Creek. Beaver Creek then ran to the south and west until it ran into the Great Spirit River, the Great Spirit River in turn ran farther to the south and finally turned to the west where it joined the Mud River. Two Elk and his people hunted and fished all the lands from their camp by the springs all the way down to the place where Beaver Creek ran into the Great Spirit River. Game was plentiful in those days and there was good variety.

Two Elk, like the others, was an expert hunter and tracker, often spending days on the trail but seldom returning empty handed. He also excelled at trapping animals and fishing with large nets in the creeks and rivers. Some of the men hunted with an atl-atl while others preferred a bow and arrow. Regardless of the tool they used, the most successful hunters were looked up to and even revered. The best hunters married the prettiest women and commanded the most respect.

Two Elk descended from a long line of better than average hunters; in fact, he descended from what might arguably constitute the finest family of hunters in the entire village. Two Elk's father White Thunder taught him from the early age of eight all the arts of tracking and hunting. White Thunder also started teaching Two Elk at a young age how to make his own hunting weapons. They traveled to the sacred hill to fetch stone to flake at least once each year and sometimes more, but by age 10 Two Elk had not yet caught on to the skill of flintknapping. Though friends and family sometimes teased Two Elk for his lack of skill in flintknapping they couldn't tease him about his hunting ability because he clearly excelled at hunting down all sorts of game. As Two Elk moved into his teenage years his father simply continued to supply him with finished arrows for hunting.

When Two Elk reached the age to marry and officially became a man in the eyes of the village, he still had not mastered the art of making stone tools. He could make serviceable tools but could not manufacture refined work comparable to his father's. For several years after Two Elk moved out and established his own house his father still brought him some of his own arrow points from time to time. When Two Elk married, his father made for him as a wedding gift, 12 of his finest arrows. These were not manufactured from stone from the sacred hill but rather an unknown source. All 12 points shone bright pink and orange in color. He decided immediately to save these arrows for only special hunts.

After Two Elk married, his father no longer brought stone tools to him in secret, but he managed to get along with his less than perfect points. What his points lacked in style he made up for with skill. As the years rolled on he stayed true to his word and very seldom brought out any of the fine pink and orange arrows his father gave him. In spite of only using them sparingly and carefully as one could, he still lost points from time to time. One he lost when the arrow sailed clean through the deer he aimed at and hid itself in the leaves on the other side. Another arrow he lost when he shot a turkey that flew away, and he never saw it again. This general trend continued for several years, and when his father finally passed away, he found himself with only one of the original 12 arrows left. Out of respect for his father he removed the last stone arrowhead from the arrow and rather than lose it on a hunt he wore it around his neck as a reminder of his father.

Two Elk raised several children and lived a long life in that quiet little valley with the springs. When he grew old and passed away he still wore that last arrowhead his father made for him all those years earlier. Two Elk's family treated him the same as all those who died in those days. First, they cleaned him and dressed him in his finest clothing, and then they carried him in a funeral procession to the bluffs high above their quiet little valley.

On top of the bluff, they built a scaffold high off the ground and placed his lifeless body upon it. There they sang songs and the elders told stories of the happy hunting grounds for three days. At the end of three days, they returned to their village and feasted. They often left the bodies of the deceased on the scaffolding until it fell down and the bones scattered. Once a generation they held a ceremony where they gathered all of the bones they could find and burned them in a great fire on the bluff top. In the end the only thing that remained of Two Elk was that single pink and orange arrowhead his father made for him, and he wore to his grave.

In 1968 a troop of boy scouts hiking the bluff high above that quiet little valley came upon that colorful arrowhead lying among the darker sandstone rocks and one picked it up.

Chapter 30: Little Hawk

A damp breeze chilled the air as Little Hawk began to break camp. He spent the last of the summer months in the thick forests in the far north along the Great Spirit River and had a great deal of success hunting elk. Little Hawk managed to kill two large bulls and two adult cows. Together, the four hides would provide enough leather to make new shirts and pants for both him and his wife. Little Hawk packed the four hides, his hunting equipment, and a large bag of elk jerky into a big dugout canoe he built the year before. He made the canoe extra-large and deep with his summer elk hunting trips in mind; but now, fully loaded, it still sat so low in the water that Little Hawk felt worried. As Little Hawk pushed off from the muddy shore of the Great Spirit River a few small flakes of snow swirled in the cold fall air.

The canoe trip lay all down-stream now, but he still found the going slow because of the large size of his canoe. The Great Spirit River often split around one or more large islands making the path confusing at times. In one stretch Little Hawk veered left around an island but ended up in muddy back waters forcing him to canoe back up stream and back down the other side of the island. Over the course of several days Little Hawk picked and weaved his way through the maze of islands and river channels finally reaching more familiar waters.

As Little Hawk floated closer to home his mind started to wander off into a daydream of his extended family, his home camp, and how happy they would be to see him with his bounty of elk hides. When the canoe rammed into a submerged log, the canoe jolted to a stop and tore Little Hawk from his pleasant daydream. The canoe started to tilt to one side at an angle in the current, and Little Hawk struggled with every fiber of his strength to straighten the canoe before the river spirits swallowed it up, a fate that he and all of his people feared more than anything. A minute later he again found himself safe and floating down the river smoothly whispering a quick prayer of thanks.

As Little Hawk rounded the last bend in the river before his home camp came into view he adjusted his posture, sitting taller in the canoe, grinning widely. But where he expected to see people going about their daily tasks at the river's edge, he found no one. His grin melted quickly into a look of deep concern. He tried to force his eyes to look farther inland and focus, but still saw no one. His heart began to beat hard in his chest, and his effort to paddle the canoe to shore doubled. On shore a dog came to the water's edge and started to bark, Little Hawk recognized the dog as one belonging to one of his uncles. The site of a living creature offered some comfort to Little Hawk, but he found it short lived. When Little Hawk made it into the shallow water near shore he jumped out of his canoe and ran up the steep bank to his camp and still found no one. The fire pits lay all cold; the bark houses looked like they had been neglected for weeks with sections of bark missing on some and the leather door flap to another torn and fluttering in the wind. A lump started to form in his throat as he headed for his own house.

Little Hawk found the leather door flap to his house missing completely, he bent over a bit at the waist and entered the dark house. His eyes struggled to adjust to the darkness and to keep the tears from blinding him. His wife's favorite cooking pot set on its side in the cold ashes of the fire pit, and the damp furs that covered their bed made the space smell musty. It became clear to Little Hawk that no one had been there for weeks. Little Hawk darted from house to house. In more than one place he found signs of struggle, broken pots, atl-atl darts lay scattered about, and some houses looked partially burned. He started to scurry about the campsite looking for any sign that might tell him where everybody went; but the winds of time had already erased all signs. When Little Hawk turned to go back to his empty house a pale colored bone protruding from the grass caught his eye, it looked like a bone that once belonged to a person. Little Hawk didn't bother with trying to figure out to whom the bone belonged, but instead let out a mournful cry and moved on. He pulled the musty smelling blankets from his house and brought in his still green elk hides and lay down to sleep.

Little Hawk awoke in the early morning hours when the night started to give way to the day. A thin layer of wet snow covered everything, and a gnawing hunger filled his belly. He poked his head out from his doorway thinking maybe he dreamed the events of the day before, but the stark silence of the hour, the lack of glowing embers or smell of smoke told him otherwise. He went to work fixing the leather door flap to his house before starting a fire. His uncle's dog invited himself into Little Hawk's bark house and seemed happy for the company. Little Hawk cleaned out his wife's favorite cooking pot and prepared a hearty stew with elk meat and vegetables.

The whole time he cooked he prayed out loud to the creator that he might still find his wife and his people alive and safe. But he knew that with every passing hour those chances decreased. In the early afternoon he packed his canoe with supplies for a long journey and kept enough open space for his uncle's dog. Little Hawk knew of another camp far down the river, past the place of many rocks; he would go there first.

By the time the sun started to set Little Hawk had covered considerable distance toward his alternate home camp. He chose a small island situated next to a place they called Spirit Island to spend the night. Spirit Island formed one of the most impressive islands in the whole of Spirit River. It rose from the center of the river with straight stone walls capped with a thick forest of white pines.

Elders said that water spirits inhabited Spirit Island and that going there could be dangerous. Elders said the small island next to it that Little Hawk camped on remained safe, but its close proximity to the other island made Little Hawk a little nervous. He pulled his big dugout canoe onto the island and flipped it on its side to use as a lean-to. He built a small fire and cut a bed of pine boughs to sleep on. His uncle's dog curled up tight against Little Hawk to stay warm.

Little Hawk awoke in a dream world. In the distance he could hear his wife crying out for him. He struggled in the darkness to find her, but his efforts proved fruitless, he merely wandered about aimlessly, unable to locate the source of her voice. When his uncle's dog barked loudly sitting next to him, he suddenly snapped into the present. Mostly awake now he sat up and stretched his stiff muscles. The sun had already climbed high in the sky. Little Hawk did not normally sleep so late. He turned and flipped the canoe and started to drag it to the water's edge.

When he went back to pick up his blankets and the dog a faint sound on the wind stopped him dead in his tracks. His head instinctively turned to the side, and he tilted his ear to better catch more of the sound. Coming and going with the wind he heard the sounds of a woman calling out. Little Hawk waited a moment and then headed straight in the direction the voice seemed to come from. He followed the noise to the very edge of the small island and out into the water around it.

Standing in knee-deep water he realized the sound of the woman sounded like his wife, and that it came from high on top of Spirit Island. Little Hawk turned and hurried back to gather his belongings and throw them into his canoe, in his haste he almost forgot the dog. A short while later his canoe butted up against the steep stone walls of Spirit Island.

He called out in a loud voice, "Summer Sun! Summer Sun! Is that you I hear calling?" The sound of the woman's voice suddenly vanished, however. He then called out again, "Summer Sun! Is that you I hear calling?!"

"Little Hawk!" came her shrill response.

Little Hawk felt shocked and confused, "How did you… Why are you…?" His voice trailed off.

"Come around to the point of the island, I think I can climb back down there," she said.

Little Hawk complied and immediately began to work his way around to the point of the island. By the time he made it around to the point of the island his wife had already started the tricky climb down the steep rock face. He wanted to jump from the canoe and help her, but he had to fight hard to keep the canoe in the right spot, the current pulled constantly at the large canoe. He finally managed to tie a short rope from the canoe to a tree root nestled into the rock face. A moment later he heard a short help and looked up to see his wife fall the last 10 feet. She disappeared into the dark brown waters in the midst of a million small bubbles and reappeared a second later by the side of the canoe. Little Hawk grabbed her by the arm and pulled her aboard.

She gasped and pulled the hair from her face.

"Why were you on Spirit Island? Where are the others?" Little Hawk asked.

She began to sob, "a war party came, a big war party. We had no chance. They killed your uncles and your father." Her head hung low, and the tears flowed freely. "They killed the men and took the rest of us for slaves. I fought the whole time. I pulled their hair and bit at them like a wild animal. I must have been more trouble than they wanted because when we reached this place in the river they, threw me into the water. Spirit Island was my only chance," she explained.

For the first time Little Hawk realized just how much weight his wife had lost and noted the poor condition of her clothes and skin.

"I didn't think I would ever see you again, I was singing my death song when you showed up," she continued. "I almost jumped into the water and tried to swim to the other shore, but I knew the water spirits would almost certainly swallow me up."

Little Hawk leaned back and tried to untie the canoe from the tree root in the stone, but the force of the current pulled the rope so tight he could not manage to untie it. He pulled his stone knife from his side and cut the rope, releasing the canoe. The canoe jolted free, and the stone knife slipped from Little Hawk's hand, but he didn't care, he felt happy to have his wife back.

Little Hawk and his wife spent that winter in their old house, and when spring came she gave birth to their first child. When the weather warmed enough and she felt well enough to travel they moved far to the west, closer to the lakes and vast prairies.

Nearly a thousand years passed before the main channel in the river changed course and left Spirit Island a lone outpost in a shallow side channel. The shallow sandy bottomed waters around the island attracted countless boats throughout the summer. A lot of people came to play volleyball in the shallow waters; others came to fish. One group of friends went there in 2008 to enjoy an early summer day outside and found Little Hawk's knife lying on a sandbar all by itself.

Chapter 31: White Stone

White Stone grew up the only son of Fearless Leader and Beautiful Valley. Beautiful Valley gave birth to him at night during a cold spring. Though the delivery lasted a long time and caused Beautiful Valley agonizing pain, both mother and child survived and lived happily. When White Stone's grandfather came to see the baby, he said that all of the stones in the Great Spirit River on which they camped glowed white because the moon shone so bright, so he named the baby White Stone. A dedicated mother, Beautiful Valley took great care in all things related to her son, and Fearless Leader harbored excellent fishing and hunting skills so that neither he, nor his family, ever went hungry for very long.

White Stone proved a very fast learner and started to speak much earlier than most children. By the time he reached the age of four he asked his parents questions far beyond his tender age. As he grew up the smart young boy became well known among their people and loved by not only his parents, but also by all the people of their clan.

Tragedy struck early in White Stone's seventh year, however. An early and unexpected thaw had threatened to flood and forced the clan to move from their bountiful river bottom land. When their usual evacuation route became blocked by melting ice they moved around to an old trail unused for many years. As they crossed near the mouth of a feeder stream the thin ice gave way and swallowed White Stone. Fearless Leader, who knew the water did not rise past his waist, jumped in to rescue his son, but the current there was very swift and had already swept White Stone far under the ice.

Fearless Leader and Beautiful Valley let the rest of their clan move on without them that spring and chose to camp on the river in that spot instead. Both of them, though accustomed to tragedy, were terribly affected by White Stone's loss. They searched the shoreline for miles downstream day after day when the ice melted away in the hopes of finding their son so that they might give him an appropriate burial. In spite of constant searching they never found White Stone. After several weeks passed and the weather grew warm, Beautiful Valley told Fearless Leader that he should go out into the forests or out on to the plains and find a new child to replace White Stone. In the days of Fearless Leader and Beautiful Valley replacing a child who died with one taken from another tribe was neither rare nor frowned upon. Several years prior to the loss of White Stone one of their clan's children went missing when he strayed too far down the riverbank on his own.

The taking of a replacement child from another village could, in some cases, cause problems in the form of retaliation if villagers caught you, or even all-out war. So the council had to approve such action. In mid-summer Fearless Leader walked to the place where he knew his people made their summer village, and in the presence of the council pleaded his case asking for permission to seek out a child to replace White Stone. Fearless Leader's people respected him and knew he loved White Stone so they granted permission under the condition that Fearless Leader travel to lands so far off that the tribe could not track him back to their village. The council suggested Fearless Leader seek his child far to the east where rumors circulated that a new pale-skinned tribe lived. Fearless Leader agreed, and with the help of Beautiful Valley immediately went to work gathering things he needed for the long trip.

It took him three days to gather everything he needed. He arranged for Beautiful Valley to stay with his brother while he traveled, and if he did not return he instructed her to remarry. Early the next morning Fearless Leader laced up his boots and slung his bag and bow over his shoulder before heading out. He walked for several days before he started to encounter lands unfamiliar to him. On the ninth day he came to a Su-has-ni village, friends of his people for many generations. After they invited him into their village, and he smoked the sacred peace pipe with their council.

During their meeting, he explained in great detail all the events which led to him coming there. They seemed to sympathize with him and said little. They did say that they knew about the strange new pale tribe in the east and one among them claimed to have met them. They told Fearless Leader that these pale people looked sickly and weak, and he would be better off to find a child from another tribe. Fearless Leader remained committed to the idea however and soon departed walking to the east with the rise of the sun.

Fearless Leader walked for three more days to the east before coming to Spirit Lake; from there he followed the shoreline of the lake far to the south. Near the southern end of the lake he came close to a village of people he did not recognize. They wore clothing completely different from his own and even though he remained at a great distance, he thought he heard them speaking a strange language. He waited in hiding until deep into the night before skirting around their village and continuing on to the east once again. Over the next two weeks he slowly continued making his way east and twice more skirted around villages of strangers in the middle of the night. Late one afternoon, in a land so far east he feared he might not ever find his way home again, he caught a hint of smoke in the wind.

Fearing he might unexpectedly approach yet another strange village, he slowed down and moved quietly and methodically through the forest. He moved carefully to leave no signs of his passing and to make no sound. Traveling so far from home and looking to steal a child didn't feel like a game, and his pulse quickened as he slowly approached a large opening in the forest. Here he encountered a strange sight. Before him lay no village, but instead some kind of strange building made from many trees stacked sideways upon one another. From a stack of red stone in the roof came a thin wisp of smoke telling Fearless Leader that somebody inside tended a fire.

All around the strange house he saw big fields filled with corn and some plants that he did not recognize. To the side of the house he encountered a number of birds that did not fly away as the birds he knew did, but rather seemed content to stay close to the strange house scratching and pecking away at the dirt there.

Fearless Leader remained there hidden at the edge of the forest for quite some time observing a number of strange sights. Then suddenly some movement caught his eye just beyond the strange house. Two men and a young boy walked back to the house from the woods opposite of where he hid. One of the men carried a large and oddly shaped stick and the other man carried a dead turkey. The two men disappeared into the house, but the boy remained outside and seemed content to play with imaginary friends all around the place. Fearless Leader observed this boy closely and noted that he looked healthy and perhaps seven or eight summers old.

The boy, like the two men, looked very pale indeed like the Su-has-ni had told him these people looked, but he did not think the boy looked particularly weak or sickly. As he squatted there in the edge of the woods the boy came closer to him, swinging a stick at invisible creatures and yelling out in a strange tongue. Fearless Leader realized this might be his best opportunity to steal this boy, even though he had just arrived in the area.

Fearless Leader carefully considered the situation and drew an imaginary line in the field. If the boy came past that line, he knew he could run out and grab him before the men in the house would even know what happened. He feared if he ran too close to the house to grab the boy the men inside might see and fire arrows his way. He did not need to wait long, however, because as he watched the boy noticed something in the woods close by. At first, he couldn't figure it out, but when the boy dropped his stick and headed almost straight for him, he realized the boy headed right for a giant patch of wild raspberries just a stone's throw from where he hid. By the time the boy crossed Fearless Leader's imaginary line in the field he began to run full out yelling and laughing.

Without any further hesitation Fearless Leader seized the opportunity and burst forth from his hiding spot and ran straight at the boy. He reduced the distance by nearly half before the boy saw him and froze in his tracks. Fearless Leader thought the boy looked scared like a rabbit standing there but just before he grabbed the boy he ran and yelled. The boy proved no match for Fearless Leader's speed though, and he quickly caught up to him and snatched him up with one arm while at a dead run. When Fearless Leader turned back toward the woods his heart nearly burst when he found a different pale faced man emerging from the woods to investigate all the yelling. He immediately thought that he should have been far more observant and careful to make sure there weren't any other Pale Faced Ones around, but now it was too late. He stopped and threw the boy down to the ground hard hoping to make him slow in getting up. When the boy popped back up he delivered a terrible fist blow to the boy's face and knocked him out.

As Fearless Leader drew his bow back and started to close the distance to within a reasonable striking distance the Pale Faced One took a stick from his back and aimed it at him. Suddenly he heard a loud thunder clap and a great cloud of smoke erupted from the man's stick. Fearless Leader suddenly felt anything but fearless because he now realized these Pale Faced People possessed great powers and might even be spirits themselves. He dropped his bow and began to run back away from the man toward the safety of the forest.

As he ran he now saw the two men from earlier emerge from their strange stick house; they too now aimed their terrible thunder sticks at him.

Suddenly he felt as though someone punched him with a giant invisible fist, and he fell hard to the ground. When he tried to get up his body failed him, and he noticed a great deal of blood coming from his mouth. After a few moments he managed to get his feet under him again and staggered rather than ran toward the woods. Before he could reach it however he heard another shot; and Fearless Leader's life left him.

Almost 400 years to the day later a man climbed down from a road grader to take a lunch break. He had been working on widening the road through that particular part of town for the better part of three weeks now. As he approached his pickup truck parked off to the side of the construction zone he just happened to come across a beautiful little arrow point turned up with all the road work. It was from one of the arrows Fearless Leader dropped as he fled from the Pale Faced Ones.

Chapter 32: Funeral Pyre

Four Winds and his fellow hunters were almost always on the move. Wherever the herds went, and wherever the waters rippled with fish they headed there. As the seasons changed and the fish and animals moved, so did Four Winds. They roamed from the land of ice and snow in the north all the way to the great river valleys in the south and from the great lakes in the east to the endless prairies of the west.

Their world seemed boundless and rich, but also filled with dangers and magic. They took great pains to appease all of the spirits so good fortune would smile upon their small band of nomads. In most years their offerings seemed sufficient. Not only did they make regular offerings to the spirits, but they also heeded their warnings and that of the shaman who regularly made the small group go long distances out of its way to avoid "bad ground" as he called it. While no member of the tribe publicly opposed any decision the shaman made, most of them grumbled about the regular inconveniences posed by him.

In early spring the elk herd that Four Winds had tracked all winter started to head north to their summer feeding and birthing grounds. The annual move north behind the elk always came as a welcome event after a long winter because they could take the elk with relative ease during the birthing season and Four Winds, as well as all the others, knew they would soon feast on fresh meat. They followed the herd all the way through the Oak Savannah and the prairies to the lake country before their shaman suddenly grew ill during the trip. Three times in two days he asked the group to stop so he might seek guidance from the spirits and to make offerings. With the annual elk hunt and feast just days away the entire group felt seriously irritated by the constant stopping. Four Winds, like the others, feared taking too much time to get to the elk might cause them to miss the calf birthing time at which point they would no longer find the elk easy prey.

When the shaman made the group stop yet again in mid-morning for the third day in a row Four Winds finally voiced his concern. Though the group possessed no official leader, Four Winds was by far the strongest and best hunter among them. Most looked up to him, and few considered him a peer. The shaman took a long time to answer, appearing to study Four Winds first. Finally the shaman indicated that the reason he asked them to stop so many times was because he experienced a vision in which their greatest hunter, Four Winds, fell ill and died. Four Winds countered by pointing out that they were almost upon the birthing grounds and that he felt fine, not only that, but that the group all hungered for a feast. When Four Winds asked the shaman if he had no stomach for the task, several people in the group laughed audibly. In the end the Shaman conceded but warned that he could offer no protection if they continued.

By late the next afternoon Four Winds and his small band approached the elk birthing grounds and found they arrived just in time. By nightfall they had more meat than they could dry or eat, and everyone slept well with full stomachs, even the shaman. They stayed there for two weeks feasting upon the surplus meat, even after the elk herd delivered all the calves and moved on, the hunters remained. After every member of the group ate their fill and everyone dried and smoked meat until all their bags were full, they decided to move on.

The morning they broke camp, Four Winds started to feel sick. When the first pains started in his side he said nothing but fear instantly filled his heart. As much as they needed the feast and enjoyed it he knew going against a shaman's advice was risky business. The group headed due west to a place they called Sun Hill where they could also resupply their hunting weapons with a beautiful stone they called sunstone.

By the time they reached Sun Hill and some started to flake new points for their spears Four Winds could no longer hide the pain he felt in his side. As soon as it became apparent the entire group grew silent and concerned. They all knew the shaman advised against it and even warned Four Winds specifically about continuing the hunt, but they ignored his advice.

The shaman, in spite of his previous warning, spent all of the evening and that night praying and giving medicine to the now gravely ill Four Winds. In the middle of the night Four Wind's appendix ruptured, and by morning he died. The small band of hunters all sat stunned and felt exceptionally scared because they knew they had forsaken the spirits and ignored the shaman's advice. Now here lay proof that the shaman indeed possessed great power. Four Wind's body had not even cooled to the touch when the others began to build a funeral pyre for him following the custom of those days.

The shaman went into a trance as the group collected a large heap of brush upon which they planned to burn Four Winds' body and set his spirit free. They had not even completed the pyre yet when the shaman suddenly came out of the trance telling the group that they all faced great danger and needed to leave this place as soon as possible. Without the usual ceremony and songs, they threw Four Winds' body upon the heap of brush and lit the fire. His family placed two of Four Winds' spears on the funeral pyre. It had barely begun to burn as the small devastated band disappeared over the horizon to the south. They did not build the funeral pyre big enough and it didn't burn it well enough to completely dispose of Four Wind's body. Two of the spear tips survived the heat of the fire. What his friends did not do to dispose of the body, the wolves did. And they scattered his remains all over the area.

Over 8,500 years later a farmer subjected the spears to fire again when he burned his field to eliminate some stumps near the edge. He worked with a shovel to expose the roots all around the stump as it burned in order to burn it completely, as he did so he inadvertently dug up one of the two spears laid on the funeral pyre by Four Winds' family.

The farmer put it in his pocket but never noticed the tip of the other point that lay exposed just a few inches away. The other point wound up broken by farm machinery many years later and the pieces of it still occasionally turn up in that field to this day, unnoticed.

Chapter 33: Twins

Spring Winds and Red Earth were twins, born just minutes apart. Their father White Eagle, was the clan chief. According to custom among the forest people in those days the chief's first born son would become chief. Nobody among their clan could ever remember twins born under such circumstances, and a considerable amount of debate took place about how they would decide which of the two boys would take over as chief when the father died. Some people thought whichever son actually entered the world first should become the next ruler. While others thought they should share the rule. In the end however the decision became White Eagle's.

White Eagle was not the sort of person who rushed into making any decision and especially not one of this much importance. He knew his two boys might grow up to be very different men, and that one might make a much better chief than the other. So he didn't want to pick one or the other based on anything yet. Instead he decided to wait until the boys grew to an age when he could compare them based on competition. A few days later White Eagle addressed all the people of his clan and told them when the twins, Spring Winds and Red Earth, turned 12 summers old he would devise a competition between them. The winner would become the next chief after White Eagle. As usual, his clan seemed pleased with the chief's wise and careful decision.

The chief among the forest people held much prestige at that time. The chief decided when and where to make camp, when to break camp, when to wage war, and when to run. The chief settled all disputes among the people, and he had his pick of eligible women for marriage. Because of the chief's great importance to the people, the people endlessly conversed about which of the two boys should rule. Seldom did a day go by in which the merits of one or both of the boys weren't a topic of discussion at great length at the various family hearths. It even became the subject of conversation around the sacred communal fire from time to time.

Because the subject became such a regular part of conversation, the boys grew up in an environment in which they quickly became aware that one day fate would pit them against one another. They began to mimic the fight they imagined would happen one day at a very early age. By age seven or eight they were already prone to frequent fights and wrestling matches, all of which were carefully watched by anyone in the vicinity. In spite of all the fighting and competition between the two boys, they remained very close, almost inseparable.

By the time the boys were in their 11th summer two distinctly different personalities emerged, each with his own group of fans and supporters. Spring Winds repeatedly proved himself stronger and more durable than Red Earth, winning most wrestling matches between them. Red Earth on the other hand proved far more cautious and witty, frequently making his brother look foolish with words alone. Many of the men in the clan valued strength and bravery above all else and thus hoped Spring Winds would one day become chief. While many of the women and elders found Red Earth's careful thought and sharp tongue a more attractive quality. White Eagle remained largely impartial, loving both of the boys for who they were.

By the spring of their 12th year, the boys and all of the clan looked forward to the competition White Eagle devised. Though many people came to him in hopes of learning some small detail about what he planned, he said nothing. White Eagle announced the competition would begin on the first full moon of the summer season at a point when that time remained only a few days away. Though White Eagle just announced it, he had in fact already planned the event quite some time earlier. After thinking about the situation for several years he concluded he would let nature choose the winner by taking a stone knife all the way to Spirit Rock in the north woods.

The place was well known to all of the forest people because legend said that it was at that spot the thunder spirits defeated the water spirits at the beginning of time. Once every few years they all traveled to the place for a special ceremony. What made the place most unique for the purpose of the competition, however, was not so much the destination as the method of getting to it. The forest people's camp and Spirit Rock lay separated by a huge lake named Thunder Lake.

The trails on the west side of the lake leading to Spirit Rock provided relatively easy traveling across mostly flat ground with mixed forest and prairies. But it constituted the long way around. The trails that ran to Spirit Rock on the east side of the lake were much shorter, over all, but covered dangerous ground that included a number of swamps and the traditional hunting grounds of their dreaded enemies the Hak-a-notten.

By daybreak following the first full moon of summer most of the clan lay awake and waiting for White Eagle when he emerged from his house. There, in the cool morning mist he announced the rules to the boys and clan in general. White Eagle left a fine stone knife on the very pinnacle of Spirit Rock in the north woods. The first boy to get there and retrieve it and bring it back to him would win the contest. He would hold a feast before the boys left, and the competition would start with the shooting of a flaming arrow into the night sky.

Right after the announcement, clan members scattered excitedly in all directions to bring food to share in the celebration. Some started to immediately play the drums while others began dancing and singing. The boys were both wise enough to spend this time resting. White Eagle went to both, individually, and wished them good luck before tying a single eagle feather to a lock of hair on each boy. Then their mother shaved all of their hair except that single lock which held the feather. The medicine man came to them during the day and painted their bodies with symbols of good luck and protection. Before dark they gave each boy a spear and small bag containing a handful of supplies. Under normal circumstance the trip, whether one went east or west, took about one week. Racing, the two boys hoped to make the trip in as little as two days.

When darkness finally fell, everybody gathered at the edge of the camp. White Eagle made a short speech explaining to the boys that the loser was bound by this just as the winner was, and that neither should hold any ill will after the decision was made because this was his wish. A short while later, a friend of White Eagles launched a single flaming arrow off a hill out into a marsh. When the boys saw the arrow launch into the sky, both of them sprinted off into the darkness. Some of the young boys of the village ran after them laughing and yelling for a short while, but the boys soon left them far behind. The trail heading north branched off to the east and west some way north of the village, so no one among the clan knew which way the boys went; and some even wagered on it.

The night remained cloudless, and the moon provided enough light for the boys to see fairly well except in the areas where the forest grew exceptionally thick. Both Spring Winds and Red Earth ran nearly side by side, but Red Earth eventually started to drop back slightly before reaching the split in the trail, he wanted to see which way his brother went before making his own decision. Spring Winds however showed no hesitation and sprinted down the trail that ran along the west side of the lake, over the easy ground. Red Earth, seeing his brother choose the west route followed suit but only ran for another hour before lying down between the lake and the trail to sleep. Spring Winds ran all through the night and well into the next day, constantly looking over his shoulder. Spring Winds had challenged Red Earth to enough races over the past few years to know that he, Spring Winds, ran the faster of the two.

Of course Red Earth also knew he could not outrun his brother, but he had other plans. On the morning of the first day he worked on a trap of sorts. He wandered the forest gathering several lengths of vines before returning to the trail. Then he walked up the trail slowly studying it, eventually he found a spot where the trail narrowed and gave way to a marsh on one side and the rocky lake shore on the other. If his brother returned down this same side of the lake like he assumed he would, he would have to pass through this very spot.

Red Earth carefully tied the vines to a tree just off the path on one side of the trail and then hid the vine under leaves and dirt across the trail, on the other side he built a well-crafted blind behind a fallen tree where he could hide himself yet see for some distance down the trail. When his brother returned with the special stone knife their father had placed at Spirit Rock he would be waiting to trip him up with the vine and then pounce upon him to get the knife for him. Red Earth was familiar with the trail and the distance and knew that he would have almost a full day to rest by the lakeside and perhaps even catch a few fish.

Spring Winds approached Spirit Rock at a steady run and felt rather pleased with his time; he knew already that he would make the trip in just under the two days he thought it would take. He began to imagine his brother miles back running but knowing already that he'd lost the race. He also began to daydream about the things he would do as chief and of the women who he would surely marry. Spring Winds found the stone knife his father placed by the rock with no problem in just the spot his father described. He briefly admired its craftsmanship before turning and running back south again.

As he ran he felt the knife flopping back and forth in the leather pouch that hung by his side and realized that if he wasn't careful the knife might cut through the leather and he might lose it from the pouch. So, instead, he decided to carry it the rest of the way in his hand. In between daydreams of being chief he briefly considered the idea that his brother might try to ambush him as he ran back, but he dismissed the idea because, like racing, he knew he could also beat him at wrestling or fighting.

In the late afternoon of the second day Red Earth made himself comfortable in his blind alongside the trail. He kept mosquitoes at bay with one hand but always kept the other hand wrapped around the vine that now lay hidden across the trail. He did not need to wait as long as he thought before catching a glimpse of movement coming down the trail. He saw his brother, Spring Winds, running right for him. He noted that Spring Winds ran somewhat slower after having run so far, but was still moving at a good pace; and he admired his brother's fitness.

As Spring Winds approached the trap Red Earth was careful to not make any movement lest his brother see him. Spring Winds grew close enough that Red Earth could see plainly that his brother held the knife in one hand as he ran, and he smiled because he had been worried about how to wrestle the knife away from him. Finally the moment came and Red Earth pulled the vines hard just a moment before his brother crossed. Spring Winds saw when his brother sprang the trap but didn't even have enough time to figure out what exactly was happening. The next thing Spring Winds knew, he hit the ground hard, and the knife slid down the trail. The trap had been so well sprung that Spring Winds didn't even realize it was a trap, but instead thought he tripped on a root. He had just started to push himself up slowly when Red Earth burst from behind the blind and ran out into the trail grabbing the knife.

Spring Winds ignored the pain and pushed himself fast now to give chase to his brother, but it was no longer a fair race. He'd been running almost continuously for two days now while all that time his brother rested. Red Earth beat Spring Winds back to the village by a safe margin and was instantly declared the winner and the next to serve as chief.

Spring Winds eventually forgave his brother, and admitted it had been a well-placed trap. When White Eagle passed away Red Earth became chief and the forest people lived out long and healthy lives under his guidance.

Two thousand, five hundred years later a new hospital was being built just south of that same lake. As the footings were poured a cement finisher happened to notice a small but perfect little arrowhead lying in the sand. He instantly recognized it for what it was because he often went looking for artifacts in his free time. What he did not know

of course was that it was the arrow which signaled the beginning of the race for Spring Winds and Red Earth.

Chapter 34: Sleeping Bear and the Dowry

Sleeping Bear was born and raised on the northeastern corner of the prairie lands where the prairies carried out an age old struggle with the forests. The land between the prairies and forests flourished with game and provided more than enough food for not only Sleeping Bear, but also for many generations both before and after him. He got his name because he angered slowly, but once truly angered found it difficult to stop. Several times during his life he fought bravely against intruders into his people's lands.

Once, when he was just 15 summers old, he nearly beat one of his peers to death when he found him stealing from the old widows who followed their clan from camp to camp. After he married, he and his wife raised three children to adulthood, all girls. Two of the three married young warriors of the clan at an early age and busily raised families of their own, but Sleeping Bear's youngest daughter, Dances In The Rain, experienced a birth defect that caused her to grow a severe curvature of the spine.

Though food abounded and their lands remained mostly peaceful, Dances In The Rain found her life far from pleasant. Her peers relentlessly taunted her because of her condition. Sleeping Bear nearly beat more than one child for abusing his beloved daughter over the years. She turned to him for support when she grew old enough to marry. Sleeping Bear knew his daughter possessed a pure heart, and he loved her more than anything in the world. But he felt fairly helpless to find a husband for her. He often times could hear her crying quietly in the dark after their hut's fire died for the night. Things only grew worse when Dances In The Rain's mother passed away.

Rather than spending time trying to catch the eye of some boy or work on her favorite hobby, making baskets, she obligingly took over her mother's tasks and prepared hides, made clothing, cooked meals, and many other miscellaneous tasks. After her mother passed away Dances In The Rain slowly became more and more withdrawn and depressed. Sleeping Bear saw what was happening, and his heart hurt for her.

He spent that first winter after his wife's passing working on a fine little axe for his daughter. It would make harvesting the basswood strips for her baskets much easier.

Sleeping Bear spent countless hours that winter pecking and grinding the river cobble into the desired shape. Of course his work came as no secret to Dances In The Rain as they shared a small hut, and the constant clacking together of the rocks made an inescapable noise.

When spring finally started to melt the winter snows Sleeping Bear finished the axe. He told Dances In The Rain that he would go with her to the river to help her gather some strips of wood for her baskets since she had not made any all winter. Quietly and without any display of emotion she conceded that she would like that.

Both Sleeping Bear and Dances In The Rain set out the next day, walking the quarter mile to the creek where they found a number of tall, straight basswood trees. After walking around and carefully examining them they both decided on a single tree about a hand's width across at the stump. They built a fire around the base of it and fed it as much small, dry twigs and pine cones as they could find.

By midday the tree fell, and they put the axe to work for the first time trimming the branches from the trunk with much less effort than normal. After Sleeping Bear cleared the branches with the little axe, he handed it to his daughter who took no time to handle or appreciate the piece but rather went straight to work with the poll end of it, using it like a hammer to loosen the bark all up and down the tree.

Sleeping Bear smoked a pipe in a sunny spot along the creek bank as he watched his daughter work with skilled hands. She used the axe to lightly tap the tree trunk all up and down its length and slowly increased the force she used. When the outer wood layer had separated from the tree, she used a small flake knife to make long ribbon cuts up and down the log before pulling each thin strip of basswood off and putting it in a pile. No sooner had she finished one layer than she started the next, again lightly tapping it all up and down the log gradually increasing the amount of force. By late afternoon she had made enough thin basswood strips to make several baskets, and they both headed home.

In spite of his gift of the little axe to her, and in spite of his many pep talks, she remained quiet and depressed. Sleeping Bear decided he might find a husband for his daughter if he offered a big enough dowry. He immediately took inventory of his belongings but soon realized he did not have enough wealth to offer a good dowry, so he began to actively collect things of interest, making some things, and saving extra hides. When the spring fish runs were over and summer was in full swing he set off for Bloody Hill where he spent several days making the largest and best stone blades he could manage. In late summer he killed a large black bear, and he made a beautiful necklace that any hunter would feel proud to own, using both the teeth and claws. When his friend asked for help building a canoe, Sleeping Bear agreed. His friend offered him two large strings of shell beads in thanks, and Sleeping Bear added these to the growing dowry collection as well. That winter Sleeping Bear made a second larger axe, one fit for a man to clear forests with; this too he added to the dowry pile.

Eventually Sleeping Bear started to hear people talking about his growing dowry. Some people remarked that it would take an impossibly large dowry in order to marry such an ugly girl, but he simply ignored them and carried on. The larger his stock pile of wealth and goods became the more he heard people talking about it. Several times the potential suitors came to his house but they turned away upon seeing the girl. By late fall Sleeping Bear had amassed a truly impressive pile of goods, one which he felt would surely be enough to attract a fine husband for his beloved daughter. Around that same time he announced to the clan his intentions to marry off his daughter and allowed potential suitors to view the impressive pile of goods. He noted the wedding ceremony would be held on the first warm day of spring. News of the large dowry and wedding spread quickly, even reaching families of the clans who lived long distances away from their central village. All the excitement seemed to pick up Dances In The Rain's spirits a little bit; and both she and her father seemed a little happier that fall.

Not long after the snows began to turn the late fall into the heart of winter Dances In The Rain became sick. She coughed so much that she grew hoarse. Her father waited on her every need giving her medicine and hot tea at every opportunity; but she developed a fever. Just before dawn one morning as Sleeping Bear finally fell asleep due to sheer exhaustion Dances In The Rain stopped coughing. He didn't notice immediately after waking up but rather took a few moments to rekindle the fire. Then he noticed how quite she lay. When he looked over at the ashen face of his now deceased daughter he started to weep. He screamed in anger and pain so loud people could hear him at a great distance.

Though many of his fellow clansmen offered to help, Sleeping Bear insisted on preparing for his daughter's funeral on his own. He removed the hearth from his home and in its place he dug a shallow grave. He lined it with fresh pine boughs and laid his daughter down upon them. He placed all the hides he had saved for her dowry over the top of her. Many people commented that it was a waste to put so many fine hides in the ground like he did, but Sleeping Bear met their criticisms with a sharp eye and they knew enough to keep quiet.

All around the shallow grave he placed the items from her dowry, the bear claw and tooth necklace, all the fine stone blades he had made at Bloody Hill, and many baskets of food they stored for the long winter ahead. Then, with painstaking persistence he filled every available space in and around the grave and dowry items with small twigs and firewood until every inch of his former house had been filled. At daybreak the next day many of Sleeping Bear's friends and family came and stood outside in the freezing air just before dawn to light the house on fire. There they stood and sang songs and said prayers as the home and grave burned.

By late in the day little remained but a big circle of burning coals. The slight mound in the middle where the hides were piled so thick over Dances In The Rain's body failed to burn all the way through. Most people had gone back to the warmth and comfort of their own homes, but Sleeping Bear stayed there all day and all of the following night to keep the fire burning, adding all the firewood he could find. As time went on he began raking in the circle to make it smaller and taking some dirt from around it and raking it in toward the middle as well. When he finished there was a small mound perhaps three feet high of dirt mixed with charcoal and burnt remains of his home. Over this he placed cobbles from the river so that no animals could ever dig into the grave. Three days after the funeral Sleeping Bear walked away from the camp in the cold of the night and no one ever saw him again.

In the spring of 1971 a young man and his daughter were walking a farm field looking for arrowheads when the dad spied a small but wellmade axe peeking out from the dirt not far in front of his daughter. Rather than point it out, he held his breath in nervous anticipation as his daughter approached. As he hoped, her face lit up when she saw it lying there in the dirt. It became the first of several axes she found in the fields of that area over the course of her lifetime. It was the same axe that Sleeping Bear made for Dances In The Rain to help with making baskets more than a thousand years before. Sleeping Bear and Dances In The Rain inadvertently left it by the basswoods where they always went to work to get wood for baskets, but neither of them ever made the short walk back to find it.

The End

Get these great history books also by Paul Schanen.

Oversized paperback

Amazon Kindle Ebook